NOT TILL THE
RED FOG RISES

NOT TILL THE RED FOG RISES

Derek Raymond

LITTLE, BROWN AND COMPANY

A *Little, Brown* Book

First published in Great Britain in 1994
by Little, Brown and Company

A CIP catalogue record for this book is
available from the British Library.

ISBN 0 316 91014 7

Typeset in Plantin by Solidus (Bristol) Limited
Printed and bound in Great Britain by
Clays Ltd, St Ives plc

Little, Brown and Company (UK)
Brettenham House
Lancaster Place
London WC2E 7EN

For John, Charlotte, Henry and Owen

For he shall dance
And he shall sing,
And he shall turn his face to the wall.

Old ballad

1

The streaks running down the stucco front of the Palmyra were black, but that wasn't surprising because it was bang in the middle of the rough end of Earls Court, and everything was black round there. Once, like the others in the street, it must have been a family house, but as far back as people could remember it had always been known as a hotel called the Palmy, the last two letters of its name having tired and dropped out of the game. Weeds sprouted out of the cracks in its roof and raddled Victorian portico, and it looked what it was, a fifth-rate rooming-house with a heavy turnover in transients much frequented by bailiffs, plain-clothes filth and debt collectors. It was the kind of place where the week's rent always fell due the day the rain came down, when depression drifted into the room like smoke under a door and the money ran out.

Young men mostly lodged there, fit and from a dry climate thousands of miles away, but they soon found that the London damp was an experience that no love of outdoor sport could temper. They would discover this on arriving at the flooded entrance of Earls Court station at two in the morning when there were no more trains and there was nowhere to go but the Palmyra whose hall light leered through the mist. Most of them paused, decided against and kept going, but some were young enough to feel that here was hell: quaint, cheap, with the kind of atmosphere they had come to see, so they crossed the road and thumbed the night bell.

Only one or two imaginative ones, wiping the rain off their faces once they were inside, felt vague doubts and wondered if, no matter how cheap, the place was really worth staying in after all as they watched the night clerk put the cork in his bottle and reach for the register. There was nothing about the Palmyra in any guidebook; the tourist board didn't advertise it, and even black-cab drivers scratched their heads when asked to go there; but there it was, waiting across the street like a bitter old actress perched at the singles bar, with a habit and a silicone implant, still wearing the dress from her last big part.

But that was what the Metropole was doing too, teetering a hundred yards further up the road (but on a less grandiose scale of drabness), also the Europa and the Tropical – each with a card in its glass door at the top of the steps saying they were full. What the card really meant was that the state sent the homeless there on a B & B basis, and that the living dead on the top floor were best left to themselves.

And why not? The Palmyra *was* dead. It was an extremely depressing place to be in, and that was why, like so many false economies, a room there only appeared to come cheap. It was also why not everybody who stayed there survived.

But these features, even the unending roadworks at the entrance, were accepted as typical of London by people on their first trip there, for what did the trans-world visitor care? All he wanted was to plunge into strange waters, and he was soon laughing as hard over the Palmyra's ground floor toilet as anyone else, since it was one of the few where there was always a queue of men outside the ladies; knowledgeable frequenters referred to it as the cocktail bar. It was a feature the apprentice tourist mentioned with exclamation marks in his first postcard home, because that was where they met the girls from the call-out agencies for a knee-trembler; in fact, what reputation the place had was stuck on the ground floor as firmly as the night porter and the broken-down lift. The rooms were clean except for the cockroaches in summer, but the top floor was three bunks to a room and cold water; there was the occasional suicide too, mostly in sunny weather. People spending forty a week and looking for somewhere even cheaper didn't mind that; they hardly gave it a thought. But anyone who was vulnerable had to be pretty desperate to stay at the Palmyra.

Except Sladden.

Sladden was not vulnerable, and he had been there since half past ten that evening. Room fifteen was second floor back and zeppelin-shaped, its peeling walls curved so that none of the furniture stood quite flush with them; it was also airless in there because the window was jammed shut.

He squatted inside the wardrobe with sweat pouring off him, stripped to his jeans and T-shirt, listening for the occupier's footsteps, which was difficult because of the deafening noise throughout; there seemed to be a party going in every room. But someone finally halted at the door around one o'clock; the key turned, the door opened, and the light came on. As soon as Sladden was sure that the man was on his own he emerged from the wardrobe with a .25 automatic.

'Hullo, Bogdan.'

The man froze at the end of the gun barrel, then his eyes slipped towards Sladden's. 'What do you want?' he said. 'I don't know you.'

'Doesn't matter,' said Sladden, waving the gun about, 'this'll do as an introduction.' He patted the man down, but Bogdan wasn't armed. 'Try and pretend the gun's not there,' he said.

Bogdan found that pretty difficult.

'In fact why don't you just go over and lie down on the bed? Relax.'

'I can't with that gun in my face.'

'Just do it,' said Sladden. 'Right now would be a good time.'

The man naturally did as he was told. 'That's better,' said Sladden, and looked Bogdan approvingly up and down. He was younger and prettier than in his photographs, which had been taken in black and white without his knowledge and showed him going furtively in and out of office-blocks. But in the flesh Bogdan's face under its smooth dark hair had what Sladden called class. Here was someone he could have taken to any of the clubs he used and in spite of themselves the regulars would have been impressed, wondering how Sladden could ever have made him; they would have watched enviously as his new conquest followed him to the bar, wondering if they couldn't perhaps nick him themselves for a spin in the Bentley and a half-timbered weekend in Surrey. In other circumstances Sladden could have gone a bundle on him, and he didn't think there would have been much opposition.

Pity.

'What is all this anyway?' said the man. 'Why the gun?'

'No need to get in a state. It can all be settled.'

'All what?'

'It's like this, you're leaving us, Bogdan.' Sladden sighed, fighting down his sexual urges with difficulty; they didn't like being said no to. 'Don't look so worried, I'm just the courier. I'm your ticket home, be happy.'

'Home where?'

'It's an open ticket.'

'I don't want to go back to Moscow. Who are you, anyway? Immigration?'

'Aliens' Office,' said Sladden vaguely.

'But I hold a British passport.'

Sladden felt like saying that so did Father Christmas, but instead he remarked, 'There are some irregularities.'

'Like what?'

Sladden ignored that. 'Happy in Britain, are you?' he said. 'You ever feel threatened at all?'

'No,' said Bogdan, 'only by that gun.'

'Nothing you've ever done that might make you feel unwelcome? No? OK. Anyway, I'm pretty reasonable, and I'm running your file, in fact I'm running your whole life just now, so let's be friends.' He winked; it made a sex deviant look like a teen in a soft drinks ad.

As he talked with the gun in his hand he was moving Bogdan about on the bed, trying to get him to look natural. Bogdan submitted passively; he had stopped asking questions and his eyes followed Sladden round the room with resignation. Now and then Sladden stepped back to judge the effect, twitching the pillow and counterpane with the precision of a studio photographer until he had him how he wanted him. When he was satisfied he went over and reclined on the bed too, putting an arm round Bogdan. 'There,' he said. 'How does that feel? Comfortable?'

'Is that all you want? If all you want to do is make love I'll get undressed.'

'No, don't bother,' said Sladden regretfully. That would never have done; one sight of the naked body would have driven him over the top and screwed everything up. 'Let's just take things as they come.'

'Why are you making me pose like this?' said Bogdan. 'Are you going to take pictures of me like that with my clothes on? I don't see any camera anyway. What are you? Some kind of pervert?'

Every kind, thought Sladden, *except the kind that answers questions*. 'I don't know about you,' he said, yawning, 'I've had a long day, I'm tired.' Still holding the gun he cuddled Bogdan up to him in a smelly embrace.

Bogdan looked small and helpless in Sladden's powerful arms. 'You don't come on right to me,' he said. 'You look a bit off, you're not normal, and if it's my body you're after, why's the gun still showing?'

'Because I like guns,' said Sladden. He added: 'Necrophilia turns me on too.' His member shoved its head around in his grubby underpants and it was a case of give in to the urge or get on with it, so he made an effort of will. He sat up, nudging Bogdan. 'Look at that!' he muttered. 'Up in the corner there. No, not there, stupid, on top of the wardrobe.'

Bogdan followed Sladden's pointing finger. 'There's nothing there.'

'You're dead right there isn't,' said Sladden. He put the pistol against Bogdan's temple and blew his brains out.

The crack of the .25 wasn't audible above the rest of the uproar in the Palmyra but the bullet made a good deal of mess on impact all the same, most of which hit the wall. Some of it flopped back onto the bed, and Sladden skipped hastily down onto the floor before too much of it landed on him.

The incident had to look like suicide, so he wiped the pistol, closed the cadaver's hand round the butt, then took the gun away again, using a Kleenex, and threw it on the sheet into a puddle of matter.

He patted the dead man softly on the testicles. 'Present from Gutteridge,' he said. 'Bye-bye.' The corpse stared at him, returning him the kind of smile a star uses on a wannabe he doesn't want to know.

Sladden got his anorak out of the wardrobe, putting it on over his bloody shirt, and waited till the corridor was empty. He was in no hurry, and when he did leave, what with the singing of the New Zealanders on a rock-'n'-Fosters binge in the room opposite, no one heard him go.

He went downstairs, nodded at the night porter who was asleep, and whistled as he walked down the street to his car.

2

It took its time reaching a verdict, but in the end the coroner's jury decided that the man had definitely shot himself in the head in room 15 at the Palmyra, so that was all right; Draper could stop sweating. But now, not a week later, here was this second man, and he was just as dead as Bogdan; a dumper truck from a demolition site had upended him with ten tons of rubble on a north London tip. The driver was just having a smoke watching the load come off when down came the body, white with cement dust and one of its legs tumbling after it, and what made the coroner and his jury scratch their heads, as Draper knew it would, was that both men were Russian.

More of Sladden's sloppy work! Draper thought furiously, because that wasn't in the least all right. This second Russian death coming on top of the first was just the kind of angle that got the press going, never mind the fact that the pathologist who examined the second body had found what he termed 'oddities' about it.

The pathologist was a morgue-hardened man who smoked too many Gauloises and never said no to a spliff. In fact his work disgusted him so much that when he was off duty he never said no to anything, which caused him problems – in his case a girlfriend whose brains lived where her bum was (if it had been the other way round she would have been someone different, of course, but that was metaphysics); she kept threatening to run off with a rock guitarist from Hammersmith and sometimes did. His opinion was that the deceased had been dead of three gunshot wounds long before he had found his way onto the truck, and that was what he said in his report.

When the heroes from the local police station got out to the tip they taped it off and looked at the body, unsure what to do about it. Used though they were to dealing with corpses they didn't come across many Russians on their patch, certainly not Russians in several pieces; in fact, they didn't even realise the body was Russian until the detective searching its clothes found a note in the same pocket as a new British passport, which muddled things up even more. Not that the passport photo was any use as identification; the man's head was no thicker than an *A–Z* guide, and what was left of his face told them less than rolled pastry.

Needless to say no one at the station knew any Russian, not even the chief inspector, so ultimately, after a lot of telephoning, Draper was sent for. Draper took one look at the passport and flew into a state of barely suppressed rage. Grabbing the passport, and the note, he signed for them and marched out of the station, saying curtly that his people would deal with the whole thing.

It was serious; why hadn't Sladden searched the body, taken the Russian note, the British passport, and brought them back? Draper looked glum because he knew the answer: Sladden had been so pleased with his handiwork as usual that he had forgotten the other essentials.

In any case Draper was beside himself at the police being involved with this second body at all; the whole point was that it was supposed never to be found. The Palmyra affair had turned out all right, just. But even there the margin had been too narrow; there could easily have been a verdict of murder by persons unknown which would have been extremely embarrassing, while in this second case there had been no margin at all, which was horrific.

Of course there had to be inquests on bodies found shot in hotel rooms or dumped on builders' skips; it was procedure, worse luck, and had to be carried out. But it upset him. In these matters Draper liked to control every detail. He was the maestro, and he resented finding himself in any situation not of his own making: rather as an ambitious conductor might feel if he woke up to find himself playing the triangle, the jew's-harp, or something virtually inaudible right at the back of the orchestra: the very idea gave him nightmares.

Besides, the fact that the second body had turned up the way it had, and then, worse still, been taken to a police station, invited the kind of public spotlight attendant on any balls-up, whereas the only publicity that ever made Draper happy was no publicity at all.

When he got back from the police station, still seething, there was a fresh-faced athletic-looking man in his thirties waiting in his office.

'What do you want?' Draper snapped.

'Name's Ricky.'

'Oh yes, you're the replacement for Gutteridge, good. At least I hope you're good, people say so. Anyhow, you'll be working with me and Sladden; there's just the three of us. Don't let Sladden wear you down, by the way, that's your first hurdle; he wears down most people, you'll soon see what I mean. So what do you know about this Russian business?'

'What I've been briefed.'

'Did they tell you we'd got problems?'

'They told me about Bogdan.'

'Well there's another one now called Oleg.'

'The man on the dumper truck.'

'You're not supposed to know that,' Draper shouted. 'Security on that's as tight as a loan shark's fist!'

'They told me about it upstairs all the same,' said Ricky. 'They didn't sound very happy; said it was a Sladden special, whatever that is.'

Draper winced. 'The trouble with Sladden is that he thinks he's sane. I'd replace him if I could, only there's nothing in the budget. Well at least you know about Oleg, which saves me having to tell you. Only I like controlling any information myself; I hate leaks. Still, it's simple enough. Oleg was working with Bogdan; they both had to go before they could tip Yuri off.'

'I've only heard about Yuri. You'd better tell me something about him.'

'Ex-colonel-general Gatov was KGB from disinformation,' said Draper, 'and we've been after him for a while. It's his connection with major British villains working from Turkey that brought us in, also the kind of business they're running. Read this.'

It was a cutting from a month-old news section of the *Sunday Times*: 'Alan Summerfield, 47, a Turkish-based British businessman, is being held in connection in Ankara with an alleged plot to supply seventy-five million dollars' worth of Russian weapons in breach of United Nations sanctions. He faces up to seven years' imprisonment over accusations that he and three associates plotted to ship guns, tanks and anti-missile systems from Russia to Angola, Iraq, Iran, Kuwait and Yemen.'

Looking up Ricky said, 'I like the way it says anti-missile systems; they mean warheads.'

'Yes, but we obviously had to tone that down. If the public knew what was really going on everyone would be running for the shelters if there were any.'

'Summerfield,' said Ricky. 'Summerfield, name means nothing to me.'

'We can't prove it, but we know he works with a man called Gates who'd rather make one pound bent than two straight,' said Draper. 'He's like Summerfield, involved with really successful villains, but we've never managed to hit him yet. He specialises in putting up capital for international strokes, and Gatov's right up his street. Logically Gatov should have operated from Germany or eastern Europe, except that too many Stasi people know him there and he was frightened of getting his head shot off, that's one reason he's started up in the UK. As for the warheads, they're sitting around in the Caucasus, 7th military district, and Gatov wants to sell them. What he's trying to do is set up the business end here, get paid in hard currency, and then ship the goods overland out of Russia. It's easy for Gatov with his KGB past – any problem with the officers at the base, he's got a dossier on them. Not that he needs dossiers. Show me the general who enjoys being on the dole. As for 7th district, that's new; before, all the gear used to be from the 4th out in the Urals. But we know that this time at least two Wallop missiles with chemical capacity have been moved from the 7th; only our problem is that of course we don't know where, and that's what we've got to find out before the fucking things get fired at someone, which could be us. Although looking at you, that doesn't seem to upset you much.'

'I've got no imagination,' said Ricky, 'that's my trouble.'

'Do a crash course on it. Meantime, getting back to Gatov, he's got no dependable contacts here, which helps. London isn't like Berlin, Prague or Warsaw; they'd have been happy as pigs in shit over there. But the nearest they've got to agents here are villains, and villains are something we all know about here: I didn't do sixteen years with the Met for nothing.'

'OK,' said Ricky. 'Mind, there's one bright spot. The people these things get sold on to never manage to fire them; they forget to order bits, or they find there's an embargo on them, or else it's prayer week, or else they put them together the wrong way round. Like as not if they did pop one the fucking thing would go straight up in the air and come down on the karzy.'

'That's a chance we're not taking.'

'No, all right. By the way, what happened to Gutteridge?'

'He overdosed with lead on some waste ground.'

3

Gust woke up in his DSS hostel in Allison Road, which ran parallel with the Kilburn Thames rail-link. He was only forty-four, but there were black stains under his cheekbones and he looked down at himself thinking, *Christ, you ought to be in the tomb, mate,* and the shadows falling across his body confirmed it.

A storm was brewing up and he didn't feel like going out, but there was always some bloody thing to do. Today it was the probation officer, so he started getting dressed to go down there. Being only two months out of jail he had to keep all that kosher, because he had the rest of his sentence waiting for him the first time he forgot to chalk his cue. He washed, throwing water over his head, pulled his trousers on and went over to the window.

The night before, coming back from Soho on the midnight train, a fat young man sitting opposite him with a briefcase and a plastic bag of LPs on his knees suddenly leaned forward between St John's Wood and Finchley Road and was sick over Gust's shoes. Gust wasn't pleased, but he thought, *It's only beer, after all; I've seen worse than that splashed about.*

Yesterday a despondent autumn sun had shone on the street, but this morning that had given place to heavy rain. It was a depressing outlook, though nothing could ever depress him again the way the view from his cell had done. This side of the railway two black and white checkered flags flew above the tyre depot opposite, hammering in the wind under a black sky. Dark clouds, bulging and swinging about like the breasts of a fat woman in a fight, had advanced on the city all week from the north-west; as for the flags, the depot was a new business struggling in the recession, so they were cheap flags, and would soon be ripped to pieces like anything that was half price. They were flattened horizontally outwards on their masts away from the storm concentrated over Brent Cross shopping centre.

While the two flags snapped, howled and argued with the weather, Gust looked out at the street. Now the rain was pissing down even harder, sweeping the pavement at a wicked angle and driving sheets of old newspaper up into the trees like a madwoman spring-cleaning; below him a young man soaked to the skin with his foot in plaster and an aluminium crutch hobbled in the direction of the tube station. The wind increased its fury as Gust watched; now the masts which carried the flags were bent over like two thin, complaining men, leaning towards each other or else whipped at random in opposite directions as the wind turned momentarily into the drab wall of the storm. Gust imagined folk shaking their heads and making for the Railway Tavern or back to the Barnet asylum, depending on which financial level they had reached, to spread themselves against some tepid radiator where they could dry out and explain their case to a fellow-traveller who had fallen asleep anyway with a can of Tennents Extra sticking out of his pocket.

His attention switched to the car parked opposite, a dirty white Jaguar, L registered; he recognised it because it had been there all day yesterday too. Not even the heavy rain had cleaned it off. Inside it sat two men, one of them big.

The law didn't often go in for L-registered Jags, but

villains did. He didn't like seeing it there, nor what he could see of the two men. They could have been watching for anyone in the building, of course, but his instinct was that they were looking for him. He went over the possibilities. Whoever they were they couldn't be Manny's people; Manny had nothing on him. Hijacking the passports had gone off sweet as a little sewing machine: no one had got hurt and he had been paid. All the same a bad taste came up in his mouth and he sat down on the bed.

After a while he crossed the room, shaved, and went back to the window; the Jag was still there. He picked up his walkman and pressed the play button; it came up with 'Fixin' To Die Blues'.

When he was ready he left the house by the back door that no one used with its notice tacked to it, Keep This Door Shut Against Rats, Landlord. It led to a tangled garden filled with dustbin lids, rotting wood slats and dead weeds three feet high. He walked through the rain to the low brick wall at the end, squirmed over it as easily as a snake, and dropped over onto a building site which fronted another street; then he walked towards the Underground with his head down against the weather like everyone else.

He didn't think he would go back to Allison Road again for a while, if at all.

4

When Draper got back from the inquest on Oleg he sent for Sladden and Ricky. 'There'll be a few lines in the press about him tonight,' he said, 'the basics. It'll tell Gatov he's lost another man. He gets the British papers every day, and if this doesn't bring him over nothing will.'

'He's too bright to go for it,' Sladden said.

'Oh yes?' said Draper. 'I've just heard he's picked up his nice new passport, so for all we know he could be on the next flight to Heathrow.'

'Don't bank on it,' Sladden said gloomily.

'He either drops by or else stays put and watches his operation collapse,' Draper insisted.

Ricky wasn't convinced. 'He's lost two men, why should he want to be the third?'

'Greed,' Draper said. 'Everything's coming unstuck for him and of course he doesn't like that, he wants to know why. He still reckons he can swan over here whenever he likes, take us for a load of burks, only this time he's got a big shock coming.'

'No,' Ricky said, 'I agree with Sladden. That passport's too obvious.'

'That's because you know it's bent.'

'You play too much seven card stud,' said Sladden, 'that's your trouble.'

16

'And I take your money off you,' Draper said. 'Still, you're right; poker is what this is.'

'Well I'm not happy,' said Sladden. 'And another thing, I want Gust dropped. Into the nearest jail'd do.'

'What you can't stand about Gust is him taking the piss out of you,' Draper said. 'But cool down. You won't be dealing with Gust this time. Right now I want you to go and have a word with Harry Ford, make sure he stays on the rails. That ought to give you job satisfaction. Then when you've finished meet us over at Heathrow. And don't forget the camera.'

Sladden made for the door.

Ricky addressed Draper: 'I've still got a few questions.' Sladden stopped to listen.

'Well?' Draper said testily.

'Slaying those two Russians,' Ricky said. 'Forgive my sarcasm, but that was really brill, that was.'

'What's the matter with you all of a sudden?' said Sladden. 'Something gone off in the fridge?'

'It was over the top, there was no need for it.'

'Why don't you take up Bible studies?' Sladden jeered.

'They were just men Fridays, the commercial end.'

'No they weren't,' said Draper. 'Bogdan hit Gutteridge, but they both had to go anyway. Besides, it was a way of opening the game up. And as for the risk, Bogdan and Oleg must have known you don't make the kind of money Gatov was paying them for spending all day in the pub.'

'And what's done is done, anyway,' said Sladden. 'Everything went fine the first time round. My meet-up with Bogdan, that was very elegant.'

'I'll bet it was,' Ricky said. 'I'll bet you murmured comforting words, held his head steady for the bullet and everything; I only have to shut my eyes and I can see it.'

'You looking for bother?

'And then Oleg.'

'Oleg didn't fly straight, I admit. Faced with the almighty suddenly like that he kicked up a fuss.'

Ricky's voice took on a patronising tone. 'I don't suppose it ever occurred to you, but maybe he didn't want to die.'

'He shouldn't have been in the game then, should he?' Sladden said defensively. 'And he shouldn't have gone for his gun when I jumped him either. He wasn't meant to do that; it wasn't in the plan.'

'Plan?' said Ricky. 'There wasn't a plan. The whole thing was a cock-up from start to finish.'

Sladden flushed an angry red. 'You cheeky bastard. It's all right for you. You talkative burks are all the same, you're always the ones that weren't there. Anyway, we're covered.'

'Let's hope,' said Draper, 'because there could still be trouble upstairs. I nearly did my pieces over Oleg, he wasn't meant to be found.'

'No,' said Ricky. 'Especially not trundled in to the law in two pieces.'

'You think you could have done it better?' Sladden jibed.

'Cut it out,' said Draper. 'As long as we get Gatov we'll cab our way out of the rest. And as for cock-ups, as in all cock-ups, you don't waste time trying to eliminate them, you just limit the damage.'

'Let's hope we can,' Ricky said soberly, 'because I don't like to think of those warheads being sold on to some fanatic somewhere the other side of the planet.'

'You ought to get a job as a lifeguard on Margate beach the way you come on,' Sladden sneered. 'You're pretty enough.'

Ricky looked down at his hands. 'Don't make me have to use these, you're too old.'

'I don't want any more of that talk,' Draper said quellingly. 'We're a team here. As for Bogdan and Oleg, there are always options in this business and you can easily pick the wrong one; the politicians do it all the time. Now let's get on with it.'

'All right,' said Ricky, 'I only wanted your opinion.'

'You just got it,' Sladden said.

When they had both gone Draper gazed at the wall opposite, musing on a couplet that he had formulated for himself during his years in the department:

'In government nothing gets done for so long,
That when anything is done it's always done wrong.'

5

Sladden went round to Harry Ford's in Frith Street. It had gone half eleven; the pubs had turned out and Sladden reckoned Ford must have been turned out with them if he could still walk. He went up to the door on the corner marked Sunbite Properties next to the El Flyover pizzeria. It was the grungy building on the corner covered in scaffolding; the landlord was having it scrubbed to make sure the tourists appreciated the other flats where his girls operated. Sladden went to ring the bell marked flat two, then changed his mind and opened the door his own way. The cheap lock didn't like it much and broke, but Sladden didn't care about that.

Ford came downstairs, frightened by the noise; everything frightened him these days, and today had been bad. All morning he had been dying for a drink, but he hadn't been able to get over to the Diadem till the end of the happy hour because he had to go to the supermarket following Clarice up with the trolley, which had taken till lunch-time. She had got stuck at the Unguents shelf, hooked on the glow from the bottles. She liked the green ones best, and he watched her spending more and more money on them, which was a dead waste, because the bottles lost whatever allure they had the moment she stood them on the grimy bathroom sill, and the stuff smelled horrible on her anyway, like a chemistry experiment.

'Who is it?' he croaked from the top of the stairs. When he saw it was Sladden he groaned.

'That's right,' said Sladden, 'it's me, so make with the hospitality, Harry. Let me in and put the wood in the hole, we can't talk out here.'

'What have we got to talk about?'

'You.'

'I thought you'd finished with me.'

'I've never finished with you.'

'All right,' said Harry in a whisper, 'but don't wake Clarice, she's gone to bed with her stomach – she thinks it's the menopause. I've just settled her off with aspirins. How did you get in at the street door? That was a new lock.'

'I broke it.'

'You mad? Any passing maniac could jump me now.'

'You've got Clarice to look after you.'

'You paying for the lock?'

'Fuck off, and get in through that door.'

It was a small flat, but Clarice had only ever taken the hoover to it once. 'What a filthy hole,' said Sladden; they were always his first words whenever he visited. 'You ought to be ashamed, the money you're making.'

'What is all this?' said Ford. 'And I'm reminding you, no noise.'

'I'll be as noisy as I fucking like.' Sladden went over to Ford's chair, which had once been the throne in a production of *Richard III* and dropped his two-hundred-and-fifty-pound weight on it. A piece of wood flew off one of the legs with a shriek and the chair tilted sharply to one side.

'Easy with that,' Ford bleated, 'Clarice says it's an antique.'

'Well you and I know better. We know it isn't. You and I know it's just a rotten old chair without any bottle, like you. Now get me a beer.'

'I'd have to go past the bedroom to get to the fridge, and what about Clarice? It's the noise.'

'Fuck Clarice. Get the beer, otherwise I'll go in there and fuck her myself. And you're not having any, I want you on full chat making sense.'

Ford came back with a can of Holsten. Sladden popped it and began to slurp noisily.

'I don't know what you keep coming back here for,' Ford complained.

'Because you haven't finished your homework yet, and I want to put some starch in you. That's why I come round from time to time, to make sure you're holding up.'

'I'd hold up better if you just left me alone.' Harry's eyes were on the tightly shut bedroom door.

'I know what you're thinking,' said Sladden, 'and if you say one word to that fake platinum bitch of yours, just one, I'll know it.'

'I wouldn't do that.' It was part of the deal I wouldn't.'

'I know what the deal is all right, I'm just making sure you do.' Sladden drank some more beer and stood up suddenly. 'Here,' he said, 'let's have some fun. It's like a funeral in here.'

'Fun?' said Ford, bemused. 'With you around? What sort of fun?'

'I'll show you. Anything to liven up this scene.' Sladden felt in his pocket and found a battered-looking tape. 'Here,' he said. 'This looks cheerful. Jazz. Old stuff.' He waved it about in the stagnant air till he spotted the ghetto-blaster in the corner. He jammed the tape into it, turning the volume up full, and the opening bars of 'Trucking All Night' roared out.

'The noise!' Harry implored.

'Bollocks,' said Sladden. 'Get dancing, Harry, this is great!'

'Clarice!'

'Get jiving!' Sladden twirled Harry around under his stinking armpits. 'Rap back to it, come on now, let's see those trainers of yours in action!'

A faint moan issued from the other side of the bedroom door, but before Harry could complain Sladden hurled him away on the beat of the music so that he thudded into the panels. 'Let's have her out here!' shouted Sladden. 'Why not?' He battered happily on the door. 'Come on, missis! Mauve nightie, blue rinse, bath foam, false teeth and all. Come on, Harry, get her out here, let's party, man!'

'No! She won't come out while you're here, but once you're gone she'll go fucking insane!'

'You live with her, masochist,' Sladden sneered, 'I don't.' He pumped Harry up and down by the arm, making him look like some kind of oil-rig. 'You call that dancing?' he shouted. 'I could do better than that just slapping my prick along the deck!'

But Harry had broken away; he was reeling about in the middle of the room gasping, the breath rattling in his lungs, his hands pressed into his midriff.

'No fucking stamina,' said Sladden, 'you little criminals are all the same.' He shoved him backwards onto the throne; it grunted, and one of its barley-sugar legs splayed out. 'OK,' he said, switching off the music, 'let's get back to that money we paid you, how much do you still owe the bookies?'

'I'm clean with the bookies, that's straight up.'

'Bollocks. You still owe them four grand. Pay them off, you can afford to. You're my investment, Harry; I don't want these people coming round now and beating you to death.'

'All right, if I owe them it's because of Clarice. She likes clothes, jewellery, stuff like that, you know.'

'What I know is she's a fucking liability, and as for jewellery, she doesn't know the difference between Ratner's and Asprey's, her mind's shallower than a fucking soup plate. Where do you find them, Harry? Waterloo?'

'Anyway, I tell you I haven't said a thing to anyone. Clarice or anyone.'

'Well you keep it that way, because otherwise you can make your will. Above all if you talk to Gust.'

'I know how to handle Gust.'

'No you don't. You don't know anything until I tell you.'

'Gust doesn't scare me.'

'Yes he does. You're shit scared of Gust. You're shit scared of me, shit scared of the bookies, shit scared of Clarice, who aren't you shit scared of?'

Ford stood up. 'I think I'll just go and strain the greens.'

'I'll tell you when you can have a piss, just sit there till I've finished,' Sladden snapped.

'What more for the love of Christ?'

Sladden crumpled up his empty can and dropped it on the floor. 'More beer.' When Ford came back with it he said: 'So how are things with you and Manny?'

'Manny and I are fine, we're always fine, we're practically blood brothers.'

'You'd be blood brothers all right if he knew you were talking to me,' said Sladden, laughing. 'There'd be a lot of blood about, Harry, yours, and it'd be all over the floor. You'd be a dead blood brother. The same as you would be if I dropped you in it.'

'You wouldn't do that, though.'

'Well you keep it buttoned. You just keep doing your part of the deal and you'll stay healthy.'

'All right, only just don't go on and on.' Ford's voice was beginning to quaver tremulously.

Sladden went on: 'There's another thing about Gust. He's going to be under a lot of pressure now, he's liable to pay you a visit; don't let him in when he does.'

'Why should he see me?'

'Because he's suddenly going to find himself very short of friends, he's even going to be pushed for shelter, man.'

'He'll get nothing from me,' said Ford. 'He won't get the skin off my shit.'

'Make sure he doesn't, or you won't need a shit.'

'Look, I've done my bit, I'm squared away with Manny, he's swallowed it, everything's kosher. What I want to know is, is everything going to work out all right my side?'

'You can only hope it does, can't you?' said Sladden.

'What do you mean? When we agreed the deal you made it all sound OK then.'

'Then that's what you've got to pray for. You just cross your dirty little fingers that it stays OK, because you're in so deep it's the only thing you can pray for. I always come out sunny side but you never do, Harry, looking at your record; only this time you'll probably come out right way up because your interests are our interests. But you can never be quite sure, Harry, and you won't find out which way it's gone till the night.'

'That's not what you said before. That's not what you said at all when this started.'

'That's right enough, you're at a terrible disadvantage,' said Sladden. 'You're working with people whose motives you don't really understand, and at the same time you're taking our money. That's not my fault; you agreed to it. But things develop in ways you don't expect as the game plays through, and there's nothing I can do about that either.' He heaved himself out of the chair and a spring popped out of the upholstery for a look round.

He went to the door and opened it. 'Pay off the bookies, Harry, I tell you again, and don't go back, that fat tart you've got in your wanking-chariot there's not worth it.'

'Look, just answer me one question,' said Ford. 'Will you be back? That's what I want to know.'

'I might. Why not?' Sladden turned at the top of the stairs. 'By the way, now you can afford it, why don't you buy yourself a new face? The one you've got looks like a corpse's.'

'Don't say that. Saying things like that's unlucky,

and I'm scared enough as it is.'

'I'm what you've got to be scared of,' said Sladden, 'and don't you fucking forget it.'

He left, slamming the street door, and bits of lock tinkled behind him in the hall.

6

What Gust told Petal later wasn't entirely what had happened with Sladden at the time. The first Gust knew was when a man caught up with him as he left the probation office.

'You don't know me but I know you,' said Sladden. 'That's nice, isn't it?' He fell into step with Gust and they started off down the street together.

'Nice?' Gust said. 'It's lovely. Tastes like a shit sandwich, what do you want?'

'I want to make you a lot of trouble,' said Sladden. 'You and I are going to have a talk, Marigold.'

'Well behave like other people then,' said Gust. 'Polite.'

'I don't know why, but I've never mastered that trick. Still, you'll get used to it.' Sladden scratched his orange stubble, also the shreds of ginger hair on his head that went with it. He added: 'And I'm not other people.' Close up to him the way he was, Gust saw what he meant; he certainly didn't smell like other people.

'You don't half pong,' said Gust. 'They say you can't smell your own shit, but you ought to think of others.'

'I'll forget you said that,' said Sladden. 'Now let's find a quiet pub and have a drink, because you're going to need one.'

'Me drink with you? You're not serious.'

27

'I'm serious enough to get you into a lot of fucking bother, as if you weren't already in it.'

Gust didn't like the sound of that. 'What are you? Law?'

'No,' said Sladden, 'worse than that.'

'Nothing can be worse than the filth,' said Gust with feeling, 'and anyway you're not fit enough to be one of them.'

'I could floor you with one arm, son, and no bother,' said Sladden. A pub loomed up and he urged Gust inside; at that time of the morning the place was nearly empty. 'Get that table over there,' he said, 'I'll buy us a pint.'

When he brought them back Gust said: 'How did you get on to me, anyway?'

'People like you, in and out of probation offices, easy.'

'So where do you fit in?' said Gust. 'As if I fucking cared.' He pushed his beer away and stood up.

Sladden shoved him back in his seat. 'Sit down, arsehole. You and I are going to work together and believe me, it's really going to function.'

'You're one thousand percent wrong, gasbag. I'm giving you nothing at all, so get your brakes off and start pedalling.'

'I don't have to tell you who I am,' said Sladden. 'I don't have to explain anything to a slimy mobile problem like you, but there's no fucking end to the questions I can ask. You're a cockroach of society, you know that? In fact I can't think why you're not still in the nick.'

'You telling me I'm not clean, is that it?'

'You're hardly back on the street and you're at it already.'

'My probation officer thinks I'm clean. He's dead chuffed with me.'

'Probation officers'll swallow anything, and a lot don't even bother to check, but I've got proof you're on a scam, otherwise I wouldn't be here. So by the time I've

finished with you you'll either be nibbling out of my
hand like a tame rabbit, tough boy, or I'll send you back
where you came from, one easy movement.'

'People who talk like that, they're all just piss and
wind. Every time.'

'Well this is a different time. Each piece of this shit
I've got here weighs around half a ton, sunset, you'll see
when it hits you.'

'You really think I'm going to work with you? You're
way out. Look at you. Anyway look at you. You're
sloppy, dirty, you're running to fat, you wouldn't go one
round with a basket-case.'

'It's a pity we've got to work together. However,
maybe we'll meet up at the back of the lot one day and
we can work it out then, what you just said. Meanwhile
I've got all I need to fix you up, so don't try my patience,
I haven't any.'

'Then learn some. Try spending ten years on the
difficult block, you'll wind up with a whole load of it.'

'You're going to cooperate,' said Sladden, 'so get used
to it.'

'Cooperate on what?'

'If it was cooperating over nicking the devil's breakfast
it would be all the same to you with your record.'

'Record?' said Gust. 'Talking of records I bet you've
got one somewhere too, and I bet it's not shit-hot
either.'

They looked like two earnest men deep in a business
discussion, and what they were saying was inaudible six
inches away.

'All right,' said Sladden, 'never mind all that, you're
handy, and I'm going to use you, so let's get down to
that end of it. What I've got on me guarantees you the
five years you've got hanging over you plus a lot more;
so you go on the way you are and you'll be back playing
leapfrog with the lifers.'

'Maybe,' said Gust, leaning over the table. 'But before
that happens do you see all these teeth of mine next to

that fat ear of yours? I could bite it straight off in one, so whatever you've got in your pocket, sweetheart, don't try and be fucking clever.'

'You're insane.' Sladden moved his chair back sharply. 'You're definitely mad.'

'That's what long-distance porridge does to you. You don't expect anyone to come out of that normal, do you?'

'No I don't, and you're not, but this time you're going to do as you're told.'

'All right,' said Gust, 'let's have it, what is it you've got on you then, wankers' snaps?'

But that shot backfired on him. Sladden produced an envelope and began to deal out its contents across the table. 'Here,' he said, 'have a look at some of these then, grungy.'

Gust only had to look at the first print to see what Sladden meant, but Sladden was also watching everything his face did, so Gust made sure it did nothing.

'Nice, aren't they?' said Sladden. 'I can even see the bristles where you missed with the razor, but my own favourite is this one of you, Manny, Harry Ford and the man from the passport printer's all leaving Manny's flat together. Ex-con out on a ticket consorting with known villains, that's serious, Gust. Serious for you, I mean; myself I think it's fucking hilarious. It's passports we're talking about. A thousand of them, brand new, worth a lot of money on the street to the right punter. Only something's gone wrong, see, and here's the proof on the table. The man from the printer's isn't one of yours, he's one of ours – at least he is now, because he suddenly lost his enthusiasm for the whole scam and grassed you.'

'Nothing's gone down yet,' said Gust.

'Makes no difference. The charge would still be conspiring to commit a robbery; you'd go down just the same, and with your old five on top, my darling, and no remission you'll go down with a thundering great bang.'

'All right then. Why don't you just nick me and have done with it?'

'Wouldn't I love to,' said Sladden, 'but no, so don't tempt me. What's going to happen, you're going to pull this caper, only we're pulling the strings. You're going to deliver the gear to Harry Ford. Harry's going to do what I fucking well tell him to do. And that arsehole Farb will pay for your whack. And all you three wise monkeys have to do is stay shtoom. Permanently. And that way we'll forget about the rest.'

'No,' said Gust. 'A great scream would start up if I did that, which I wouldn't like.'

'Who gives a monkey's what you like?' said Sladden. 'Who even told you to open your yap?'

'Something tapped me on the shoulder.'

'You just concentrate on doing what you're told, and do it right.'

7

The three men spent a long time hanging round Heathrow. On the second afternoon, as the four o'clock plane arrived from Moscow, they changed position slightly like lizards in the sun, because they saw Gatov walking through the Aeroflot landing gate.

'See?' Draper said. 'I told you.'

'I know,' said Ricky, 'but I still don't believe it.'

Gatov was middle-aged; he was wearing a new suit, a burberry, a new hat and highly polished black shoes, but those were not the only details about him that Sladden didn't like. Sladden didn't like any detail about him; but then he never liked the details about anybody anyway except young men. On the surface Gatov looked brisk and carefree, but to Sladden, a practised watcher if ever there was one, he behaved like a man in need of a stiff shit. A briefcase was all he carried, and he reminded Sladden strongly of a nervous two-year-old going round a paddock before its first race. He hissed as much in Ricky's ear and added, 'All he needs is a stable lad to stop him flinging that stupid chin of his about.'

They watched the sad story unfold. Gatov reached the immigration control point. Sladden set up his camera and started filming. He muttered to Draper, 'He comes on really cheeky. What does he take us for? Amateurs?'

'Why not?' said Ricky. 'The whole country's run by them.'

'What did you expect him to do anyway,' Draper said, 'open up with a Uzi? And mind he doesn't see you filming him, Sladden, because if you're a Japanese tourist I'm widow Twanky.'

'I don't care if he does. Give the bastard's nerves a jolt.'

Gatov produced his passport and started going through what should have been routine, but it quickly became obvious that it wasn't going to be routine at all; in fact things started going wrong right away. To begin with, the man on the desk was new, someone Gatov had never seen before; this official studied his passport for a long time, flicking the pages over. In the end he said, 'I'm going to have to question you further, Mr Gregory, so would you mind just standing aside?'

Gatov lost his temper, something the watchers could well understand. 'What are you talking about?' he shouted. 'That's a British passport! Everything is in order, I'm entitled to go through!'

'You're not entitled to anything,' said the official, 'and by the way, what's your English like? Can you under-stand what I'm saying to you, or do you want an interpreter? It looks as if you're going to need one.'

'I speak perfectly good English, everybody knows that!'

'I didn't,' said the passport officer. 'I must be deaf.'

He turned his attention to the other passengers, but Gatov still wouldn't leave the queue, and carried on blustering, 'Let me through!'

'You don't give the orders here,' said the passport officer, 'I do. Now get out of the way.'

Gatov changed his tone. 'All right, no problem.' But he still didn't move.

Another official had got hold of Gatov's passport by now and Sladden watched him through his camcorder, tapping the serial number into a computer.

'All this is really just to knock him into shape,' Draper said. 'The man on the desk there isn't from immigration, he's one of ours, all this moody's just to rattle him.'

'It's working,' said Sladden, filming away.

Gatov was still in the queue and the other passengers were getting restless; someone behind him, trying to speed things up, trod on his new loafers. Gatov swore viciously in Russian and a nasty little scene developed; then the airport police arrived and got into the game.

'Makes you want to pray for him,' said Sladden, as Gatov was led out of the queue.

'I've never seen anything like it,' Ricky said. 'I've seen them go down often enough, but this is like a Punch and Judy show.'

Without moving from the camera Sladden said, 'See that?' Of course they couldn't. 'He's really bothered now. Hey, look at the sweat leaking out through his hatband. I lap it up when they do that.' He took more pictures. 'These are beauties. You should see his face.'

Ricky was checking a tape recorder inside his jacket. 'Yes, good,' said Draper, 'we'll need that. We might get a few names, because these people are all the same – once he gets started he'll be babbling on about the people he's going to get hold of to shit all over us. He can't take it in that the lot's collapsed on him. That's a year's work justified, lads, it's wonderful.'

Sladden muttered into the viewfinder: 'Look at me will you, you bastard! Christ, I wish I could keep some of these for my collection, have them to thumb over when I retire.'

'You've got to stay alive to retire,' Ricky pointed out.

'I'm going to,' said Sladden. He stopped to load more film and said to Draper: 'Wait till we've broken him, that's when the big fart'll go off. Though it'll be unlucky for some. Gust, for instance.'

'Don't worry about what's expendable,' Draper advised him.

'Me?' said Sladden, crestfallen. 'No one ever accused me of doing that before.' He pointed the camera in Gatov's direction. 'Turn your face to the camera, dickhead, that's better. There, what a sequence, beautiful.'

'There's nothing heroic about Gust,' said Draper, 'so just film and keep your mouth shut. You're worse than an old virgin with a fuck on her conscience.'

'That burberry he's wearing doesn't help him,' Ricky commented. He stared at Gatov isolated on the wrong side of the barrier with a copper each side of him. 'What he should have done was look inconspicuous.'

'He's too high and mighty for that,' said Draper. 'He thinks he's fireproof.' He whistled at the passport officer: 'We'll let him go through now.'

The passport officer let Gatov stew until all the other passengers had gone; then he beckoned him over.

'Staying long?'

'A week.'

'Pleasure?'

'Pleasure, also business.'

'What sort of business?'

'Personal business,' said Gatov. But his voice didn't carry its old conviction; it was the voice of someone who realised something had gone badly wrong. Gatov knew all about making things go wrong; no one knew better than he did how wrong things could be made to go.

'Look at that bloody chin of his flying up again,' Sladden was saying. 'I tell you, he's like a racehorse; he'll be foaming at the mouth next. They must've put the wrong bit on him, he's too high-strung by half. Jumpy little sod, you wouldn't get my money on him.'

The passport officer finally okayed Gatov's passport and was handing it back to him. Draper said: 'Right then, let's do it.' He dropped his Westminster, and they followed Gatov as he made for the exit. They drew level with him halfway across the concourse and waited till he was in a space clear of people; then they surrounded him like a welcoming committee, which in a way of course they were.

'Well here you are at last, Yuri my old son,' Draper said. 'Had a good flight? No point your putting that passport away, I'll have it. It belongs to us anyhow. I see it's made out to a Mr Gregory, but never mind, Yuri'll do.'

'Who are you?' Gatov shouted, only his words didn't carry because the three men, smelling of tobacco, chewing gum and the Underground, pressed him against them tight, stifling his voice in their stomachs. In fact his face was jammed into their bodies so hard that his hat fell off.

Sladden kicked it out of the way.

'Anything wrong here?' inquired a young priest who was walking swiftly past. He stopped, picked the hat up and offered it to Sladden. His face was that of a compassionate man ever alive to our suffering human condition, but he was also in a hurry.

'No,' said Sladden. He dropped the hat and trod on it. 'But that could suddenly change, so keep moving.' The young man coughed, blushed, looped up his cassock and very sensibly strode on without looking back.

'Holy busybodies,' said Sladden. 'I shit 'em, they're as bad as the clerks.'

Meantime the process of stripping Gatov had begun; besides his hat he had already lost the contents of his pockets, jacket and burberry. His shirt had been ripped open to the waist; he had been felt, palmed, squeezed and poked all over. Sladden specially enjoyed the game; he even got his hand down the back of Gatov's trousers and stuck his finger up his fundament.

It was all over in less than a minute.

'And so, Yuri, welcome to sunny Britain,' said Draper. 'You're in for a long stay. This all the luggage you've got?'

Gatov pointed at his briefcase, which was under Ricky's foot. He hadn't got to grips with his situation yet; he even managed to crack a joke. 'Sure! How do you say here, he travels fastest who travels light.'

'That's right,' said Draper, 'but what happens if he hasn't any legs?' They formed a phalanx round him and propelled him towards the back of the concourse.

'Where are you taking me?' Gatov asked. 'I don't want any problems.'

'You won't have any,' Draper said. 'Your problems are over, Yuri. When you're finished with us you're going to make a field study of the British people, the part of it the tourist never meets. You'll be off on a minimum thirty-year trip to Parkhurst in the sunny south, my old darling, what's the problem about that? It's lovely, it's bracing, it's near the sea. They say you can watch the yacht race while you're painting motorway signs – you'll have a terrific time.'

'This is crazy,' said Gatov, 'it's like a bad dream.'

'You know just what kind of a dream it is, Yuri,' Draper said. 'You've been responsible for them often enough.'

Suddenly Gatov reverted to the hectoring bluster he had used on the customs officer. 'I insist on knowing who you are,' he shouted. 'You're new. I always deal with just the police. Are you police?'

'Not any more,' said Draper, 'we've moved on. We've graduated from being coppers, we've moved sideways, upwards.'

'Downwards, even,' Sladden added.

'I can see that,' Gatov said bitterly. 'Not even Russian police behave the way you do. It was the Met I always used to deal with.'

'I know,' said Draper, 'but that happy period has come to a sudden end.'

'I want to see your authority.'

'What people see depends on who they are,' Draper told him, 'and you aren't anybody.'

'I don't understand. Where are you taking me? Are you arresting me?'

'Arresting you?' said Draper. He sounded dumb-founded. 'How can I arrest you when you've dis-appeared?'

'Vanishing's the same as being as free as air,' Ricky said helpfully. 'It's the same as being dead, there's lots of advantages.'

'Billy and Dave could get me out of this,' said Gatov. 'Where are they? They off sick or something?'

'You mean Detective Inspector Holt and Sergeant Dickinson?' said Draper. 'They've anticipated their retirement; they've decided to take a long holiday, concentrate on the *actualitay*, if you know what I mean.'

'He means they've been suspended,' said Sladden.

Draper patted Gatov on the shoulder. 'Your nerves are in bad shape, Yuri, you need a long rest. You've been out on the town too much, making too much whoopee, knocking out too much money, there's been too much wining and dining, sex orgies and the rest of it. We're very puritanical here, you know. But never mind, that wickedness is all over now; they'll soon put the roses back in your cheeks at Parkhurst. Spartan diet, plenty of exercise, good company, morally uplifting; Lenin would approve. In fact I'll see if we can get you into B wing with the heavy mob.'

They doubled him down one empty corridor after another so fast that Gatov started to limp.

'Slow down, can't you?'

They didn't take any notice.

Gatov changed tack. 'Look, we ought to get to know each other better, we ought to have a good talk.'

'We're going to,' Draper said. 'We've got hundreds of things to talk about, Yuri. For instance, what about this republic you're setting up?'

'That's right,' Gatov said eagerly. 'I want to open up markets here. Trade. Buy and sell.'

'Buy and sell what?' said Draper.

'Consumer goods, you know. Vehicles, washing machines.'

'Washing machines?' Draper was laughing. 'You mean the kind you fire through a two hundred and fifty metre barrel?' Now everyone was laughing except Gatov. 'I'll tell you what, my old darling. We've got washing machines galore of our own, and what we'll do, we'll put you on one of our special hot spins; the shit'll come flying out of you. And even if you aren't cleanest clean first time round, we can always put you back in.'

'No, I want to cooperate. There are a lot of things you don't understand.'

'I know,' said Draper, 'and you're going to tell us all of them. And then when you've done that there's going to be a trial, and it's what you're going to say at that trial, that's what we're going to have a very long rabbit about.'

'Now listen,' said Gatov, 'my slogan's always the same, I'm ready to do business with anyone. There's plenty of money in this, so what does it matter if you people are brand new?'

'You're way off beam,' Draper told him. 'Everything in this deal's brand new except you; you're looking very tatty.'

'Even so,' said Sladden, 'it's nice to know you're loaded. You and I could hit the town and go mad on your lolly; I know a place in Soho that'd turn your wig grey.'

They stopped in front of a steel door marked Airport Police and Draper unlocked it. The door opened into an empty room painted apple-green. It wasn't much of a room. It was the sort of room where people waited to be told if it was cancer, but whatever scenes it might have witnessed had drained off into its featureless walls. A metal desk and two chrome chairs caught the sunlight filtering through the slatted plastic blinds, and that was it.

Sladden got hold of Gatov. 'I've got a surprise for you, Mary. I'm gay, I'm HIV positive and I want to have a look at your sunburnt Black Sea bollocks immediately,

so get into that room there. Look, I'll give you a hand.'
He did that, hard, and Gatov skidded down the room on
his hands and knees.

'You can't do this to me!' he shouted, picking himself
up.

'That's what all the villains say,' said Sladden. He
kicked Gatov's feet out from under him and he fell on
the floor again. It was a tiled cement floor, and this time
Gatov had the sense to stay there, hugging his kneecap.

'Why are you treating me like this?'

'I don't know really,' said Sladden. 'I just feel like it.'

'I'm ready to talk.'

Draper intervened. 'No, this can't be a quickie. We
want the full version and it's going to take weeks. You
know better than most how these things work, Yuri;
anyway, if you've forgotten you'll soon get the hang of it
again once you've been under the lights for a while. And
don't make a fuss. The more you moan the worse it'll get
– they're your own methods, you know.'

'Your methods, Yuri?' Ricky chipped in. 'You bet!
We've got film of you taken by your own staff jumping
up and down on people's bellies, screwing them doggy-
fashion in interrogation rooms. You're bi, aren't you?
Men, women and kids, you give them all the same
treatment, you're a real Romeo.'

'Search him again,' Draper said.

Sladden said to Ricky cheerfully as they got going:
'It's like playing the piano four-handed, Rawicz and
Landauer, isn't it?' Gatov's clothes flew off him like
leaves in an autumn gale. Ricky jabbed his fingers into
his liver and Gatov squealed.

'These two men you've lost, Yuri, what were you
going to do about that?' Draper said.

'I'm here to find out why they died, of course!' Gatov
shouted as they went over him. 'I want their bodies back.
I want to take them home.'

'I don't think any airline'll sell you a ticket now you've
got no passport,' Draper said.

'Stories about love and friendship are very romantic all the same, though,' said Sladden. 'They really get me going, Yuri. Why don't you tell me about it while we're having a screw, murmur it into my shell-like?' He put a huge arm round Gatov. 'I hope you don't catch anything.' He kissed him on the mouth. 'I know I shouldn't do this,' he told him, 'but it's no good, I've been going for advice about it for years. I'm not very pretty either, so I have to take what I can get, but the old zob, I just can't keep the thing buttoned up. It's probably how I got sick in the first place, kerbing round King's Cross.' He unzipped. 'So how would you like it, buttercup? You want to eat me? Look how big I am! Toothpaste fashion or the other way? I'm not fussy.' When he saw Sladden's dick Gatov shrieked, and it was true, thought Ricky, it did look iffy.

Gatov tried to break away from Sladden. He screamed at Draper: 'This man's an animal, get him off me!' but Draper shook his head.

'There's no controlling him at all when he's like this.'

Ricky watched Gatov yelp and gobble, Sladden encouraging him with a serene smile on his face, his vast hands clapped to the back of the Russian's balding head, watching Gatov work out what he would do to Sladden if it ever came round to his turn.

'Somebody take that denture out of his mouth by the way; it looks expensive, and I wouldn't want my Annie bitten in two.'

'That's right,' said Draper, 'and we ought to take a look in his mouth anyway.'

Ricky drew his pistol and put the barrel up against Gatov's teeth. 'Open. Come on, hurry up or I'll smash the lot in.' Gatov tried to say something, and Ricky used the pistol as a lever to open his mouth the rest of the way. He extracted the bridgework, probed around the real teeth with the point of his knife, examined the gums, and handed the bridgework to Draper. 'Nothing there,' he said. 'Beluga, toast, some beef and pork. Usual airline lunch except for a lot of Sladden.'

'Good,' said Draper. 'No capsules, we don't want him topping himself now, though I might try it if I were in his place.'

'I don't see what the fuss is about anyway,' Sladden said. 'Here I come.' He pushed Gatov's head down to his crotch. 'Come on, then, Mary, suck away. Oh dear oh dear, can't you do any better than that? I'm disappointed in you. Considering what you did to people when you'd got them under the cosh, I can't understand you turning up your nose like this; I thought you'd be longing for it.'

When Sladden had come he buttoned up while Gatov stood wiping the excess gear off his face; he looked crumpled.

Draper said: 'All right, Sladden, you've had your fun. Now, Yuri, you in a fit state to listen to me? These two men. You had them killed, we know that, you shouldn't have done that.'

'I don't know anything about it!' Gatov screamed.

'That's murder,' Draper continued. 'You can't get away with that here.'

'All I know is, they're dead,' Gatov shouted. 'It was in the papers.'

'We'll leave that for now. We've got all the time in the world. Next, what about this passport you were carrying? It's stolen, and that's a very serious offence, you realise that.' Draper walked backwards and forwards over Gatov's bare feet several times.

Ricky got bored. He picked up Gatov's briefcase, took it over to the window and turned it this way and that. It had a coded lock but that didn't bother him; he just carved into the leather with an American knife which leaves the blade in the body while the handle stays behind and gets back to work as a knuckleduster. He gave the papers in the briefcase to Draper, who stuffed them in his pocket. That left Ricky with nothing to do, so, as he had the knife out anyway, he went over to Gatov and slit the waistband of his trousers. 'Christ, did you see that? Went through that material like newspaper, and it's Harrods too. And look what he's got for undies!' He whistled. 'Black boxer shorts with his initials on.' He slit them down the front and the shorts fell off.

Without his teeth Gatov's face had fallen in, so that he looked pretty dead anyway. He tried to speak, but nothing emerged except a mumble.

'He can have this lot back now,' said Draper, giving Ricky the bridgework.

Gatov put his teeth back in. 'I want a lawyer.'

'How would he know where to find you?' said Draper.

'I've got rights!'

'The dead don't need those,' said Draper. 'So go on then, what happened to those passports? A thousand went missing.'

'You tell me! I've never heard of any passports. I never had them.'

'What do you mean you never had them?' said Ricky. 'You were the punter for them.'

'And we know where one of them went all right, Mary,' said Sladden. 'You've just travelled on it.'

'I don't know anything!'

'You know a man called Manny Farb?' said Draper. 'South London villain.'

'No.'

'We know you know him.'

'No.'

'Lenny Williams, calls himself the Hammer. You know him? You should do. He's one of your accomplices, works for Farb.'

'Never heard of him.'

'Harry Ford then.'

'I've never heard of him either. I've never met any of these people.'

'You're lying. What did you have to do with that hijack when the passports went missing?'

'Nothing! Sounds like petty crime. Why should I be interested in that?'

'But you admit that the passport you were carrying this afternoon was one of those passports? You admit you knew that?'

'I don't admit anything! I collected that passport in Moscow, bona fide.'

Draper sighed. 'We could go round the houses like this all day, Yuri. You're going to have to do much better than that.'

'Don't you worry,' said Sladden. 'I fancy him rotten. I've got the short cut to Yuri's arsehole and we're going to have hours and hours together in the sack. I'll give my little Mary singing lessons, I'll have her crooning like a little nightingale. You leave her to me, I like old bird.'

'Look,' said Gatov, 'let's behave like grown-ups. I don't need this hassle. I'm a businessman in a big way, I've got a lot of deals in the pipeline.'

'Don't choke on them, Yuri.'

'Now you've got a price, I've got the money.' There were traces of desperation in Gatov's voice. 'I've got a figure in my head right now, already. I always pay dollars. I can give you a lot of money straight away on account as soon as we get to London, so why don't we cooperate?'

'It hasn't sunk in yet, has it?' said Draper.

'What hasn't? There've been bent coppers before.'

'Yes, and look what happens to them. They wind up doing bird like your mates Holt and Dickinson.'

'You wouldn't be running any risk at all!'

Draper turned to Ricky. 'You got all this down on tape?'

'There are one or two things, maybe I'd better scrub them.'

'Why bother?' said Draper. 'The only people it'll upset will be the clerks at the MOD; and that way they'll get some idea of the horrible way we make a living.' He looked at his watch. 'OK, let's get him into the motor.

I'm tired of hanging around talking to this piece of shit. Where's that poxy driver?'

'You're down on me because I'm a Russian!' Gatov shouted. 'You're a racist!'

'Wrong,' said Draper. 'My attitude to the human race is dead simple. I divide it into people I like and people I don't like, and I don't like you which is your fucking bad luck.'

They doubled Gatov to a back exit from the terminal building, passing a few airport staff on the way, who turned to look back at the strange figure clutching at its waistband as it was rushed along barefoot.

On the way into London Gatov asked where they were going.

'Factory for a start,' said Sladden. 'Book you on a holding charge.'

'Factory?' said Gatov. 'What does that mean? Are they going to tin me?'

'You're spot on,' Sladden said. 'It's where they grind villains up for sausage-meat.'

'There must be a way out of this.'

'There was,' said Draper, 'but you missed it at Moscow airport.'

'There's going to be trouble when people find out what's happened to me.'

'Well, it's trouble you won't be in, Yuri,' said Draper. 'You'll be in a cell.'

'And you'll be about ninety when you leave it,' added Sladden.

'I thought Britain was a democratic country.'

'Democracy these days is just a show,' Draper told him. 'Something people go and watch on a stage, period stuff. Up in the West End people pay thirty quid for a seat, but they put on some good productions at Park-hurst twice a year for nothing, so you won't miss out. Homegrown productions of Ray's A Laugh, stuff like that – you'll split your sides.'

They passed the Guinness brewery at Park Royal.

Sladden eyed it longingly. 'Now there's a factory I could do with. Every time I set eyes on that place it gives me a thirst. Christ, I could murder a pint.'

'You drink too much, Sladden,' Draper said. 'I'm always telling you.'

8

Round about midnight two men, one tall and one short, came into Marly's club, looked around, then came and stood up against Gust at the bar as close as they could get, one on each side. The place was packed, and after a while they started talking across him, taking the piss, laughing at him as if his cock was hanging out or something. It was a night when Gust didn't want any aggro, because he had a lot to think about, so he paid no attention to the men, which got them choked; finally the shorter man gave him a shove. Whether the shove was intentional or just the effect of drunken dancers bumping around, Gust wasn't sure. He took a good look at the man, whereupon they both turned their backs on him, but not in a way that indicated they were bothered at all.

It was their lookout, but Gust reckoned that in their place he would have been seriously bothered, even though they looked heavy. The taller man had red hair, acne, a love/hate tattoo on the knuckles of his left hand, and an open eye weeping a tear of blood on the back of his right; the shorter one had thick brown hair, prominent front teeth and eyebrows that met across the bridge of his nose like Rudolf Hess. They both wore jeans and trainers that were not exactly on their first lap round the track and Gust had never seen either of them before; the only thing he felt sure of was that they had both done bird.

Redhead turned towards Gust and shoved him again. 'You Gust?'

'That's me. What about it?'

'Well, it's like this. It's nothing personal. We'd like to let you live if we could, only we can't, so instead we're going to give you a terrific beating, see; then we're going to take you outside round the back and kill you, would you believe?'

'Is that right?'

'Yeah, that's right.'

'Someone's in for a rough ride then, because I just don't feel like dying tonight.'

'Tough,' said Rudolf Hess.

'Well, OK,' said Gust, 'have a go if you want it that bad. It'll be cheaper than a work-out at the gym.'

He didn't move, except to put down his glass. He waited to see what the others did, in case they made a mistake. In any case there was no room to move; people were squashed against them watching the dancers, and the singer was punishing the mike so hard that you couldn't have heard a lion roar a foot away.

Rudy put his lips to Gust's ear. 'Pain,' he whispered. 'You got any idea what pain is?'

'You bet,' said Gust. 'It hangs around too long the way you do.'

Redhead stared at Gust, astonished, and a reverent look came over him. 'You've just asked to be taken apart,' he whispered. 'Massacred.' He had eyes the colour of old shit.

Meantime the place was hotting up still further. Marly was singing now. Two trannies up on the stage were having a cuddle by the gold tinsel curtain behind the piano and some tourist who didn't know any better photographed them; the flash and an asti spumante cork popped together. A minder came over and ripped the film out of the camera; they didn't like photography in there.

Marly was drunk. The song he was belting out chain-sawed through the crowd, and when he had finished it he sat down hard and went to sleep. Some punter on a trip got the block put on him at the door and burst into tears on a bouncer's chest; outside a squad car shot a set of lights with its siren going. The Colombian dealer with the Rolex and thousand-pound suit left suddenly with his driver and the scene was set; the music was tuned all the way up for trouble.

Just then the phone on the bar rang. A waiter naked except for a pink apron and high heels scooped it up and stood on tiptoe, looking inquiringly over the massed heads. 'Chris?' he piped, 'anybody here called Chris? Phone call for Chris.' No one wanted to know, so he banged down the phone and confided to an old queen nearby, 'My voice, this sort of work's killing it. My voice is the same as it was when I was ten, did I ever tell you? Did you know it's never broken?'

'Working in here'll break your heart, darling,' said the old hasbeen, stroking a beard the colour of ginger ale, 'never mind your bleeding voice.'

'You doing this for money?' Gust asked Redhead. 'Yeah. Well, I'd charge plenty then if I were you, and make sure your insurance policy's well up to date with a clause for funeral expenses. Your girlfriend'll find it was money well spent.'

'It's not just money,' said Rudolf Hess. 'I get my jollies off and this is a knife, see?' It certainly was, a flick knife at that, and it was pricking a point right on top of Gust's liver.

'OK,' said Gust. 'Well, I'll just go to the karzy first. I read somewhere it's unhealthy, dying with a full blad-der.'

'No you won't,' Redhead snapped.

Gust decided to get down to specifics. 'Has this stupid scenario got anything to do with a delivery of docu-ments? Such as little brown books?'

They didn't say it hadn't.

'I don't know what the fuss is about,' Gust complained. 'The gear was all delivered.'

'No it wasn't,' said Rudy. 'And that's the trouble.'

Gust thought of him as Rudy because of his eyebrows.

Redhead was getting impatient. 'Why bother rabbiting on anyway, let's just do it.' He sneered at Gust. 'At least you'll die with money on you. We know you're running around with a load of it, and that's our wages you've got there. So you won't mind when we whizz it, will you, because you'll be brown bread by then anyway.'

A girl from the Tiara patted Gust's shoulder as she went by. 'Hi, Gust, how are you?'

'Terrific,' said Gust. He came in on Rudy suddenly; ducking straight under the knife. He stamped on Rudy's foot, bringing his metal-tipped heel down on the arch, and wasn't it lucky Rudy enjoyed pain so much, because here he was getting as much of it as he could possibly want.

'You can't run away now, can you?' said Gust. He smiled and stamped on Rudy's other instep. Rudy went floorwards squealing like a badly felled tree and dropped the knife. Gust kicked it across the dance floor while Rudy fell on the floor howling and clutching his feet.

Redhead tried to bust him with a right but Gust blocked it, kicked him on the tibia and heard it snap.

'What you want to do when you get out of hospital,' Gust told him, 'is get properly shod. I know a place.'

Redhead had dropped to one knee in front of Gust like a suitor in a Restoration play. His lips were parted, he gazed up at him as if in adoration; then, as the pain bit into his leg his expression changed to the sneer of a poisoner asking the post office about his victim's mail.

'I somehow knew you and Rudy were no good at this,' said Gust, looking down at the short man. 'They ought to have sent someone heavy.' He thought the short man really could have got a job playing Hess in this new TV war series they were doing, and he would have had a word with a director he knew if Rudy had been a mate of his. But, as he wasn't, Gust kicked him in the stomach as he tried to drag himself up with the help of the bar-rail; then he turned to have a look at Redhead.

'How are you doing then, sweetheart?' he said to him. 'Kosher?' He took one of the man's ears in his thumb and forefinger. The ear was small considering the size of his head; it had little hairs inside and it was dirty. Gust found a used cocktail stick in a glass on the bar and jammed it into the eardrum as far as it would go. When he pulled the stick out again it was red, except that up at the end there was some grey stuff there as well. He shouted: 'I think I just broke your leg!' But Redhead had his hand clapped to the side of his head. He was dribbling, swinging up and down from the waist. He wasn't making sense any more; he was just crooning.

Or maybe the music was too loud.

Redhead fell on the floor. He made no sign of getting up, and Gust knew he had put the stick in too far.

Now Rudy tried a new stroke. Although he only had one hand free because he was using the other to hang onto the bar-rail, he smashed a glass.

'No no, Rudy,' said Gust, 'not that way.' He stopped the glass on his forearm and stamped on the man's right foot again. This time he definitely felt the bones go; Rudy screamed and let go of the rail. But instead of letting him fall Gust took him round the waist, ripped his fly open and searched inside his knickers till he found his testicles, which he yanked out into his hand. They smelled fetid, like left-overs from a canteen lunch, but Gust wrung them like the devil having a go at a set of wedding bells all the same until Rudy was shrieking on the same D minor as the music.

'As you said, Rudy, it's nothing personal,' Gust told him, 'but I'm afraid you're going to have to learn to fuck all over again.' He pulled Rudy's face towards him and drove his nose in with a Glasgow kiss. The music boosted into E major on a key change and Rudy doubled up under a bar stool.

'Buy yourselves a drink now why don't you?' said Gust, moving away. 'Enjoy.'

The waiter whose voice wouldn't break rushed up, holding his apron to his mouth. 'Oh!' he shrieked. 'Oh my God!' That was all he did but at least it was something; nobody else did anything at all.

'Don't break your heart over them, Daphne,' Gust told him. 'They just won't be wanting the other half that's all, maybe a minicab.'

'A hearse more like,' the waiter sobbed. 'I saw you!'

Gust prodded him in the chest. 'You watch that little tongue of yours, Daphne,' he said coldly, 'you didn't see anything, isn't that right?'

'I faint at the sight of blood!' the waiter moaned.

'As long as it isn't your own,' said Gust, 'you can count your fucking blessings.'

The waiter's friend appeared just then and took his hand; they disappeared sobbing through the staff door.

Rudy had managed to sit up meanwhile with his back against the bar. He had got one of his trainers off and sat alternately holding each of his feet in both hands. Gust could have told him that taking the trainer off was a silly thing to do if he meant to try and hobble away. He would never get it back on again; both his feet were fractured.

The manager arrived; Gust used to bounce for him. 'What's going on?' he asked. 'Trouble?'

'I don't think you'll get any more now,' said Gust. 'Not from them, anyway.'

The manager looked briefly at the two men. 'I don't know either of them. How did they get in here?'

'Don't ask me, I've never seen them before.'

'You see what happened?'

'No, wish I had, but it looks like they really had it in for each other.'

'It's just a fight. These cunts get tanked up and can't

hold it. I'll clear them away later, who gives a shit, anyway?'

'That's right. By the way, you've got a waiter crying his heart out in the rest-room. He's got a rather hysterical outlook on life, thin and a treble squeak for a voice, net stockings and a pink apron.' Gust slipped the manager a fifty. 'I'd just have a word before he makes a silly phone call.'

'Sure.' The manager took the money. 'I'll deal with it.' He went back to his table where he was drinking iced champagne with friends and playing hi-low.

The law arrived latish and looking relaxed, because Marly saw to them every month sharp on the thirtieth. But Gust made for the exit just the same, pushing through indignant dancing couples. 'Sorry,' he muttered, 'just need some fresh air, feeling a bit sickish.' That parted them like the waters of the Nile.

As he left, Marly waved to him across his vodka. 'You leaving, Gust? Stay for a last one.'

Gust shook his head. 'No, not tonight. Maybe tomorrow. Incidentally, I haven't been in tonight, Marly.'

'No that's right,' Marly agreed. 'I've not seen you.'

'Anyway you've got visitors.' Gust nodded at the law marching three-handed towards the bodies on the floor.

'Shit,' said Marly, 'some twat must have belled them, and it's that inspector too, not my nice Sergeant Rawlings. Well, goodnight, then.'

'Night,' said Gust. He left surrounded by nine or ten other people, and seeing that he'd just been with Marly the law didn't say anything.

It was two-thirty when he got outside. The bitter rain was dying out, foxtrotting round the corner into Brewer Street, the wind that carried it making the dead leaves patter with a noise like a last friend running for a cab.

He ended up at the stop in Regent Street, but no night buses came, nor did a taxi. Besides, Allison Road was out, so that he didn't even know where he wanted to go, except away from where he was. It was bitterly cold. An old woman wearing two overcoats dozed on the pavement, surrounded by Waitrose bags, and another woman, fat, about forty, went past raving, shaking her fist and spitting on the walls. *She's on crack, she'll wind up in the hard place*, Gust thought absently. His knuckles were sore after the fight and he sucked them, leaning against the bus stop and watching the street bend away northwards like an icy scimitar towards Oxford Circus, its edge serrated by an endless row of to let signs, all part of the government's green shoots.

The sound of running steps echoed in the silent streets and Gust wondered if the two men in Marly's had any back-up. A man shouted in the distance, there was a pause, then a woman screamed abuse. Presently it began to rain again, the scattered drops smarting with the sting of ice.

He had to move, but all he had on him were half ton notes, seventeen thousand quid's worth, and he didn't see how, even if a bus did come, he could pay the fare and expect change on a near empty vehicle. He hadn't anything small on him except for a single pound coin; he had knocked all his change out at Marly's. He separated a fifty out all the same, then decided against using it; the note would only help the driver remember him.

And that was the last thing he wanted. What he wanted just then was to be forgotten, ignored, to go unnoticed as if he had never lived, never been seen or heard of, never existed.

9

Gust went round to Harry Ford's and banged on the door.'Hey! It's me! he shouted, then muttered under his breath, 'Come on, fuck you.' There was no answer, though he was bloody sure Ford was in there. But Harry always looked after himself. He never liked answering the door at night; he was afraid it might be the bookie's man or that he might find himself being pushed upstairs by some maniac with a sawn-off.

Like a good many other people, Gust had never thought much of Harry.

In the end he gave up knocking and went round to the call boxes in the avenue, getting a fifty-p piece off a tramp in return for the pound coin BT wouldn't take. The tramp couldn't believe it. 'Fifty p for a quid? It don't add up.'

'No, it's your lucky night,' said Gust. He dived into the booth, slamming the door and holding it shut with his foot. He dialled Harry's number and it rang for a long time before it answered.

When it did Gust said furiously, 'It's me, Gust. That was me banging on your door just now; why the fuck didn't you open up?'

'How did I know it was you? And you're not supposed to be ringing me anyway, have you gone mad?'

'I've got nowhere to go, that's why I'm ringing. I need

to spend the night, the floor'd do.'

'You can't stay here,' Ford shouted. 'Clarice wouldn't stand for it. What's the matter with your place?'

'I can't go back there, it's being watched. Something's gone wrong, fuck knows what. Anyway I've got to clean up, get my head down.'

'How do you know something's gone wrong?'

'Because two men in Marly's tried to kill me an hour ago. But there's more to it than that. There's all sorts after me.'

'Why?'

'The men just now said they hadn't got the merchandise. That's one reason.'

'That's impossible.'

'Whether or not, that's what they said.'

'Well, you've been paid, anyway, so what's your beef?'

'I don't like people trying to kill me, Harry, that's my beef.'

'How do you know they're not lying about the merchandise?'

'Don't be stupid,' said Gust. 'Nobody sends the wrong half of London after you for no reason.'

'Well, as far as I'm concerned everything's kosher. If anything's gone wrong it's not down to me.'

'Listen, it isn't a case of who it's down to, it's a case of people trying to knock me off. Now come on. I can't stay here all night, the money's running out, so let me in.'

'Sorry, no can.'

'Now look, I've just had one fight and while I'm not greedy for another I'm telling you, either I get you in your listening mode or I'll come round and smash your door down and your fucking face in. So which is it going to be, Harry? How do you want your head, on or off?'

'You're crazy. You could get us both nicked.'

'Right now that would suit me. Right now buttons and a foot of cement between these folk and me would be good news; it'd feel a fucking sight safer than the street. And I'll make sure you come with me. I mean it, Harry.'

'All right, then,' Harry said grudgingly, 'you'd better come round.'

'That's better. At last.'

When Harry let Gust in he was barefoot with just a shirt on, and Gust thought no one had ever been less pleased to see him. Harry looked big out in the street with his smart clothes on, he looked and came on tough; but without them he looked like a bass drum balanced on a couple of sticks. He met Gust at the door and led him into the sitting room, where there was a single light on. Ford sat on the edge of the sofa and Gust pulled up some kind of sagging throne in the corner.

'Easy with that,' said Harry, 'it's got a theatrical past.'

'Really?' said Gust. 'Well it's got a broken leg now, it only runs to act three.'

'Keep your voice down,' Harry muttered. He spoke in a hissing voice like a leaky water pump, intended not to wake Clarice next door. 'She goes bananas if she's woken from her deep sleep, and that's now.'

'OK, then find me a drink, maybe that'll keep me quiet, but I'm not promising.'

'There isn't any drink, and listen, you're not even supposed to be here. If what you're saying is true these people who are after you could be after me.'

'And you wouldn't like that, would you?'

'Who fucking would?'

'So now you know how I feel.'

Gust thought Harry looked even more frightened than usual and wondered why. He had come a long way down from the confident manner he had worn the day in Manny's flat when he had sat next to the Hammer while Manny put the deal; already that seemed a long time ago. Gust had watched Harry through the cigarette smoke that afternoon and thought, *You've got no bottle, you never had*. At the time it hadn't seemed to matter, Harry was just the go-between. But now that the deal had gone sour everything suddenly mattered.

'I'll have to sleep here for tonight,' Gust said.

'I told you, no way.'

'I've got nowhere else to go and look at the time, it's gone three. What do you expect me to do? Sleep rough?'

'Why not? You've done it before often enough. Anyhow, you're one of those people, you only come on tough when things are going your way.'

Gust kept his temper. 'These people aren't after you, Harry,' he said patiently, 'they're after me. It's not your life on the line.'

Harry yawned. 'Well, the lord giveth, the lord bleeding well taketh away. Anyway, Clarice'll be wondering what I'm doing and I don't know about you, but I'm going to get my head down.'

'Look, just because you've made some money, Harry, it doesn't mean you have to float off the edge of the planet; you're losing your sense of values.' Gust still spoke in a soft reasonable tone; indeed Harry had never heard him use any other tone, but he must have noticed some change in him all the same because he started paying more attention. 'For the last time, Harry, I need to sleep on your floor.'

'No,' said Harry. 'I keep telling you, it isn't safe.' Gust didn't respond. 'What's the matter? What are you looking at me like that for?'

'I wasn't looking through you, not at you,' said Gust. 'I was just thinking what a wanker you are, and asking myself why you remind me of a sheet of wet newspaper that's been used on somebody's arse. I know we're on the same side of course, don't I?' He paused. 'I think I know that, don't I, Harry? I *do* know that, Harry, don't I?'

'Know it? Course you do!'

'Well then, don't be deliberate.'

'Course you know it!'

'You wouldn't grass me to anyone, would you, Harry? Would you? Would you ever do that, Harry?'

'No!'

'No. You wouldn't, and you haven't, Harry, have you?'

Harry went white. 'Has anybody said I'd grassed you? I'll kill the bastard!'

'No,' said Gust, 'nobody's said that. It's more a matter of my making up my own mind.'

'Grass you? That's a fucking lunatic idea! Christ, no!'

'Good. That's very good. It's good to know I'm working wih a mate, good to know you're straight up, Harry, twenty-four, a diamond, because if not, you see these hands, they're friendly hands right now, but they do terrible things to people when they're not.'

'I know that,' Harry whispered hoarsely, 'course I do. Shit, I've seen you go over the top.'

'Of course you have, so you remember how it was for the other feller. And it cuts both ways, of course. I'd have looked after you if it was you that was in shtuck.'

'There's no need to go on about it,' said Harry. He grinned suddenly. It looked as if the weak were about to rebel.

'What are you grinning for?' said Gust. 'Had a happy thought?'

'Yes. I was just thinking that at least I've come sunny side out of this even if you haven't; still, that's the luck of the draw.'

Gust said in the same even tone, 'You've got a lot to learn, Harry.'

'You should have done your own learning maybe,' Harry retorted. 'You've had plenty of porridge to do it in. Anyway, at least you've got money.'

'Banknotes aren't bullet-proof,' said Gust. He stood up. 'Talk about learning, Harry, I've learned that much.'

Harry went to the door and opened it.

'So that's it,' said Gust. 'You're throwing me out. You're saying I can't even clean up and kip down here for a couple of hours.'

'That's it,' said Harry. He put his finger to his lips.

'Now for Christ's sake leave quietly on account of Clarice.'

'I don't believe this,' said Gust. 'I just don't. It must mean there's someone around who frightens you even more than I do.'

That was true enough; Harry was much more frightened of Sladden than he was of Gust. But he felt brave now that Gust was at the open door. 'I'll tell you what you can do, Gust,' he said, 'if you want my advice.'

'Yes, you bet I'd like that. I can't wait for the info from the man who knows it all, Harry.'

'What you can do is run. Start running now, keep going, and don't come near me again, ever. Understand? Now piss off.'

'All right,' said Gust. 'I've got it. Thanks, Harry. As I say, what it is to have a mate.'

He went out on the landing and Harry looked happier still, really bold. He made to pat Gust on the back. 'So look,' he said, 'so it went wrong, you'll get over it, just don't worry too much.'

'No, you're right, I won't waste my time doing that. Instead, what I'll do, I'll give you a tip, Harry.'

'I don't want any tips. All I want to do is get back to bed.'

'Well take this with you,' said Gust. He smacked him in the face hard with the flat of a hand about as yielding as a cricket bat. 'That's just a warning. That's how it goes when you let a man down, my old son, now make sure it's a lesson that stays in your head. Goodnight and sweet dreams.'

Harry stumbled back into the flat, holding his head and shaking it, then slammed the door. Gust stood there on the landing, listening to Harry going back into the bedroom and shutting that door as well, as if that would somehow keep him safer. He wondered if Harry had ever found out about him and Clarice in the old days; he hoped so.

The timer on the landing light snapped out as he went downstairs. Guided by the gleam from the fanlight, he went out into the street. Round the corner the Dial Club was still open; at the entrance lights flitted round the neon dial over the shapes of a bare woman, a life-size poster of a girl in a black bra with her thighs spread at twenty to four, and Gust made for it. He felt that she had probably never indulged in romantic dreams; she would have come down from the north at fourteen in laddered tights and gone straight to work. Trouble was no mere bad dream once you were in it, and it came naturally to those who had nothing else on tap. Trouble had the condensed reality of a nightmare, and the real nightmares were the ones that came for you when you were awake.

The girl he was really thinking about was Petal. In the months he had been out he hadn't seen her yet, and couldn't make up his mind whether or not to bring the pain back and try. *No pleasure without pain, Petal. Do you ever think of me?*

But he had been away a long time.

Some of the bouncers in the Dial still knew him, though. He had worked with them in the past between jobs, and the girl who was singing put the mike down amazed and left the piano when she saw him come in; so it seemed she remembered him too.

'Hullo, Lynn.'

'Have a drink,' she said. 'I'm buying.'

He shook his head. 'Not tonight. I've got things to think about.'

'Pleasant?'

'No. A little treachery somewhere.'

'It goes with the lifestyle,' she said. 'Tell me if you change your mind. Any time.'

He bought her a bottle of champagne, a Scotch for himself. 'Go back and sing,' he said. 'Sing "Just One More Chance".

'Sing that.'

She talked to the pianist, who gave her the opening bars, and something came over him as she went into the song that made him feel about ninety years old.

He worked out why at the bar, over his whisky: right tune, wrong girl.

10

He slept in Soho Square for a few hours during the morning, then had breakfast at Valerie's and crossed the street to a pub called the Flower, where he thought he might find Sholly. But before he could get inside the pub a man in a bomber jacket and a head like a forty-watt bulb came running after him.

'Hey! You!'

Gust turned round. 'You shouting at me?'

'Yes,' said the individual. 'I'm Pacey, detective constable.'

'Oh yes?' said Gust, 'I thought you were the dustman, let's see your card.' He read it over. 'All right, get this straight right away. I don't like people running around shouting at me like that in the street unless it's a mate, I'm liable to go completely cyclonic, OK? Now, what do you want?'

'I'm from Poland Street; there was a fight down at Marly's last night, did you hear about it?'

'No.'

'Well it was pretty bad. There were three fellers involved, and there's an idea going round that you were one of them.'

'I see, an idea. Why me?'

'There were people in the place said you were there at the time and that you knew about it. Well, do you?'

'People are always asking me if I know about things, like have I got the Queen's phone number. What people, anyway? You got any statements? Witnesses?'

'No one who's prepared to go into court, no.'

'Well you'd better dig some up, hadn't you?' said Gust. 'Till then, bye-bye.' He turned back to the pub.

'Wait a minute. I'm still asking you if you knew about it, that's what I'm doing.'

'No,' said Gust, 'I'll tell you what you're doing. What you're doing is just making aggro, picking on me because I'm an ex-con out on licence. What you're thinking is, I'm the smart young copper from the arsehole of nowhere come down to the smoke, and I wonder if I can't just fit this individual up for something that'll put him back in the nick because here he is as handy as a dish-rag, and the answer is it'll take a lot more than that, sweetheart, and no you fucking can't.'

'I wouldn't even be bothering with someone like you if I hadn't been talking to people at Marly's. You're not someone I'd ever talk to from choice.'

'Well that goes double for me,' said Gust, 'and I'll tell you this. It sticks out a mile that they've only just let you out on the street round here. You're a half-wide mug, you don't know Greek Street from your left bollock yet.'

'You watch yourself,' said Pacey, 'I'm doing my job.'

'That's not a job, that's just wasting public money. What you call a job is listening to some pisspot who's talked to another pisspot who's talked to ten more pisspots about some fight, so you chase down to Marly's, pop your head round the door, tell everyone you're a copper, as if they were likely to take you for anything else, and then you listen to a load of crap, and if you call that a job why have we got unemployment here? I'm mystified.'

'Your name came up.'

'It's always doing that. So it's happened again and so straight off you're saying I was in Marly's last night, fighting? You'll have to be able to prove that.'

'I'm not saying anybody said that outright, though it's true I'm looking at the state of your knuckles, which of course you cut opening a tin of beans.'

'Thanks for the line, but in fact I got them caught in the street door.'

'What they said was that you're one of the few people round here capable of beating up two men that bad.'

'That's not the same thing, is it?' said Gust. 'As your governors will very quickly tell you, never mind a lawyer, so don't try and improve on your arrest record this time, give it a day off.'

'Talking of records,' said Pacey, 'there's yours.'

'It's what I'm saying, the ex-con automatically gets the winning ticket. And is that all you've got? Go away, you've got a fucking nerve even talking to me, you haven't a leg.'

'These various people said they thought they might have seen the three of you talking up at the bar together, it was kind of animated.'

'Thought they might have seen, and that's it, is it? You listen to crap like that and then come straight round looking for me? That's very bold, that is, in fact it's dead cheeky.'

'I can make life oh so hard for you, Gust.'

'Don't you threaten me. Instead of bothering me, why don't you go off and find out if they didn't do it to each other, which sounds likely. Or better still, go and tell some Japanese tourists the way to Piccadilly Circus. Or else get your knees brown round here; then you'd find that people say lots of things, and would you believe, it turns out in the end they never saw a dicky-bird and what's more they will stand up in court and deny having said anything like what you thought they'd said. Particularly in Soho. Anyway, sounds as if it must have been a busy night down at Marly's.'

'I suppose you were in bed at the time, reading and watching the telly.'

'No I wasn't, though what business it is of yours I

don't know. However, I hadn't thought of that, being in bed, but why not? Sounds like a good idea. Or else maybe I was right the other side of London stoking the boiler.'

'Stoking the boiler?'

'I reckon you being married, living out in the sticks with two kids, you wouldn't know what stoking the boiler means.'

'Well, whatever it means, reading and stoking boilers isn't what these people say you were doing.'

'I keep asking you, are they going to stand up in court and say what they think I was doing?'

'I've told you no. They didn't say they were going to do that.'

'Good, because it doesn't sound to me as if they're going to say anything, and why should they, since the only thing any of them probably saw was pink elephants? Now listen, you people are undermanned and under-paid and you've got serious villains to run after, so I'm surprised you're not doing something about that right this minute instead of wasting public time on me. You coppers come expensive, do you know that? Have you any idea how much an hour you cost the taxpayer?'

'Don't start because I haven't finished,' said Pacey. 'One of the men involved finished up with a hole through his eardrum into his brain, also a fractured tibia; the other one's bollocks are up the spout and he'll never walk straight again, he had the arches of both his feet smashed.'

'His shoes must have been too small for him, but I don't see why I have to do porridge for it.'

'It's not just that. The fractures are one thing, that's only GBH, carries next to nothing these days, but the man who got the hole up his ear, he's dead, so someone's going to be done for murder.'

'I should hope so too. Whoever did a thing like that must be really sick, so if you can catch him, get at it, it's disgusting. Hole in his ear, you say? How did that happen? Someone have a gun?'

'No, it was done with a cocktail stick.'

'A what? For fuck's sake!' Gust started laughing. 'I'm sorry, but I can't help it. A cocktail stick? You mean one of those things you eat little bangers off?'

'It's nothing to laugh about.'

'Well it is. I mean just look at me. So what was it down to, after all? A couple of brown-hatters having a spat?'

'I tell you there were three of them,' said Pacey, 'and you should have seen how far that stick went in.'

'Maybe it was down to politics. The whole country's very uptight just now, I suppose even you read the Sun or something from time to time. It was probably fans of Woolly John and Duggie Turd discussing government policy on a night out with too many gins and naked male waiters in frilly aprons around, it must've gone to their heads. Look, I'm practically doing your work for you.'

'They were a couple of heavies from out of town.'

'There's people going around calling themselves heavies who'd be better off in carpet slippers making mum a cup of cocoa.'

'It's still murder,' said Pacey, 'and don't take the piss.'

'Well, you know the answer to that. If you don't want the urine extracted out of you, my old darling, don't offer your cock around all over town.'

'Easy. People don't talk to me like that, and you've not got that many friends that you need enemies, especially not us.'

'I don't know. There was a detective-constable about your age up for murder just the other day, strangled a pregnant woman behind a supermarket. Still, lend me five ton if you like to show you're honest, then you'll be halfway to being my mate.'

'There was a flick knife found on the floor afterwards when they were sweeping up. Over the other side of the premises from where the fight was.'

'Someone probably had the sense to kick it out of the

way, and as long as it was found on the floor and not in someone's belly it didn't do any harm, did it?'

'It's still an illegal weapon.'

'You'd better find out who it belongs to, then. You get any prints off it?'

'Only off the man it belonged to.'

'Well that wasn't much of a result then, was it?' said Gust. He looked up at the clock on St Anne's tower. 'Anyway, I've got to wander.'

'You can't help me with this at all, then?'

'No, I can't, and the way you tell it I won't be the only one.'

'If you hear anything.'

'Yeah, but I never do, because I never listen, which is good advice round here.'

'Where are you living right now incidentally?'

'Wherever my probation officer says I'm living. Ask him.'

'Where did you spend last night, for instance?'

'Doorway of a bookshop in Charing Cross Road, full of horror stories. Well out of the rain, found a nice cardboard box, good kip once I'd cleared away the beer cans and what else do you want to fucking know?'

'A lot,' said Pacey, 'it's all too pat.'

'Pick a hole in it then,' said Gust, 'only do it in your time, not mine, I'll catch you again.'

He pushed through the door into the pub, and Pacey didn't follow. Sholly wasn't in there but Gust bought a pint just the same and after a while one of the barmen came over and gave him a note. Gust opened the envelope and read the scrawl:

Wait while I get out of this hospital you bastard you reckon yourself as an amateur prize-fighter, you had a few drinks and killed my mate, I no all about you, you killed my friend what were you doing anyway you bastard you wont get away with that again you dirty low bred scum they make you out a Hero *on the manor do me a favour place your head in a gas oven or jump under a Heavy Vehicle you and your halfbred Chinese-puzzle girlfriend I pray for your death you bastard you will not go to that club in a Hurry again they should have EXECUTED you you scum when you read this you'll laugh you are on the spot you'll die soon.*

He put a match to the paper and watched it burn.

11

When Gust left the pub it was late afternoon and he walked north up Dean Street to the Tiara Club still looking for Sholly. Sholly was there all right at a corner table, and Gust gripped him by the shoulder inside the fur coat he wore that gave his shoulder a greasy feel like cold lamb. Sholly jumped.

'No need to do that,' Gust whispered in his ear. 'It would've been a jump too late if I'd meant it.'

Sholly was no hero. Nobody even knew if Sholly was his right name. It sounded something vaguely like that, and it went with the endless deals he conducted in bars with his fur collar turned up, even in hot weather. He wasn't forty yet, but with his past he could never have looked anything but old, and he didn't. When he first appeared on the manor years back he used to work Soho for the KGB in return for a resident's visa and a few quid a week, though he had been so badly trained in Smolensk that he couldn't tell a gay MOD clerk with revolutionary ideas from a life peer on a night out. He was so fake that he even told people he played cricket, adding that he had been a colonel after his eleventh pint. But now that the USSR was no more he had gone into business for himself, there being no other business.

'What do you want?'

'A gun, of course,' said Gust, 'what did you think I

wanted, your address book? I want something small, no rubbish and none of your nine millimetre Russian cannons, I don't want to bring the chandeliers down.'

'A twenty-five, then.'

'No, not a twenty-five. I want a thirty-eight with no past.'

'I can do it of course,' said Sholly, 'but it'll cost you. Unfired, two and a half ton. It'd be three, four on the street.'

'You robbing bastard,' said Gust, but he knew it was the going rate. 'What's that you're drinking there? Water?'

'Fuck the water. You want the shooter, I want to see some snow on the ground.'

'You will when I get the thing in my hand. Not before, and I want it now.'

'Now?' Sholly shouted. 'You mean like this minute or something? What do you think I am, a fucking gun-smith?'

Some people at the bar in suits turned to look at them over the perpetual refresher.

Gust took hold of Sholly by the finger he was pointing at him and bent it back in his face. 'You want me to break this?'

'Give me my finger back!' Sholly yelled. 'That's torture! What do you think you're doing?'

'You raise your voice like that with me again,' Gust said, 'and you can leave your false teeth to your granny, understand?'

'I understand you're a maniac.'

'I'm a maniac about security, and with the business you're in so should you be. So calm it with the voice, this isn't the fucking Bolshoi.'

'Look, all right, but what I'm telling you is that what you call now means tomorrow night earliest. What do you expect? You expect me to get hold of new shooters just like that? Pull them out of a hat or something? Keep a range of them under the fucking table?'

'Tomorrow's too late.'

'Too bad then.' Sholly shrugged. 'It's a sale I won't make because I can't do it before.'

Gust was screwed there; there was no one else who could get it for him any faster. 'OK then, what time tomorrow night?'

'The Eclipse at ten, and I want a ton and a half in my hand now.'

'A ton and a half on two and a half? You ought to be more trusting, we've dealt before.'

'I don't trust the skin off my shit, any more than you do.'

'All right, only it'll be your head in the gutter if there's any mistake.'

'There won't be. I like my head where it can't look me in the face.'

Gust sorted out three fifties in his pocket. 'I don't have to remind you what happened to one or two people and I'm reminding you very seriously, Sholly, because there are stories going round that your memory's got hazy.'

'There'll be no mistakes.'

'Good, because otherwise . . .'

'The piece will be what you ordered, and the round'll go where you put it.'

'OK,' said Gust, 'then we can relax.' He bought Sholly a double vodka to see what he would do with it. It went down in one. He wondered if Sholly was likely to drop him in it – he wasn't so amusing these days. He was making too much money and his looks were melting down with the rest of him, what with the perpetual Stolichnayas, the yuppie Porsche and his general life-style. Gust knew his place, a ground-floor maisonette in Balham with Ikea furniture and truly horrible wall-lamps with blinding hundred watt bulbs all over the living room, but it didn't pull the birds any more the way he said it did and his expensive clothes didn't make up for his belly any longer either; only an idiot would ever have thought they would. But the dangerous thing about him was that his liver was shot and his nerves with it. He was in a permanently bad temper now and unsteady about taking risks, though he was as ready to run them as ever, so that anybody dealing with him needed to do it quickly. So it made sense not to tell him anything he didn't strictly need to know, and even better sense to tell him only half of that.

One way and another Gust didn't give Sholly very much longer on planet Earth, and no bookie would have given any odds on him at all.

12

Gust went over to the Eclipse. He took his drink to a table back from the floor and sat down to watch the few dancers. There was something restful on the tape for once because it was early, and he sat drifting with the music; then Petal suddenly turned up on the edge of the floor with a man, pausing to pick up the beat. The effect her appearance had on Gust was of someone switching on a light, cutting out everything but her, which was why he hadn't tried to find her, besides knowing she was living with another man, and knowing that when you go down for ten years relationships go to the cells with you and usually stay there.

A spotlight circled the floor, picking her out. She was wearing a red silk Chinese dress edged with gold and seemed younger to him than when he had seen her ten years before, and that was the image he would take with him from now on, her straight black hair framing blue eyes in a Chinese set with a half-smile which never betrayed what she was thinking. She hadn't seen him in the shadows yet and he still couldn't quite believe she was there, but the sight of her took him back to his cell at night, where he used to gnaw his hands on waking in a sweat from the dreams he had of her. But the dreams always ended the same way: just before he woke she would turn away from him saying, 'Why didn't you look after me?' until he could have screamed, and he did scream one night; his cellmates had to deck him and then kneel on him to stop him trying to batter down the door.

He wrote to her when he hadn't been inside long. It wasn't his first spell in that nick; the walls and the courtyard were the same as they had been the time before, the sky above the purpose-built buildings the same icy blue. He knew that letter by heart, written on the ruled paper which treated an inmate as if he were a half-wit unable to write across the page straight, but he did write straight across it in a way he never had before:

220 Gust P. House 5, HM Prison Wayland.

Well, they took a van-load of us away at dusk, Petal, and we have ended up here, so I am looking at fifteen, and all I can say is that I hope the years we had together were worth it despite all the ups and downs.

The fact I'm inside means I've failed, though once the cards are down you can't do much about it. I'm not moaning, but when you draw a bad hand that's what it is and nothing else. It's like dealer's choice and you know when you pick it up that you're going to wind up beat on the table; there's nothing you can do about the aces you don't hold. So what do you do? Stack or play it out? I've always been an optimist, always thought I could win, but I wish I'd been a realist now instead, in which case I wouldn't be in all this shit, and you neither.

There's something I want to tell you that keeps going round in my head. One evening the week before I was nicked I was on a night bus at four in the morning; it was the last N16 and packed and I was standing on the top deck. Turning round I noticed this old man slumped in his seat. He looked really tired, worn out, and he was in the arms of this young girl. I don't know, maybe she was his daughter, she was young enough to be, but she was behaving to him more like a wife, a mother even, although I doubt if she was eighteen; she held him close to her, there they were in each other's arms. But though I had my own worries I thought, something looks wrong there; I even wondered if they were going home to kill themselves. Of course I didn't do anything about it, but now that I'm in here I find myself thinking about them, remembering those dark streets going by and the two of them not moving, the old man with his plastic sandals and grey hair and she with her face in his shoulder, half sleeping, half watching over him.

So then I began thinking about you of course, and all you did for me, which will help me keep my brains straight better than some of these poor bastards, particularly the first timers; some of them are pounding their fists on the concrete already and head-butting the wall. That's the way downhill in a place like this; you just knock yourself out and get nowhere.

I think that, because of the publicity my case got; and from what I have heard, they are well choked with me, so I expect to stay in hard places like this a long way from the smoke, in which case I mightn't get much chance to have visitors. It's no use being sentimental, so I'll say straight out that if you don't want a V.O. I will understand, and I also want to say that if you decide you don't want to see me again, at least let's remember the good times. The years we were together might not seem long to you, or else you could think of it as I do; it seems to have been both to me, the past sometimes flying by and sometimes standing still.

Well, once again I'm getting used to life here. The secret is to refuse to turn round and round like something in a cage; you've got to learn to 'settle down', though of course if I got a chance to go on the hot-cross I'd take it. There's three of us banged up in here and the other two don't talk much, which suits me. What I can't stand are the ones that bang on telling you they're lonely and trying to make a pass, or talk in their sleep or start telling you their nightmares etc. They're the worst. Christ, who needs it?

You being in court when they took me down, and waving to me when they snapped the steel on: that will keep me cheerful, but what I have to face up to is that when my appeal comes up next month I'm going to lose it, so I will be facing this very serious amount of porridge, and I have to put it like this, Petal, a minimum of ten years in the slammer is a big slab out of anyone's life, too long for me to expect you to be waiting at the gate when I'm released, so I'll understand if you remake your life while I'm away 'on my holidays'.

I've realised that the true lovers are the desperate ones. People have got to be desperate for each other if they're going to give each other everything; many people don't understand that. So what I want is for you to do what you feel you have to do with your life, but still spare me a thought at times so that we stay friends. Because when my parole date does come up, when you've been in for a long time you need every friend you have, so that it would be nice at least to have a drink.

Well, I'm running out of paper now, but I just want to say I love you. All right, I'm in for armed robbery and it's true the driver was shot, but even the police and the court accepted it wasn't me. I'm no two-a-penny killer, Petal, and no one in here judges me as one.

Well, you will always be the centre of my thoughts and so even if this is a letter of farewell I will still seal it with a loving kiss.

I'm having to write this up the side of the page but no, definitely don't visit me yet till I'm straightened out, but think of me as I do of you. Our love won't run away, love doesn't know what it means to run away.

As ever, regards to everyone on the manor.

He remembered every word of it, but it hadn't said what he had really wanted to say. What he had wanted to tell her was: *We live in a nightmare world of treachery and deceit.*

He remembered what had happened one grey rainy

day just before he was busted. He had come in that
evening. There had been no messages for him, and he
decided he couldn't stand another of their silences,
which were becoming longer and longer. He was restless
as well, because he was waiting for the collar, so he said,
'I'm going out.'

'It wouldn't break my heart if you didn't come back,'
she said.

He thought she was joking. He didn't realise she
already had someone else, had decided to leave him; that
didn't come out till she wrote to him after he had been
inside for some time. Even now he hadn't absorbed the
pain. Watching her on the floor now, dancing with the
man, it was as bad as it had ever been.

She still hadn't seen him and he thought, *Why don't I
just go over and have a word?*

He had a good look at the man she was with. He was
overweight, in his thirties, and wore a five hundred
pound suit with a tired carnation in the lapel; he spotted
Gust looking at them and he didn't like it. Gust thought
he must have taken her out for a candle-lit and reckoned
her for a one-nighter, which was why he was looking
around in case someone tried to take her off him. But
the Eclipse wasn't like the darts match at the local, and
Gust doubted if he knew much about dirty fighting. He
looked as if he might play amateur football at weekends,
his bottom wobbling in his muddy shorts as he went
back to his four-by-four after the match, then home to
mum and back to the City on Monday morning. After
work Friday night he probably got pissed in a wine bar
and then cabbed his way up to Soho, so that by the time
he found himself at the Eclipse he wasn't too sure any
more which way his hands went round the clock.

Petal wasn't turned on by him, he could see that; she
was staring into space somewhere past his ear. It upset
him to watch her moving listlessly around the floor like
that, so he left his table hardly aware he was doing it and
went over.

She saw him as soon as he stood up.

'What are you doing here?' she murmured. 'I didn't even know you were out.'

Her date was angrily trying to read the situation. Petal said to him, 'Why don't you go back to the table and order some champagne?'

'I've already bought two bols. What are you doing talking to him, anyway? Is he going to be hanging around all night?'

'For as long as it takes, Crispin,' she said.

The man didn't like that, particularly when she started walking off with Gust. He followed them shouting, 'Who is this burk, anyway? He's who did he say he was again?'

'I didn't,' said Gust.

'You're dead right,' said the punter. 'I'm telling you. Get lost.'

Gust took Petal round the waist. He laughed.

Crispin said, 'Don't fucking laugh when I'm around. Who do you think you are?'

'Relax,' said Gust. 'You might have been in your school boxing finals, but that won't do you any good in here. So look, you're well shlonked, do yourself a favour, piss off, you don't want to be the balloon that went pop at the party, do you?'

'Look, I bought her two bols of champagne.'

'And that's all you bought,' Petal said.

'So there you are,' said Gust, 'you've heard it from the lady herself, now split.'

'I want value for money!' he shouted.

'Work for a bank then,' Gust suggested. 'I might drop in for a loan.'

'You want to look out. I know a few people round here.'

'Buy them a drink then, and give us a rest.' Gust took Petal over to the bar. 'You certainly give them a hard time.'

She shrugged. 'I just won him anyway, he picked me

up at the Tiara. You buying?'

He nodded at two empty stools. 'We'll have them here.'

But Crispin wouldn't let it drop; he came and stood with them at the bar, swaying. The few other people dancing were bored, so they started taking an interest as well.

The barman put down the glass he was polishing and his hand kind of strayed towards the phone.

Gust shook his head at him. 'Don't bother with that, it isn't worth getting the fuzz in for.' He decided he didn't feel like having to take Crispin the distance. 'Listen, friend, I'll pay for the champagne, now just let it ride.'

'Don't fucking patronise me,' said Crispin. He grabbed Petal by the arm and started twisting it.

'Oh Jesus,' said Gust. Crispin took a swing at him which he blocked. He told the barman, 'Don't worry, this is just the one I keep for the kiddies,' and smacked Crispin on the ear. Whether it was just for the kiddies or not Crispin went down with a terrific bang that astonished everyone, including himself.

'I've left you one ear,' said Gust, 'so use it to listen with, now make smoke.' With some effort Crispin got up and went away to the back of the club. Gust watched him going to the payphone.

'Have I spoiled your evening?

'You've certainly changed it.'

'I didn't think I was going to run into you.'

She said abruptly, 'You want something, I know you. What is it?'

It was something that had just come into his head. 'You could do me a favour.'

'Get this straight,' she said. 'You and I are washed up, I'm living with someone else now.'

'So I'd heard. Who is it?'

'Connor.'

'Connor? You don't mean French Connor, used to be

into long-firming, drinks Löwenbrau?'

'That's him. He's doing really well now.'

'He looking after you all right?'

'Better than you ever did.'

'Yes.'

They sat silently staring into their glasses.

'What was this favour you wanted, anyway?' she said at last.

'I need a roof. Just two or three days.'

She thought it over. 'Well I might,' she said finally. 'Connor's up north as it happens. There's just one thing, though, and don't laugh. As long as that's all you want, you know what I mean.'

'No, just the space, nothing more.'

'I really ought to hate you,' she said slowly, 'and over the years I've tried hard. How long have you been out?'

'Two months.'

'Thanks for not telling me.'

'I thought as you were with someone else I'd better not.'

'You always come unstuck when you think,' she told him.

With a snap the electricity was back inside them again, and he realised she knew it too; he felt that if he were to touch her sparks would crackle out of their hands. She moved away from him, then dug into her bag.

'The keys.'

'Why, they're my old set,' said Gust. The silver tag she had put on them with his name engraved on it when they moved into Berwick Street was still there.

Gust.

'I'd forgotten to take that off,' she said, reddening. 'You can keep it if you like. The tag, I mean.'

'It'll only make me dream all over again.'

'I can't help that.'

As they talked Gust was watching Crispin as he returned from the payphone and went back to his table.

He looked satisfied and sat watching the entrance expectantly.

'Your man there still doesn't know when to leave off,' said Gust.

After a while the street door opened and a big man walked in and went over to Crispin's table. They talked for a while, the big man nodding, looking across at Gust a few times, and presently he came over.

'Hullo,' said Gust, 'you looking for me?' He stood up.

'Yeah, you were pointed out.'

'That's nice. Makes me feel famous. And what do you do for a living?'

'Sometimes I'm a professional boxer, and then again sometimes I might go round and kill someone.'

'Let's hope you're off duty tonight then.'

'Well I'm not,' said the boxer. 'Fact is I've dropped by to teach you some manners, son. So go easy with the mouth. I warn you, I'm tough.'

'I should think that must have been a long time ago looking at the way you are now.'

'How's that, then?'

'Like a tub of flat beer.'

'Well, I don't know what you look like, except a cunt. In fact you must be a cunt, because nobody else would come on like that, not with me.'

'OK,' said Gust, 'so I'm a cunt, so now what do we do? Sit around and juggle with that thought all night?'

'No we don't. You've given my friend over there some hard titty, and I've come round to deal with it.'

'You won't find that too easy.'

'No? I don't think I'll have any bother at all, so would you like to step outside?'

'No need,' said Gust. 'I know all the folk in here. The barman can referee, he's just seen Crispin getting a smack, so he's had some practice. There's plenty of room on the dance floor and it'll entertain the punters.'

'There'll be a lot of damage,' the boxer warned him.

'No there won't, there won't be time.'

The boxer thought that over.

'It's logical to do it in here,' said Gust. 'Have a fight in the street and we're both nicked; fix it in here and who's the wiser? No one'll call the law.'

'Rate yourself that high, do you?'

'With you?' said Gust. 'You bet I do. A tenner you don't go thirty seconds, the barman can be timekeeper. You good for a tenner? Well get it ready.'

'Look, you were seriously out of order with the lady.'

'You'll have to prove that the hard way.'

The boxer thought some more. He was short and solid with small hands which he constantly brushed together; he also made ducking and feinting movements the whole time which Gust thought made him look really silly.

'All right, now I don't want to give you a real spanking, sonny,' the boxer said finally, 'so if you're prepared to apologise to my friend over there and if the lady will return to his table I might let it go, but if not I shall have to tune you right up.'

'And a nice tune it is too,' said Gust, 'like Westminster chimes. You must've heard them often when you've been flat on your back.'

The boxer didn't reply to that at once because he hadn't any answer ready. The dialogue shouldn't have turned out like this; in fact there shouldn't have been any dialogue at all. It was meant to be an action picture, but somewhere down the line there'd been a script problem.

'Well, make up your mind,' said Gust. 'I'm sick of everyone picking fights with me, and this one isn't even yours. And stop dancing about like that; it makes you look like a budgie with a wooden leg.'

The boxer looked at Gust again. He had been just about to hit him, but at the last moment he put his hands in his trouser pockets instead. He realised this man was ready to back his words up; no one but a madman would have come on like that otherwise, let alone back himself with a tenner. 'Maybe you're not what I took you for, after all,' he said. 'I thought you were just a yob.'

'Go on,' Crispin yelled from the background, 'hit him, will you, for Christ's sake!'

'So you don't want to get hurt after all,' said Gust.

The boxer said that was right. Thinking it over, he didn't really feel all that inclined.

'Pity,' said Gust, 'bang goes my tenner.'

'What's more, I'm going to a wedding over at Tooting in a couple of days,' the boxer confided, 'so I want my face looking reasonable. I've got an idea, why don't we have a pint instead?'

'Oh for God's sake!' Crispin shouted. He jumped up, crashed into his chair and stormed out.

No one paid any attention to him except the barman, who shouted, 'The bastard hasn't paid his bill,' and prepared to vault over the counter.

'Don't sprain an ankle,' said Gust. 'The bouncer'll catch him going out.' He turned back to the boxer: 'Well, if you don't mind I'll just get back to the lady.'

And that was that. The boxer hung around for a bit, only there wasn't really anyone for him to talk to any more, so in the end he just waved at everyone and left.

All that remained was a little tableau in the dimness of the near empty club: Gust, Petal, and the barman endlessly polishing the same glass.

When they got into the flat Petal gave him a drink and launched straight in. 'All right, now we're alone, what are you up to right now? I can tell you're at it.'

'I've got something going,' he admitted, 'but it's just small.'

'You want to tell me about it?'

He had forgotten how much she liked getting to the bottom of things. 'No,' he said.

'It can't be as small as all that, then. Anyway, it's like this, either you tell me something about it or you're not staying here.'

'It's for your sake if I don't tell you.'

'I'll be the judge of that.'

She had changed since he had been away. She had always had an inquiring turn of mind, but now he found that her curiosity was as penetrating as a Black and Decker drill and an inner voice warned him to say nothing.

'You've pulled a stroke, haven't you?'

It was no good telling her the lot, that it was far from small and that there was a lot going on in it that he didn't understand, because that would really get her going.

But he had to tell her something.

'Start anywhere, just talk,' she said. 'And no porkies, I always know when you're lying.'

'All right, well, the other day there was a man waiting for me outside the probation office.'

'Who?'

'What does that matter?'

'He must have a name.'

'His name's Sladden. But don't you ever repeat that, Petal, because you're the only person I've told.'

'Never mind that,' she said. 'So who is this Sladden? A villain?'

'Yes he is,' Gust admitted, 'in his own way; he's a blackmailing devious bastard.'

'You under the cosh to him?'

'Listen, can we drop this?'

'No. I want to know what I'm dealing with; I've got Connor and me to think of. This is my place, I don't want a load of villains or the bill come storming in.'

'It's what comes of being out on a ticket.'

'What is? I'm still waiting.'

'All right. What happened was this. This Sladden character comes up to me outside the probation office, I've never seen him before, and he says: "Hullo. You were nice and easy to find."

"Who the hell are you?" I say. "What do you want?"

"A drink," says Sladden, "and you're going to need several."

"What are you, anyway?" I say. "Filth?"

"Worse. Where's a reasonable pub round here? Quiet."

'So we find a pub. Sladden gets the drinks in and says, "You're in serious bother, Gust."

"No I'm not," I tell him, "I've done ten years in the slammer and I've got five hanging over me first time I slip on the duckboard, so I'm making double sure I keep my nose clean."

"What was that you said?" Sladden says. "Your nose is filthy, it's covered with shit."

"Wrong," I say. "I haven't missed a single date with my probation officer. You can see I just came out of there, he's dead chuffed with me."

"It's not the probation officer I'm talking about," says Sladden. "What I'm talking about is what you've got going down with Manny Farb and Harry Ford. Consorting with known villains for the purpose of conspiring to commit armed robbery, that'll look tasty on the charge sheet. And bang goes your parole."

"What are you talking about, armed robbery? And these people, I've never heard of any of them." (But I'm thinking, Petal, how does he come to know anything about Manny and Harry?)

"Don't come the acid," said Sladden. "There's no point with me."

"Farb. Ford," I say, "sorry, don't know them." I finish my drink and I say, "Well, bye now, I've got to be going, I'll catch you again."

"You just stay right where you are, arsehole," says Sladden, "and fucking listen to me. There's a consignment of blank passports coming up from the printer's to London on the twenty-eighth, and I happen to know that your job is to hijack the van; it's just the kind of caper you think you're so good at."

"I wasn't thinking of hijacking any van," I say.

"Yes you were."

"You'd have to prove that."

"I know," says Sladden, "and your bad luck is that I can, and what's more I'm going to. I've got the proof on me, in my pocket."

"Whatever you've got, it's just fairy tales."

"Well, if they are, they're informers' fairy tales," says Sladden, "and I lap those up. They cost money too, and I do like to get value. Grasses, they're every villain's nightmare, aren't they?" Then the bastard takes out an envelope and slings it at me. "Go on, have a butchers. No, I'll do better than that, I'll show you myself." So he gets these photographs out and spreads them on the table. I look at them and I go fucking spare, Petal; there's shots of me, Harry and Manny all leaving Manny's flat. "So you don't know them, eh?" says Sladden. "well it strikes me you get on fucking well with strangers is all I can say. Go on, pull the other one."

"Get those fucking things out of sight," I say. "Don't flash them in here."

"With you three," says Sladden, leaving the pictures where they are, "you, Farb and Ford, plus the evidence of the man who took the shots, of course, all the CPS has to prove is conspiracy and you're back inside, Gust, your feet won't touch."

"Who grassed us?" I ask. "Who took those fucking shots?"

"The man from the printer's," said Sladden, "with the help of a little camera we gave him. He'd bottled out of the scam and called the law, which for various reasons is where we came in." But I ask him again, and he still won't tell me where he's from.

'Anyway, he's got me, Petal. I didn't want the printer in on that meet in the first place, but Manny said we had to. I told Sladden that. I might as well, he knew everything else. "All right," I say to him, "well, let's book me in at the nearest nick, then, what are we waiting for?"

"Don't tempt me," said Sladden, "but no, we don't want to work it like that, only it depends on you, on whether you can make what we've got in mind stick. It depends if you can keep your nerve, it depends on a lot of things."

"I don't understand," I say.

"No," said Sladden, "you don't, and what's more, you're never going to. All you're ever going to understand is the bit where you come in."

"I don't go into anything blind," I said. "I've never done that in my life and I'm not starting now."

"You'll start what you're fucking told," says Sladden, "and you'll go on until you're told to stop. Have another drink, I'll get them. Think it over." When he comes back with them he says, "Well?"

"Yes, OK," I say, "I'll play." What else can I do, Petal? "I'll play fucking King Lear if I have to," I say to him. "If it means staying out of Maidstone, I'll play snooker with a hand grenade."

"That's about what you will be doing," says Sladden, "and they won't be easy shots."

"What do I have to do?" I say.

"You're going to hijack this van exactly the way it was set up," says Sladden. "The only difference is, you won't be doing it for them, you'll be doing it for us."

"Look," I tell him, "be reasonable. These people, they're heavy villains, they're barking mad; one little thing doesn't smell right and they go olympic, and you know the only way they've got with grasses; it's the way out."

"Yes, maybe you'd better just do the rest of your bird," he says. "Maybe you're right, Maidstone would be peaceful compared."

"That's just the kind of peace I don't need," I say. "I don't think you understand. When you've just come out from doing ten, the last thing you want is to go straight off and queue up for another five. And if it means screwing up Farb it so happens I don't like the bastard and never have; he grassed up my brother-in-law, got him sent up for three. I've never trusted him, and I only agreed to pull this caper because I was skint."

"And you will pull it," says Sladden. "Our way."

'So that's it, and he gives me money, five ton under the table. "That's for expenses," he says, "but I'm telling you now: if anything goes wrong with this we won't cover you, we don't know you, we've never heard of you. But you make it stick, and your other five will be off the books, scrubbed, forgotten." Well, that's how it looked right then, he had me by the shorties and I knew it.'

'And so you pulled the stroke, but not for the people who thought you were pulling it for them?' she shouted. 'You're totally mad, I ought to throw you out right now.' But she stayed right where she was. 'So tell me some more about this Sladden; I haven't finished with him yet.'

'I can't,' said Gust. 'I don't know any more and I can't even contact him.'

'And to think I asked you if you were bad news.'

'At the time I didn't know about you and Connor.'

'What's that supposed to mean?'

'I thought there was a chance that if I made some serious money and got that time knocked off we might get back together again.'

'You can totally forget that idea,' she said coldly.

'All right. Do you want me to go now you know all this? Maybe I'd better.'

She looked away from him and didn't answer. She looked down at the floor. 'Christ,' she muttered in the end, 'what a nightmare. How will any of us ever get through it?'

'Because we have to. It's because the end's there, that's the way it is.'

'I still love you,' she said. 'You know that, but why didn't you ever do me any good?'

It was what she used to say to him in his prison dreams. 'Because I never did myself any,' he said. 'I'm

on a treadmill I can't get off. I'm sick of violence, I'd like
some peace, but I can't seem to find it, and I'm tired.'

'You? Tired?'

'I'm tired of battles.'

'I can't get you out of them,' she said. 'Christ knows
I've tried.'

'I wouldn't have blown it next time.'

She turned away from him. 'That's enough of that,'
she said wearily. 'Meanwhile here you are.'

'For a couple of days.'

She turned back and looked at him pleadingly.
'Look,' she said, 'you've done ten years and now you're
out, you've got a chance.'

'Not till I've got this Sladden off my back I haven't, if
I ever get him off.'

'You do more bird now and you're finished.'

'I know.'

'That is if Farb doesn't kill you first.'

'He'll try,' said Gust, 'but it's too late to worry now,
and if I want to shoot for the teddy bear this is the only
way.'

'You'd just better pray nothing goes wrong,' she said.

He wasn't going to tell her it already had.

'At least for tonight let's say we've got a chance.'
Desire was building up in him like the fumes from damp
explosive; he had an idea that if he made a move towards
her now it would blow them both to pieces. 'Just for a
minute, suppose it was back in the old days.'

'But it isn't.'

'Well, anyway.'

'I told you. No.'

That was final enough, yet there was still something
important he wanted to settle with her if he could only
get at it. But because of what she had just said he felt
hollow and knew they would never be able to settle
anything; there was a sheet of glass between them, and
there was nothing to be done about that.

Someone next door somewhere had some old jazz

going and the woman singer was wailing:

> I had pity on you and I took you in,
> Now all you have to offer me's an inch of gin;
> Why don't you do like some other men do:
> Get out of here, and get me some money too.

'There are these things I worked out in jail,' he said.

She cut into his mind as usual: 'Even if we did it, it would only be like doing it with someone like Crispin for me.'

'I can't make a single mistake, can I?'

'Why not?' she said. 'You've made them all, what do a few more matter?'

'We've gone downhill.'

She shivered. 'You've cut off your own right hand. That was easy. It was me.'

He didn't say anything, but he thought, *You're right, I don't know about easy, but I've done it*, and the years of pain he had suffered over her that he thought he had mastered fell in on him. That was when he knew what hell was; it meant that beauty for him was now unreachable, deaf and indifferent behind that glass; it was looking at him without even realising any more that it was looking for him; it had searched for him with less and less conviction, and finally none at all, growing weaker until it died, with him standing there on the wrong side of the glass and powerless to break it. He hoped there was no such thing as life after death.

They fell over on the bed. 'We've got no chance,' she muttered. 'Don't talk about it any more. Just sleep.'

Instead, though, he held her to him and felt her resist him, but not hard. He thought, *It's the joy you can never have that's the sweetest*. They slept after making love as if it were for the first time, but of course it wasn't, and he could feel her knowing that.

Later, she said, 'Reality's what you can't deal with, and maybe that's why I think of you as dead.'

'We're not dead, we're just kids.'

That made her sit up. 'What?' she shouted. 'Kids? *Us?*'

'All right,' he said, 'once I leave here I'll never bother you and Connor again.'

'I'll hold you to that.'

'Still, I was meant for you.'

'Don't be so stupid, no one's meant for anybody.' She calmed down a bit. 'All right, maybe Connor's only a substitute. Maybe he knows it too, and maybe I do, but he cares for me, he pays the rent and I need looking after.'

'I thought you were so tough.'

'Nobody's that tough, it just suits you to think they are.'

They were trying to bottle eternity into five minutes; they were too urgent. They were two spirits talking, tangled in each other on an everlasting dance floor, together one second and insubstantial the next.

'I love you,' he said. 'Connor or no Connor.'

'No.'

'I'll prove it to you.'

'It's too late. Sleep.' Yet she kept whispering *Again, Take me again*.

'Haven't you had enough of me?' she said towards morning.

'No,' he said. 'I could never have enough of you and that's how it is.'

'It's not true,' she said. 'I tell you.'

'We could have a real place together,' he said. 'I could get work.'

'Don't fool yourself.'

'We could live together somewhere. Here.'

She just laughed. 'Dream on, you poor cuckoo,' she said. 'We'll never have a place together and you know it. How could you ever sit still anyway when you're always on the run?' She wound her fingers into his hair and dragged his head down to her again.

'We need some peace,' he said.

But they would never have any and he knew it; they had drawn the wrong cards. What could have been absolute was nothing but a few moments together in the dark; they were separate people gyrating as haphazardly as colliding stars.

The street lights switched off along Berwick Street as dawn broke and the rain started, leaving a wet rash on the pavement. Then at eight sharp her clock crew. She got out of bed. 'I'm going out.'

'Out? Where?'

'Don't ask questions; I never did.'

'You going straight away?'

'I'll leave you some coffee.'

'Wait. What are we going to do about Connor?'

'What do you mean, do about him?'

'I mean you and me. From now on.'

'There isn't any from now on,' she said. 'I told you; Connor looks after me now.'

'I thought we'd decided to change that.'

'Well, we didn't.'

'And me?'

'You?' she said, quoting his jail dreams again, 'you're the past. Last night? It never happened.'

At the centre of the pain she was giving him he experienced an absurd, negative relief, because she had just said it all without his having to.

'How about the Eclipse tonight?' he said. 'I've got a meet there.'

'I'm not sure.'

'I've got to see you again. Tonight. I feel bad when you're not there.'

'That won't last.'

'We could go for a meal. Say at the Blackjack.'

'Ring me at the club and we'll see.'

'One last time,' he said. 'Come here.'

She cried when he said *come here* but she came anyway, so that she didn't go anywhere after all, until in

the end they had to sleep, surrendering to each other in
the paling darkness, he dropping out of pleasure as she
drew away from him straight into despair, watching the
November sky with clouds apparently bolted to it and
boiled white, listening to the stallholders' voices below
in Berwick Street market. They had their stalls set up
and were already shouting: 'Green *bananas*! Who wants
my *green* bananas?'

The mens' voices came to Gust as something ordinary
that had become transfigured, much as Petal just now,
talking about Connor, had transformed herself at a
stroke from a goddess into the croupier at a game for
losers, or as the distant view of the cement works from
his cell window had sometimes looked when the sunlight fell on them in a certain way. Or, in his waking
confusion, the stallholders reminded him of bells in
some East Anglian steeple ringing a change that he
might have heard working on a prison allotment.

It was like a one-time cell-mate of his, a bank manager
done for fraud, talking about the art course he was
doing, saying how subjunctive the present is, as in
painting, where everything seen is present in the frame,
nothing to either side or behind, and there is nothing but
a suggested future, and in some pictures not even that.

He turned to Petal. He wanted to say once more *I love
you*, but thankfully the words wouldn't come this time.
She was out of bed anyhow and getting dressed.

'Will you be back again during the day?'

'I don't know.'

Against his will he slept again and she was long gone
when he woke; the coffee she had left for him was cold.
The phone rang once; he didn't answer it.

They had talked about the phone.

'I won't use it, just call boxes.'

'Like old times,' she said.

But it wasn't.

He had looked her in the eyes; they reminded him of
his grandmother's the day he had to tell her she was only

going into hospital for a minor op.

He had got three fifty-pound notes out of his pocket and given them to Petal.

'That's for shopping, whatever.'

She didn't want to take the money, but did in the end. Anyway she was gone now, and he thought how, without attaching much importance to it at the time, you found one day that love had become routine without your noticing it and then left one day, changing into just memories. What memories? Just anything at all really: random details, agreeable while you were both together but terrible when you weren't.

When it was over the face of memory turned dark and ugly, revealing fangs that drew blood.

13

Gust left the flat in the afternoon; it was really coming down. The *any spare* changers squatted as far back in the doorways as they could, motionless under their blankets, their shopping bags by their knees, eyes fixed on another planet; account executives shuffling along with the *Standard* over their heads looking for a cab.

But Gust didn't notice the rain. He had to think, and it was easier to do that outdoors than in the flat with its constant reminders of Petal. Petal represented part of the situation but there was the rest of it as well: Manny, Sladden. If he wanted to get out of that in one piece he would have to get it right.

He thought about Manny. Gust didn't like him, didn't trust him, and what he had told Sladden was the truth; if he hadn't been skint he would never have agreed to work with him. He had told Manny at the very start: 'Passports? Since when have bent passports been your style?'

'Everything's my style,' Manny had said, 'and this Euro-UK shit's worth big money on the street, especially if you've got a punter for them. I've also got an inside man at the printer's too; I've got the timetable for the van, the route, the date, the whole operation. It's all set up – it's a doddle.'

Sure.

Gust decided to pay him a visit and straighten out some details, but not alone, so he went off to look for Frankie Petrosa. He went round to Jackie's sandwich bar next to the Diadem; Jackie was Petrosa's girlfriend.

'Hi, Jackie. Frankie around?'

'No, but he should be in ten minutes, he's stuck in City Road.'

'What a life,' said Gust. 'Cabbing.'

'Keeps him out of the nick, anyway for a while, and look who's talking. Liver sausage on brown?'

'Listen,' said Gust while she started making it, 'when he gets back tell him it was me asking for him. I'll be in the Diadem, there's a bit of a hurry. Thanks.'

He paid for the sandwich and walked into the pub eating it.

Half an hour later Frankie appeared. 'Sorry,' he said, 'I got held up.'

'I know, Jackie said.'

'Fucking traffic-jams,' said Frankie, sitting down, 'and the feller forgot his briefcase at that.'

'Fancy one to Clapham, wait and return? It says in the paper they're cutting down on pollution, but I've come across some over at Marjorie Grove that needs seeing to.'

'The usual?'

'Sure, but I want you in the background. I don't know how many they'll be in there but these people seem to think it's OK to piss in my face, and if they won't see sense I might have to give them a spanking, which is where you come in. You shod?'

'Just the blade. And you?'

'Not till tonight,' said Gust, 'till tonight all I've got is my hands.'

'That's usually enough.'

'I don't particularly want to hurt them. It's more if they try putting the bubble in, we'll see. If I can manage on my own you'll get your normal whack, but if I do need you it'll be extra of course. Anyway here's a ton down, cop for it quick, I don't want anyone sussing us in here, it's a grasses' paradise.'

'Something tricky going down?' said Frankie, putting the money away.

'Could be some treachery. And that's what a traitor is, tricky.'

'I don't like them either,' said Frankie. 'I'm all for knocking them off. One fewer, that's doing everyone a favour.'

'I can't tell you what all my problem is,' said Gust, 'but I'm on the run and the trouble is, I don't know who from. I can't go back to my own place, it's staked out, but I don't know who by, and I even had the filth onto me this morning, would you believe.'

'Sounds like you're busy all right,' said Frankie, swallowing his beer. 'Let's go, then anyway, I'm on a double yellow.'

They went outside. 'This your motor?' said Gust. 'The BMW? Nice.'

'And it's new.'

'I can see it is. This what you cab with?'

'What?' said Frankie as they got in. 'This five-thirteen's my personal tuned-up set of black man's wheels; see any squad car off.'

Once they were in the car, Gust gave Frankie his instructions. 'When we get there you follow me up the stairs, it's the second floor front. If anything happens in you come, just kick and enter. If not, wait at the stairhead; it'll either be a lively afternoon or it won't. Like I say, no one need get hurt unless they're stupid enough to ask for it.'

'Who's likely to come on strong?' said Frankie. 'Anyone I know?'

'I don't think you know him, but the Hammer's the main problem.'

'I've heard of him.'

'That's enough for most people.'

'What are your views on danger?' said Frankie, starting up.

'Why ask me?'

'Because I want to know what you think.'

'If it's take a risk or go under,' said Gust, 'you take the risk. That's danger. You know that.'

'Risks is like doing drugs,' said Frankie. 'The more you take the more you want to take.'

'It doesn't have to be a way of life.'

'I think it does,' said Frankie.

'Suit yourself.'

'You can't work everything out yourself. There are times when you have to ask someone.'

'As long as you don't ask me,' said Gust. 'I never ask anyone anything, not even my mates, that way there can't be any treachery.'

'Mates,' said Frankie, 'yeah that's right, that's where the treachery can often be.'

'I don't know about that. I don't know anything much. I don't think, I just survive.'

'Ease off. I'm twenty-three; I want to see if I've got a future.'

'Of course you have, in the nick. Future? Don't be daft, we never even had a past.'

'No wonder I'm always in bother then, that explains a lot of things.'

'And, anyway,' said Gust, 'what do you mean, think? Do you mean the thinking you do at night, the easy stuff, tucked up in your chariot with a spliff and a mag and a pillow behind your head? Is that what you mean? Or the other kind, the kind you do when the dreams come?'

'I score zero for dreams,' said Frankie. 'I never have any.'

'What, never? Not even over that car-park thing down in Carshalton Beeches? You remember what happened there.'

'Where the man got hit too hard? Once something's

gone down it's over. Doesn't bother me, that. Never did.'

'Well, I hope it never does, Frankie,' said Gust. 'Anyway remember one thing, we all come unstuck in the end.'

'OK, so we come unstuck. Talking of that, you've been shot, so what do you think about death?'

'It's like a freezing wind, that's all.'

'There must be more to it than that. What about the pain?'

'Will you just stop talking for a minute,' said Gust, 'and fucking drive.'

'We'll get there,' said Frankie. 'What do you want me to do with all this traffic in front of us, motor over it? Go on, tell us about death.'

'All right, you asked for it. Look at it this way. Who cares if people die? When was the last time you really cared if anyone died? Even if it was a mate, was there ever a time when someone went down and you didn't just shrug? When did you ever say anything different from ah fuck it, people die all the time, we've all got to go? And that's fine right up till the day when it's your turn; that's the bad day, when you find yourself saying to your body, hey, you, where do you think you're going, we've worked together all our lives, and now you're on the blink when I need you, on the floor, numb all over, what's the matter with you? That's terror, that is, that's panic; it's like ripping a place off and there are the wooden-tops pounding up the street and the fucking getaway won't start. You've never had that yet, Frankie, you've just taken a beating or two which is a few days' swanning around the manor in dark glasses with little brides asking you what happened Frankie, tell us all about it Frankie, but that's nothing like the same as turning up the last card and finding it's blank.'

They reached the Battersea roundabout; there were roadworks under the bridge there leaving only one lane open, and the traffic was truly terrible.

'Nice route you've picked I must say,' said Gust. 'At this rate we'll be sat here like a couple of twats till the fucking government resigns.'

'It'd be a bloody fantastic route if there was only a road,' said Frankie. He turned off and went up Prince of Wales Drive. 'By the way, did you hear what happened in Lexington Street?'

'You mean Benny Arnold the other day?'

'That's it. Right after he copped for the reward on that big coke bust, fifteen long ones.'

'Ten,' said Gust.

'All right, ten, and then there's his mates take him round the clubs, they get him pissed out of his skull, take him home, put him to bed, pour petrol all over him and up he goes.'

'Yes, well you know what it was with Benny,' said Gust. 'He never rated as a generous man, that was his real problem. He thought not buying a round was the smart thing to do, and then he not only never gave his mates a penny, but he didn't even want to know them any more either once he'd copped.'

'I wonder what he's thinking now.'

'He isn't thinking at all,' said Gust. 'He's got nothing to do it with. I heard he looked like a slice of Danish left under the grill.'

'Remember some journalist was going to do a book on him, and Benny went round the pubs saying he was going on the box?'

'Yes, well he went into a box instead and they never did write a book about him,' said Gust, 'instead they just spiked it.'

'Maybe we're all spiked. Maybe that's why we never get anywhere.'

'Who wants to get anywhere, except out of bother? Apart from that, the place you get to's the same as the one you just left.'

'It's discouraging the way you put things,' said Frankie, 'it makes you wonder if it's worthwhile going out robbing and doing bird. In fact I ask myself if it's even worth going over to Clapham right now; why give yourself a hard time for nothing?'

'So that you can give Jackie an easy time,' said Gust, 'and as for Clapham, there are some sharks swimming around over there and I'm leaving a blood trail. It's survival. Everyone wants to survive except suicides, and even then, topping yourself, that takes bottle.'

'I'd never do a thing like that, no matter what the pressure was. I've got Jackie. I don't mean just a one-night stand, but you wouldn't think like that if you had someone like Jackie in your life, Gust.'

'Yeah but that's just it, I haven't.'

The traffic got going again, slowly.

'There's something else I want to know,' said Frankie.

'Oh for fuck's sake, Frankie, cut it out will you. You're worse than my old mother-in-law.'

'Doesn't not having a steady bird bother you ever?'

'No, but I'll tell you what does; I wouldn't mind if you put a burst of fucking speed on.'

They stopped at another set of lights.

Frankie said, 'What were we talking about?'

'I wasn't, I was thinking.'

'What about?'

'OK,' said Gust. 'If you really want to know, I was thinking that one day I'll feel shakier than the other days and find myself being helped off a bar-stool, someone saying this poor old bastard's been sick in his beer, and I was thinking, I'm never going into an old people's home, I'll make sure that never happens to me.'

'But you'd have your memories when you grew old.'

'And what am I supposed to do with them? Wank over them?'

'What's the matter with growing old?'

'You'll find out when it happens to you,' said Gust.

'Why do you make everything sound such a waste of time?'

'Because that's all we can think of to do with time, waste it.'

'How do you think you'll wind up, then?' said Frankie.

'Dead. Like everyone else.'

They were stopped at a roundabout by a church, a pub and a bank; outside the pub on the pavement the driver of a Dial-A-Ride bus was loading up with autistic patients who had had an afternoon out in the corner café and were shaking hands with people before they went back to wherever it was they kept them.

'What are you looking at?' said Frankie. 'The whores-and-sores bus? That's the weekend ride for the mentally handicapped, that's all that is. And lucky it's them, not us, mazeltov.'

What Gust was thinking of while he looked at the bus was what he ought to have been saying to Frankie: *Listen, in answer to all your questions, I've grown up and I see I've been done. I'm forty-six, I've been away ten years, I've read, I've thought, I've exercised in my cell, but now the whole fucking lot, it's coming up fast. Too bad, I'd no choice in the matter (this corner coming up, throw a left, Frankie). I keep going the same way time after time, I say to myself don't try it, you'll never get through, the road's barred. Can you imagine the end of it? It's the final bad dream. No more women, no more pints, you're a broken-down old man in one of those places for the dying shouting I've got to piss I've got to shit and in the end someone drops by. They're all right, the staff, but they're muttering, Christ it don't half pong in here, oh God it's old man Gust again, look at him, we'll have to change him, that's twice today, pyjamas and all, top to bottom, strip the bed, shit everywhere, it's enough to put you off your boyfriend, isn't it, well let's get it over with then and go down and have a Coke in the canteen, it was lovely with Ted last night Mandy, he's got lovely eyes, don't you think, they're green at times, he says he's Welsh on his mother's side, well I do reckon him, we can throw this sheet away, hold your breath now, one end each, strip the lot off and bin it, it'll never come clean it's black with shit, blankets too, there's no machine can deal with this lot, it's not fair to ask it.*

He looked at Frankie, who had tuned into Kiss FM. 'All right,' said Gust, 'we're getting near. Listen, if you do have to come in there'll likely be the Hammer there, the man I was talking about, he's Farb's minder, look out for him. He's not even an insect, he's the spineless form of a rat, he hits you from behind. I'm marking your card.' He tapped Frankie on the knee. 'This is it, this left turn off Elspeth Road. Keep going fifty yards and park where you can, we'll walk back.' He had a look as they went past, saw men up there with their backs to the window and heard rock music. 'Looks like they're all there.'

'They expecting us?'

'No,' said Gust, getting out of the car, 'they'd be playing the fucking funeral march if they were.'

They walked back up to the flats and through the street door; there was no need to ring because the lock was smashed. They went up to the second floor and Gust told Frankie at the head of the stairs, 'You stay here out of sight, OK?'

Gust rang the door-buzzer and kept ringing it till the music stopped. A big paunchy man opened up; right behind him stood another man, small, with a mac over his shoulders.

'Hullo, Manny,' said Gust. The small man was the Hammer and Gust ignored him.

He was known as the Hammer because that was the weapon he used, but it had been shortened to the Hammer now because some young villains still saw him as a face on the manor and called him the Blind Hammer because they didn't know any better. It was true he once used to be known as the Blind Hammer, but that wasn't because he was blind; it was because he had blinded a woman cashier in a bank raid by throwing acid in her face and then gone round boasting about it, which was how he had got himself nicked and been done for nine years.

Gust wished it had been thirty; he hated the man.

When the Hammer saw Gust his face lit up with the kind of joy people don't need. He hated Gust too; Gust had once told him to give up villainy and get a job as a horror film extra. Now the Hammer moved backwards into the room like a man judging his range, smiling at him like a cannibal looking forward to human meat.

'Come on in,' Manny said.

'This is far enough.' Gust leaned against the wall of the sitting room and said to the Hammer, 'You always wear a mac indoors, raindrop?'

'You're not meant to be here,' said Manny, 'but as you are, stay fucking polite.'

'I'll do better than that,' said Gust, 'I'll be frank. That'll make a real change.'

Four other men Gust didn't know were parked on the settee. They didn't speak, they didn't even move when Gust appeared, they just sat and watched him. They were smoking cigars that smelled like rugs on fire and their clothes crackled. They were probably the height of fashion in Irkutsk, and might have made the plain girls' heads turn on a slow night out there, just.

'You're not answering me, Hammer,' said Gust. He went over and looked at the mac. 'What's that in your pocket? Looks weighty, must be your prison record.'

'It's a lot heavier than that,' the Hammer said.

'Must be a fucking tank then,' said Gust, 'your yellow streak's showing. Frightened of it raining indoors, and you even wear iron to drink with.'

'You always get a party going,' said the Hammer, 'I don't know how we ever managed without you.'

The foreigners on the settee smiled, but not with their eyes.

Gust indicated them. 'These four geezers here understand what we're saying?'

'You can't tell,' said Manny, 'but I shouldn't think so really. They're foreign friends, mafia, I think, and what do you want, anyway?'

'Explanations.'

'Explanations?' said Manny. 'What have I got to explain to you?'

Gust turned on the Hammer suddenly. 'I really hate that mac of yours,' he said. He ripped it off his shoulders; it fell with a thud. Gust picked it up and removed a nine millimetre pistol from one of the pockets. 'Oh dear, look at this then, no one but an old age pensioner needs a thing this size indoors.' He unloaded the pistol and threw the magazine at the window, which was shut. Then he threw the pistol and the mac in the Hammer's face. The Hammer started for him, but Manny got in the way.

'Keep calm, Gust, will you,' Manny said when the noise of breaking window glass had died down. 'I don't want any violence in here.' In fact Manny was well known for dreading violence; it made him nauseous, and his heavies looked after all that end. The four men on the settee leaned forward intently as if they were watching the big race on TV.

'No, let the little cunt have a go,' said Gust, 'it'd be a real treat. He'll wind up looking for his head.'

'No,' said Manny, 'and what's your problem, anyway?'

'Two individuals came down to Marly's Club and tried to kill me. Was all that anything to do with you? You know anything about that?'

'No.'

'I thought maybe it might tell a story.'

'Well, it doesn't,' Manny said, 'means nothing to me.'

'Nothing seems to mean anything to you suddenly,' said Gust, 'it's funny. Anyway, about the two men in Marly's, it's probably lucky for you it doesn't, because one of them blew his tunes in hospital this morning, did you know?'

Evidently they didn't because Manny said, 'Did you top him?'

'He accidentally died. Real stroke of luck for me I admit, because I wouldn't be here if he hadn't.'

'That would have been nice,' said the Hammer.

One of the foreigners on the sofa moved slightly, felt Gust's eye on him, and just put down his cigar.

'Must have been catching too, whatever he had,' Gust went on, 'because the other ice cream's not too brilliant either.'

'You kill him too?' Manny asked.

'He never asked me, so why would I do a thing like that?'

'Because you're a fucking animal,' the Hammer said.

Gust ignored him. 'No,' he said to Manny, 'your man passed a remark so I gave him a couple of smacks, but I think he died of over-exertion myself. I think he may have been trying to dance or something but he was clumsy, tripped over himself and got a cocktail stick up his ear, kind of thing that could happen to a dog, isn't it?'

'You've got your reddies,' said Manny, 'that's all I know.'

'It isn't,' said Gust. 'It isn't all you know. Were those two men in that club yours, Manny?'

'I know nothing about them!' Manny shouted.

'Well, why did they know so much then? I mentioned passports, and they knew just what I was on about. They also knew I'd got their wages for topping me in my pocket, in cash, and I wonder who told them that. So you see, I'm not happy, Manny.'

'Then go and be fucking miserable somewhere else,' the Hammer said.

'What I'm telling you is straight up,' said Manny.

'It can't be. Nothing from you is ever straight up, and this load of shit you're giving me certainly isn't.'

'This is just friendly advice, but you want to watch your tongue.'

'It's bad advice,' said Gust. 'The other man who gave

it me, they buried him, the bits they could find.'

The man on the settee with the cigar balanced it on the edge of the glass table, then changed his mind again and put it back in his mouth.

'Who are these people anyway?' Gust said, meaning the men on the settee.

'They're not connected with you or Harry in any way at all, they're in the car trade.'

'They'll get a long way here in London,' Gust sneered. 'They don't look as if they even knew the English for a fucking sparking plug.'

'They trade abroad.'

'I see,' said Gust, 'just dealing in second-hand Trabis and Ladas, are they? Not interested in little documents at all.'

'That's right, and I'm afraid we're very busy right now, so you'll have to leave. Sorry I can't offer you a drink.'

'That's all right, I don't drink with shit anyway.'

'Then I shouldn't think you get pissed often,' the Hammer said.

Gust looked straight through him. 'Where did the delivery go, Manny?'

'That's none of your business. Where it was going was never anything to do with you. You've had your money, now fuck off.'

'Manny, I'm going to get to the bottom of this and it will be very naughty when I do, there'll be some serious spanking done.'

'I don't know whose arse you think it's going to be, unless it's yours. You're on the way out, Gust, you've lost cred; you've got too many enemies, not enough friends. Show him out, Hammer, put the wood in the hole; and Gust, don't insult people, you want to stay on the right side of me. Where would you ever find another feller like me?'

'All over the karzi walls,' said Gust, 'and the rest on the fucking floor.'

'Those are hard words, friend,' said one of the men on the settee.

'That's right, they are,' Gust said, 'and you're on the away ground, so you want to learn them by heart.'

'Let's take it easy,' Manny said. He told the foreigners, 'This is just a business conversation, he doesn't really mean it. People like Gust here are all the same; they don't make a lot of money so they get worked up over it, they get like heated.'

'Yes,' said Gust, 'all except the ones that are too greedy, they get cooled right down to morgue temperature.'

'I'm sorry if you're in shtuck is all I can say,' said Manny, 'but I'm afraid I've got to look after these gentlemen here. We've a little business to attend to and then we're off to dinner in the West End.'

'The Red Wok?'

'Why not?' said Manny, 'and what a pleasure it's been doing business with you.'

'I'm giving you a last chance to clear this up.'

'Fuck off.'

'All right.' Gust shrugged. 'If that's how you want it.'

He walked out of the flat and picked Frankie up on the stairs.

'That was disappointing,' said Frankie as they got into the car. 'I don't know how you kept your hands off that fucking Hammer.'

'Did you hear it all?'

'Why not? I'd got fuck all else to do.'

'I warned them.'

'I heard you,' said Frankie as they zipped away from the kerb. 'They ought to grow up.'

'They will,' said Gust. 'As weeds in the cemetery.'

14

Gust got to the Eclipse early; he hoped Petal might turn up. He was at the bar getting a scotch when a bald, overweight man shifted up onto the stool next to him and said, 'A word in your ear, friend.'

'Nothing today,' Gust said. 'Fuck off.'

Gust had never seen him before. He had a croaky voice, smelled of hamburger, his belly rolled out unhealthily over his belt and his round white face shone under a film of sweat. He wore jeans and an Ultra Dig jacket and did his best to look grungy; he needn't have tried so hard.

'The name's Spaulding.'

'Then go and whack yourself off a tee like a golf ball.'

'A lot of people say that, but the name's still Spaulding at the end of the day.'

'That's not my fault.'

'We need to have a talk.'

'Look, I'm straight is what I'm trying to tell you,' Gust said, 'so try getting them off somewhere else.'

'I can see why people say you're not easy.' Spaulding laid a hand on the back of Gust's; it felt like a cold hot water bottle.

'Get your fucking hand off me.'

'I was just being friendly.'

Gust took the man's arm and bent it till the hand was

110

up against the back of his neck. 'Don't ever do that to me again. Understand?' He let go of the arm.

'My,' said Spaulding. He got his arm back round in front of him, flexed it and winced. 'You really are aggressive.'

'You fatherly ones are the worst of the lot.'

'I might almost be your father,' said Spaulding, 'and rather a strict one at that, seeing I'm from round the corner.'

'What corner? I don't know what you're talking about. I'm just telling you this isn't your kind of bar. Why don't you try the street corner outside the Mutineer, or the White-Hot if you're worth a few bob? Look, I'm trying to be kind, I'm writing you off as a half-wit, don't force me to do it the hard way.'

'No need, because here's something that works all the way.'

'I don't believe it,' said Gust, looking at the warrant card. 'Detective Inspector? Poland Street? Christ, I know you all do it at the Factory, but I didn't know things were so bad you had to go shopping outside.'

'Don't chance your fucking luck, Gust. You're already hanging onto it by the skin of your bollocks.'

'No, but this is twice in one day. It's way over the top. Poland Street? I know it well. Are you by any chance a mate of a hero called Pacey? And another lovely man called Charlie Bowman, do you know him? What part of Poland Street do you work out of?'

'A14.'

'Unexplained Deaths? You investigating a death, then?'

'Yeah, two as a matter of fact.'

'Still doesn't explain why you're all following me around.'

'Because you're in bother again, that's why. Serious bother.'

'This rash I've got on my face, do you mean? I got that in jail but it's all right, it's not AIDS-related. I've been to the quack about it, so you were quite safe touching me just now.'

'You're not reading me straight.'

'I'm not trying to.'

'Change your mind,' said Spaulding. He drank some whisky.

'I see you drink on duty.'

'Yes, sometimes. What about it? You going to report me?' Spaulding rattled the ice in his glass. 'So you're surprised that here you are, being questioned by a police officer?'

'I can't think why you're bothering.'

'Plenty of reasons, all of them bad news for you, some of them worse than others.'

'None of them to do with Pacey's rigmarole about some fight in a bar, I hope. I'm bored with that, I've been over all that.'

'Pacey must have got it wrong about that fight,' said Spaulding. 'It's funny. We're not usually that badly misinformed, although mind, I don't say it never happens. You know.'

'No, I don't fucking know.'

Spaulding sighed. 'You go out of your way to be difficult, don't you? You really are a dose of what I can do without, we've got enough people like you on the books as it is.'

'All you can handle, I should think,' said Gust. 'Still, that's what you're paid for.'

'True, but you're vulnerable. Your first miscue and you don't hit the street again till around the year two thousand.'

'I know, so I'm being very careful how I go, you can bet on it.'

'Not nearly careful enough,' said Spaulding. He finished his drink and beckoned for another, but the girl behind the bar took no notice of him.

'Is it your day off or something?' Gust said. 'You going to hang around here all night?'

'Why?' said Spaulding. 'You waiting for someone?'

'My old gran,' said Gust. 'She's not very bright, of course, she's eighty-eight, but she's more fun to be with than you are, no doubt because she hasn't got a wooden head.'

'It's nice listening to good old-fashioned English,' said Spaulding. 'So many people murder the language these days, don't they?'

'That's right. Nothing lives for ever, and how did you find me here anyway?'

'Without letting you into any secrets, it was a doddle. I was strolling about on the manor and I saw you get out of a stolen BMW with Frankie Petrosa so I followed you down here.'

Gust didn't know anything about Spaulding. He had never even heard of him, but then no one can ever know them all. The jarring element was that he was from A14, and Gust didn't like that. The coppers there were not just any old detectives. They were picked for their ability to track killers; indeed they practically picked themselves. They were dedicated loners, and they had the reputation of being difficult bastards one and all, impossible to dislodge from a case. They worked out of Poland Street because the Yard didn't want them there, they wouldn't integrate, which was why they never got any promotion and didn't care; Gust knew all that.

'Drink?' said Spaulding.

'Not with you. What do you want to talk to me about?'

Spaulding clicked his fingers across the bar and said to the girl, 'Double ring-a-ding and ice, love. One.' The girl served three other customers, then blew him a raspberry in the bar mirror. Spaulding's pale blue eyes sparked with anger. He said to Gust, 'Once more with feeling, do you want to talk in here or up the road?'

'Not Poland Street in this weather,' said Gust. 'They've cut public spending again, so the heating'll be off. It's criminal to make people work in a shithouse like that, and by the way you ought to get some sweeties for that throat of yours.'

'Not for you the heating isn't off,' said Spaulding. 'For people like you it's always on full blast.'

'Makes no difference. I can't talk to you anywhere tonight anyway, I've got this family meeting in a minute, I told you. Unless you're giving me a john of course.'

'I can't do that yet, worse luck,' said Spaulding.

'Fancy, and there I was thinking that was what you were in the game for.'

'I am. I'm looking into this death at Marly's Club, among other things. That's to say two men, one dead, the other crippled for life, which will add aggravated bodily harm to murder when I hang it round the right neck.'

'Sounds more like an industrial accident to me,' said Gust, 'and anyway, I went over all that with your country boy up from the parsnips this morning, your mate Pacey.'

'Well, we're going over it again,' said Spaulding, 'so let's start by your not pretending you know nothing about it, that'll make things a lot easier.'

'You're in for a shock, because in fact I don't know anything about it at all. In fact it shouldn't come as a shock to you really, because that's what I told Pacey. So come on, let's hear some more of your patter.'

'All right, but this is something else. I've got to tell you somehow.' Spaulding scratched his cheek; the flesh came up an angry pink. 'It's hard to say it straight out, though.'

'Try,' said Gust.

'You won't like it.'

'Too bad,' said Gust. 'I never expect good news from you people anyway.' He said to the girl behind the bar, 'Large one on the rocks, Sherry, just one.' The drink arrived straight away and he said to Spaulding, 'You OK like that with your empty glass?'

'No,' said Spaulding irritably. 'It's a bar like any other

bar and not very busy at that. And I'm the same as the next man, I don't like not being served.'

'You're not the same as the next man. You're a copper, and you stick out like a spare cock at a wedding.'

'OK, well since I'm a copper let's leave what I was going to tell you and go back to this fight at Marly's. Can you account for your time over that?'

'Don't be stupid. Where would I start, seeing I wasn't there?'

'You weren't in that club last night at all?'

'No.'

'Funny, because you were seen in there.'

'This is Pacey all over again. Still, stay with it if it'll keep you happy. You've got witnesses, have you?'

Spaulding suddenly lost his cool. 'Don't try and be fucking clever with me, Gust. This is a murder case. You don't know what we've got and what we haven't got.'

'I'm sorry,' said Gust, 'but after ten years in the slammer I'm not impressed.'

Spaulding looked him in the eyes. 'All right then, we'll drop Marly's and get on with the other thing. You don't know what it is yet because you can't know, and though I never thought I'd say this to someone like you, I'm sorry for you.'

'Why?'

'Because it affects you personally. Have you got half an hour? I know you're waiting for your gran, but I think you really should spare the time and leave a message for her. This new thing happened this afternoon while you were out with Frankie.'

'Are you taking the piss?'

'No, but if you don't believe me why don't you come and see for yourself? Shall we just go and take a look at Miss Chang?'

'Petal? Have you bastards gone and fucking nicked her or something? Is she all right? What have you done to her?'

'We haven't done anything to her,' said Spaulding. 'All we've done is find her, and what are you talking about, is she all right? Was she all right would be more like it.'

'What's that supposed to mean?' said Gust. He felt his insides turning white.

'What do you think it means?' said Spaulding brutally. 'It means she's dead, of course, what else did you expect? People always die when you're around.'

Can't live without you, Gust thought; that must have come into some song they had heard together. For no reason he remembered an alarm clock she had given him for Christmas once; they were broke and they had spent all afternoon in John Lewis in the warm choosing it. It had still been there in the flat last night, which had pleased him. He had to hold onto himself.

'Shall we go?' said Spaulding. 'By the way, my hand on yours just now, that was intended as sympathy.'

'Just stop talking will you?' said Gust. 'Let's get over there.'

He took the club stairs up into the street two at a time.

'Are you OK?' said Spaulding, 'This isn't going to be nice.'

'I'm all right.'

Sombre.

15

The forensic team had gone by the time Gust and Spaulding arrived, leaving the scene of crime officer in charge. With him was the young copper called by the woman from the next door flat who couldn't get any answer to Petal's bell, and two other uniformed officers were standing around with a body bag at the head of the stairs.

'We were waiting for you, Mr Spaulding,' said the scene of crime officer. 'We've got two sets of prints besides Gust's and hers. There's blood on one of them.'

Gust stood just inside the door.

'You realise your being here is completely against the rules,' said Spaulding.

Gust didn't say anything; he was looking at what was on the floor.

'If you don't mind my saying so,' said Spaulding, 'you're not showing much emotion about this.'

Gust said nothing, did nothing.

'You had feelings for Miss Chang though, didn't you?'

'Did I?' said Gust.

'I was asking you.'

'You people are running this,' said Gust, 'not me.' He knew he was having trouble with his mouth when he spoke.

'In that case you might as well come all the way in.'
Spaulding sounded like an estate agent showing a client
around.

Gust followed Spaulding into the sitting room. Blood-
sodden, it was a different place now; not even remotely
what it had been like last night. Petal's body lay in the
middle of the floor, wall-eyed. Her eyes were almost
closed like those of a woman spurning an insult, and she
was surrounded by the shattered pieces of a mirror they
had bought together. When it sank in that it really was
her body he was looking at, and that it was her handbag
that she had tried to defend herself with lying under the
bed they had slept in the night before, everything that
had ever been in his head before was ripped apart and
replaced with a red fog.

'Not so nice to look at now, is she, tough boy?' said
Spaulding.

But Gust barely heard him. *When I fell in love with
you, long before you knew it – or did you know it? – I
stood out in the street all night watching the window of
the fourth-floor room you had then in Carlyle Street till
its light went out, wishing it had been me that had put
it out. Didn't you ever wonder – I never asked you – if
it was just coincidence that I walked into you in the street
when you came out of your door next day and that you
sent me up for being unshaven, and then we went and
had chile con carne at the Cucaracha? It was the last
money I had; that was eighteen years ago.*

He heard one of the coppers behind him say to
another, 'It's heartbreaking, man.'

Gust thought, *It's hit me. Me!'*

'Haven't you any pity at all?' said Spaulding.

Gust heard somebody choking and realised it must
be him. He wanted to leave, just get outdoors
somehow, but it was too soon; it would have been like
leaving a funeral halfway through. He saw the point
about funerals suddenly. It wasn't the priest, the
music, or the church but the impossible prettied up,

rationalised, straightened out.

Only in here nothing was straightened out; there was just the odour of cold blood. It smelled like steel, one sharp line, final, cutting everything short.

'Have some respect, will you?' he said. 'Just keep quiet.'

'Respect wears off in our job,' said Spaulding. 'It has to, otherwise we'd all be in the nuthouse.'

'I wish you were,' said Gust. He bent to look at Petal's face, but there was nothing left of it except the bridge of her nose.

'Did you kiss her this morning?' When Gust didn't answer Spaulding added, 'My bet is that she'd be alive and well now if it weren't for you.'

'If you don't button it,' said Gust conversationally, 'I'll kill you in front of your own men, do you under-stand?'

He knelt down beside her. 'They did a good job on you,' he told her aloud. 'They took a razor to you first, or maybe a Stanley knife, then the kiss-off across the chops; I think it was something weighty, don't you, Petal? Say an iron bar or a baseball bat.'

'Whatever the weapon was they didn't leave it,' said Spaulding.

'No,' said Gust. 'They were wankers, but not ama-teurs.'

'How do you feel about it then?' Spaulding said.

'You're just trying to break me, aren't you? That's all you brought me up here for.'

The scene of crime officer came over and said, 'No one we've talked to so far saw anything suspicious.'

'Of course they didn't,' said Gust. 'Everyone looks suspicious in Berwick Street.'

'You're a heartless bastard,' Spaulding said. 'I'd be surprised if this even put you off your dinner.'

'It won't,' said Gust, 'because I'm not hungry.'

'Surely you must feel something.'

'I do. I just told you, I don't feel hungry.'

'People like you, you're hardly part of the human race at all.'

'Why don't you keep that crap for the killers? When you catch them, if you ever do, then you can tell them that.'

'You're the one to moralise, is that it?'

Gust got hold of Spaulding by his jacket. 'Why don't you try feeling your way through a fog sometime? A red fog. And I hope the dead judge you for what you've done bringing me here if the living don't.' He pushed him aside. 'Let me through,' he said to the coppers.

'Just a minute,' said Spaulding. 'I might want you to come down and make a statement. There's the Marly business and now this; where are you living?'

'Nowhere.'

'You'll regret not cooperating with me.'

'Life's full of regrets,' said Gust.

He went out, and nobody tried to stop him.

He found his way down to the street. He got as far as Shaftesbury Avenue and leaned against the cinema wall, then he vomited down a drain. A woman who was passing said to her boyfriend, 'Don't look, Perry. I mean, honestly, how is the government ever going to get these ghastly people to stop drinking?'

Gust had emptied his stomach, but his thinking remained the same, heavy and confused; there was a red fog in his head. In his head he was talking to Petal when he had first met her: *I'm still young. All right, I've been in trouble with the law, that's no secret, I've done porridge – so what? I'm scarred, I get into fights, how can you help it, mixing with villains? But the people I smack need to be smacked, they're all grasses and wankers. You and I could set up together; you're happy, I'm happy, I could settle down with you; I've got a few bob over from some things that worked out and anyway you don't spend much money inside.*

Also he remembered one of his best mates, the Irishman, coming into the bar of the old Contract Club after he'd been on the piss for a week saying you got the price of a pint Gust? So Mick downs the first, gets halfway through the second and brings the lot up. Was all that really as long as ten years ago, the armoured van on the A12? Ten? It seemed like yesterday. Gust flew on the fleshless wings of the nightmares that had plagued him in jail until he dreaded sleep, back to the night the Irishman had died in the attack, the guard managing to catch him and smash him across the face with his cosh. The Irishman collapsed, spitting the insides of his head out, red, black and yellow, pieces of teeth, the whole lot spewed out, tumbling and bloody. That was all Gust's eye had time to catch in the panic of the action; then there was a blur, an explosion, and the Malt blew the guard's head off with a starting pistol. By abandoning everything they got the Irishman back to the safe pad in Hammersmith. 'Tea, tea,' the Irishman kept saying. But there wasn't any tea; all they had there was whisky.

He had lived through three-quarters of the following day, crooning, and that was how Gust got lessons in how a man spoke when he had no bottom half to his face. The Irishman cooed, too, because he couldn't scream, a sound that reminded him of a courting pigeon in spring. Gust shut his eyes by the bedside because he couldn't bear to look at the exposed tongue moving around, hunting for its lost jaw.

They took him round to the hospital in Fulham Palace Road as night fell because the whisky had done him no good; he died there an hour later and the law came for them soon after that.

He was still only just beginning to realise that Petal was dead too. He felt the roll of banknotes in his pocket as he stood at the corner of Peter Street. He said to the black sky, 'You going to murder all my friends like that, you bastard?' He shook his fist at it.

There was more vomit in his mouth and he bent over the drain again. Lines came back to him from something he must have read in jail:

You hear her
Running down the stairs on her clattering heels:
And you are deafened
By the sound of doors shutting on you.

Madness scrambled up to him through the fog in his
head and massaged him in its supple hands.

16

Later he wasn't in the Eclipse as he should have been to meet Sholly, but in the Diadem getting drunk. He couldn't face the Eclipse again yet.

Half an hour later he was still in the pub, gazing into his glass. He looked around him; existence looked filthy, like a gambler's ashtray piled with stubs. He sat trying to imagine what Petal must have been through as she died, and he still couldn't accept that if it hadn't been for him she would be dancing at the Eclipse with him right now.

He looked round, and there was the boxer from the other night sitting next to him.

'Hullo,' said the boxer, 'how's things then?'

'Not good.'

'You don't look too good. You sick? You look as if you needed a friend.'

'I do,' said Gust, 'but right now I haven't got one.'

'That's bad,' said the boxer, 'everyone needs a friend. Didn't you ever have any?'

'Yes,' said Gust, 'but I lost them in the fog.'

'In the what?'

'The fog in my head.'

The boxer moved his stool back slightly. 'You ought to see the quack about that.'

'No point.'

'Well, I don't know what you ought to do. Still, it's

123

none of my business; I don't ask stupid questions.'

'You did the night we met.'

'That was a misunderstanding,' said the boxer. 'How is the lady?'

'She'll come to no harm now.'

'I'm glad to hear that,' said the boxer. 'She's twenty-four carat, she is, a little diamond.' He got up. 'Anyway, I'd better be going, let me know if you get in any bother.' He took out a bookie's ballpoint and wrote on the back of an empty Westminster packet. 'That's the number of Paul's gym down in Wapping, they always know where I am.'

'Thanks, but I'll manage.'

'Let's have one more then.'

They had five more.

Later the boxer said, 'Take care of that fog of yours now, mind how you go.' He staggered out, colliding with the door.

The door lost.

Later on Gust was still in the Diadem. Someone tapped him on the shoulder and said, 'Man over there wants to talk to you.'

Connor was standing by the door.

'Come outside,' he said when Gust went over.

They crossed the street into the shadows.

'Well?' said Connor, 'speak up.'

'What about?'

'You know fucking well what about.'

'How did you find out?'

'The hard way. I got home and the law was there.'

Gust didn't say anything.

'What's the matter with you suddenly?' said Connor. 'You been struck dumb?'

'Yes,' said Gust.

'Is that all you can think of to say?'

'It's enough,' said Gust, 'that's it. That's all I've got to say.'

'Not even an amen for her?'

'You think she'd hear it?'

'I don't believe this,' Connor said. 'You're just such scum it amazes me.'

'I've got my memories of her the same as you have.'

'They're not worth much, though, are they, memories?'

'They'll just have to do though, won't they?'

'What happened to her was straight down to you.'

'I know,' said Gust. 'I got Petal killed because I wasn't thinking what I was doing; what more do you want?'

'I used to know you,' said Connor. He hit Gust hard. Gust didn't defend himself. He went down and Connor walked over him, especially his face. Every now and then he put the boot in it. When he had had enough of doing that he said, 'You're not worth killing,' and went off down the street, turning into the avenue without looking back. Gust watched him go from where he lay on the pavement. After a while he wiped his face and got up.

He went back to the bar and ordered a double scotch; the liquor burned his lips, which were split. People standing around looked at him uneasily, but no one came near him. He heard voices shouting through the fog: 'We don't want it like it happened to Petal! Make sure it's quick when it's our turn!'

Gust told them, 'What just happened to me will be like a kiss from the angel of mercy for the man who did it.' He said it out loud.

He sat on at the bar drinking and whistling, filling in the keys for her in his mind, the black keys and the white keys of everything he and Petal had been through, the major and the minor keys. It was the only funeral he had to give her.

He had seen people grieving less leaving a newly filled grave.

17

Sholly was angry with Gust at being late; the anger was really fear in case Gust had got his collar felt and told the law something.

When he saw Gust he shouted, 'Where the fuck have you been?'

'Busy.'

Sholly took a closer look at him. 'You look terrible. Christ, what happened to your face?'

'Never mind that,' said Gust. He sat down opposite Sholly. 'Well, have you got it?'

'Got it?' said Sholly. 'Of course I've got it. And you. Money. Come on.'

'No, bollock-brain. First off, where is it?'

'In the karzi, second shithouse inside the cistern, and don't do a runner.'

'What would I be chasing?' said Gust. 'The turds?'

Sholly was angry enough to shout why not? but he looked at Gust again and didn't.

'That's right,' said Gust. 'I've got no looks to spoil.' When he got upstairs to the men's it was empty. He went to the second cubicle, bolted himself in, got the gun out of the water tank and slit the plastic. The gun was dry, but he dried it again under the hot air blower to make sure. It was a new .38 all right, a Beretta.

He smiled at it and said, 'I've got work for you.'

He loaded it and put it in his pocket; then he went back to Sholly. He paid him the rest of the money, palming it to him under the table. 'You can count it later, it's all there. You know Petal Chang by the way, don't you?'

'The one with the sultry tits? Sure,' said Sholly. 'I used to get a load of those at the old Contract Club when she was singing there topless. Good dancer, uses the Tiara a lot. She used to be yours, didn't she? So what about her?'

'Nothing,' said Gust. 'Not any more. She died this afternoon.'

'Died? What do you mean?'

'She was killed with something like an iron bar, maybe a baseball bat, they don't know yet.'

Sholly turned the colour of wet fish. He sold death seven days a week, cash, terms even, but he himself wasn't into the hooded man on any terms at all. 'Fuck,' he said nervously. 'They got anyone for it?'

'No, but you're always on the manor, you seen her around with anyone in particular lately?'

'You know Petal,' said Sholly, 'all sorts bought her a drink.' Gust watched him trying to think up an excuse to leave. The news of her death had rattled him; bad news always rattled Sholly now. 'Day or night, people always did. If she hadn't anyone with her she'd dance with a stranger as they say.' He looked at Gust's pocket. 'Is that what the iron's for?'

'If you think about that even in your prayers, you're dead meat, Sholly; it'll be my pleasure to see to that personally.'

'Listen,' said Sholly, scraping his chair back, 'as long as it's not me you aim that at I don't care; you aim it where you want, you do what you like with it, all right? I'm off.'

'Best thing you could do,' said Gust, 'and if you get any information on Petal I'll pay for it.'

But Gust was already talking to his back. Sholly had

a file at the Home Office among other things, and he
didn't want to inflame it.

Gust went up Greek Street looking for a cab.

He half expected to find some burk waiting to try and
mug him as he left the Eclipse but, as often happens, the
more tooled up you are to deal with a situation, the more
it forgets to come for you.

It's always the situation you never thought of that cuts
you down.

18

Gust took the cab to Johnny Laray's place in Brockley. Johnny was round the side of the house feeding his greyhounds, and he answered the door carrying a bucket. When he saw Gust he said, 'Christ, have you hit a truck or something?'

'I took a beating, that's all,' said Gust. 'Can I come in?'

'Sure.'

Johnny was his ex-brother-in-law, and they had always got on. When Gust split up with Johnny's sister Cheryl it hadn't made any difference. In fact Johnny had said, 'You did well to get shot of her; my sister or not, she's a cow.'

Johnny carried on feeding the dogs while Gust watched. The dogs had racing names, but he never used them at home. 'Micky, Michelle, Vic! Vic's sprained a tendon in his off hind leg,' he explained, 'but a man up in St Albans offered me five grand for him cash just the same. For stud. Course I said no; life wouldn't be the same without him.' He fondled the dog's muzzle.

Gust looked at it rubbing itself against Johnny's legs. He wasn't into animals but he understood Johnny and the dogs all right; it was love all week long, even while the hare was whining round the track.

'All right then,' said Johnny, 'what's up?'

129

'This isn't a social visit,' Gust said. 'I haven't dropped round just to borrow a tenner; it's bad. I'll get round to telling you, but it'll take time.'

'That's OK,' Johnny said. 'Just wait till I finish up here, then we'll go in and have a drink.'

'I'll need a heavy one.'

The dogs tore round Johnny trying to get double rations. He stroked a young bitch. 'Meet Princess,' he said. 'She's the latest addition. She's really fast; she could win us a grand. I've got her in for a race Saturday week.' The dog rushed up and down, weaving between Gust's legs.

Johnny finally finished up and they went through into the main part of the house.

'So what's the news?' Johnny said.

'As bad as it could be.'

'Tell me, take your time about it.'

'I'll have to,' said Gust. 'I don't even know how I feel yet. I went out in the street afterwards and spewed up, and since then I haven't seemed to feel anything.'

'Listen,' Johnny said, 'best not talk about it yet.'

'Why? Aren't we alone here?'

'No. Knowing Shirley she won't stay long, she gets bored in the evenings, but she's in the sitting room. She's not everyone's treat, I warn you, and she's not in the best of tempers tonight, you'll see. Tonight she's red-hot on gin and women's rights.' He called out, 'Here I am, Shirl, you in the lounge then?'

A woman screamed out, 'Where else would I fucking well be?'

They went into the lounge. Someone on the old side for a girl was spread on a divan, wearing a pink skirt that started at her waist and more or less ended there. She was watching a Bruce Lee video, showing a motorway of leg, also crimson suspenders, and looked like something that had fallen off the tree at a conman's Christmas party.

'This is Shirley,' Johnny said.

She said to Gust sharply, 'Who are you?'

'He used to be my brother-in-law,' said Johnny.

'Cheryl's ex? I've never met him before.'

'You wouldn't have,' Johnny said, 'he's been away.'

'Oh yeah. One of those.'

'One of those what?' said Gust.

'One of those people who are always away on long holidays,' she sneered.

'That'll do,' said Johnny, 'cut it out.'

'Why?' she said, stirring her frillies on the sofa. 'I want to hear more. All I ever hear in this dump is foxes in the garden and doggy farts in the kitchen.'

'Drop it, Shirley,' Johnny said, 'you've had a few.'

'A few?' she said. 'So fucking what? I wish I was back trolling up at King's Cross.'

'You will be if you don't shut your yap.'

'I might as well at that. Ending up in this dump I must be dumb enough.' She made a sweeping gesture and knocked her drink off a doyly that said *Olé! España!* on it, then she opened her thighs wide, showing her pussy.

'Don't do that,' said Johnny, 'I've told you.'

'Why not? All you want is your fucking dogs and there's no one else waiting for the bus.'

Her top was so low-cut that it was practically cut out and Gust looked at her knockers; he felt he might as well, since seven-eighths of them were on display anyhow. They reminded him of the pumpkins he used to serve in his teenage days when he helped out on a stall in Berwick Street market.

She groped for her glass and threw it at Johnny. 'Here. Catch. Fill it up, and don't forget the ice.'

Johnny took the glass and sniffed it. 'That Spanish brandy, knocks you apart like an old packing case, that stuff does.'

'Fuck the commentary, just fill it up.'

'I've got a feeling I'm in the way here,' said Gust.

'In the way?' said Shirley. She picked up the TV remote control and zapped the sound off. 'You're not interrupting anything.' She tore one of her raspberry-coloured slippers off and hurled it across the room, demolishing a Portuguese doll. 'Go on, you couple of old closets,' she shouted, 'feel free, talk away, don't worry about me.'

'I just came round to see Johnny,' said Gust. 'It's nothing I want to say in public.'

'Don't be shy,' Shirley said. 'I'm not public, I'm his private life. Anyway for the moment.'

'It's for your own sake.'

'Oh it's for my sake, is it? Thank you so much.' She said to Johnny, 'I wish your past would fucking let go of you sometimes.' She snatched her drink from him and gave it a long swallow, then started zapping channels on the box again. The screen exploded into a spasm of gold leaf and cut to a monkey nibbling a nut. Then, thanks to state of the art graphics, the whole lot collapsed into itself.

'See that?' she said. 'It just blew away. Like his money.' Now she was listing on the sofa, really pissed. 'Talking of money, I'm going down to the disco now, wanker, got a ton on you? I'll get a minicab to civilisation and fuck the two of you.' Johnny took gave her the ton.

Shirley hooked a telephone in pastel lilac over with her foot and dialled a number; outside the wind moaned over Brockley Park, rattling the windows.

'A ton?' she slurred. 'Big deal. Back in the old days I might even have got a bent Diners card off him.'

After a while the doorbell went. Shirley got to her feet. 'My cab. Have a good cuddle, lovebirds, see you on the front page of *Hello*.' She reached for the back of the divan, missed it, got her balance back and moved unsteadily towards the door. On her way out she collided with Gust.

'Gust,' she said. She belched in his face, then said to Johnny, 'Why do you mix with crap like this anyway?'

'For the last time hold your tongue, Shirl.'

'Jail-meat,' she said. 'People like that bring jail fever,

let's hope it's not catching.' She shrugged herself into a wannabe sable coat and left, slamming the door.

'Understanding, isn't she?' said Johnny. He sounded proud of her. 'Anyway, she's gone now and we can talk, so start anywhere.'

'I need backup, Johnny,' Gust said. 'I need it badly and I need it now, tonight. It'll be risky, but there's no one else.'

As he spoke he felt betrayal stuck to his face like a whore's make-up, because whatever the state of his mind he recognised the lunacy of what he was going to do. It was as if he was saying to Johnny 'Trust me,' then going next door and charvering his woman. But necessity was like lust; it had to be satisfied.

'How risky?'

'Shooters.'

'For Christ's sake have a heart. Why don't you try someone else, like Frankie Petrosa?'

'I just have,' said Gust. 'Frankie's all right, but this is different, grown-up stuff.' He stopped; then he got it out in one burst. 'She's gone, Johnny.'

'Who? What are you talking about?'

'Petal.'

'Gone where?'

'I don't mean that kind of gone.'

'What do you mean then? Where's she gone?'

'Nowhere,' said Gust, 'even if she made it that far. She's been gone since this afternoon. She's dead.'

'Petal?' Johnny said. He sat down suddenly. 'I don't believe it. How did it happen?'

'It happened at her place,. She was putting me up. They cut her a smiler first, then they whacked her over the head maybe with a baseball bat. Anyway, she'd no real head left.'

'How do you know she hadn't?'

'Don't you start looking at me as if I'd done it. Why I know about her face is because the law took me up to see her.'

'What?' Johnny shouted. 'You're raving, man, the law never does that. Who was it from the law?'

'Spaulding, a DI from the Factory, A14.'

'A14, that's naughty. I don't make Spaulding, though. Anyway, he can't know a pint from his arsehole doing a thing like that. It's dead out of order, that could backfire on him. What the fuck did he do it for?'

'He wants to crack me, Johnny. It could be because I got into a fight in Marly's where a man died. Or it could be because I've been on a scam; I've only been out of the nick two months and I needed the money. I got into this thing, but before we even pulled the stroke I was nobbled by a man with photographs of us all together, so I had the choice between doing what he said or going back for my other five.'

'Who got at you?'

'No one I knew, but he knew me all right.'

'He anything to do with Petal?'

'How do I know?' said Gust. 'I don't know anything yet.'

'What was going down?'

'It looked like a simple job nicking passports and delivering them on. All I had to do was rob the van and I did rob it. Only I didn't rob it for the people who set it up, I did it for the man with the photographs, so what looked like a straightforward job has turned into ten thousand kinds of shit and I'm in all of it.'

'You'll have to do something about him,' said Johnny, 'the ice cream with the pictures.'

'I can't, he's fireproof.'

'No one's fireproof. Why's he fireproof?'

'He's from the government.'

'For fuck's sake,' said Johnny, 'what have you got mixed up in? No, wait. Who steered you into this in the first place?'

'Manny.'

'Manny Farb? What's the matter with you? Have you gone mad? Christ, I hate that bastard. Manny's a grass, you know that. You should do; it was him got me done in eighty-six. And who else? The Hammer, is he in on it too? Him and that other little wanker Harry Ford? Christ, you've got to live, you say? Jesus, any proposition you get from that load of shit you're more likely to fucking die, man.'

'When you're out after doing ten,' said Gust, 'you're pretty well dead anyway, anything else is on top; I had to take what I could get. And now Petal. Listen, Johnny, Petal and I had our ups and downs. We split up while I was inside, yes, but we stayed mates, which is why she took me in. Now, suppose you were in my place and you still loved her, fuck the rights and wrongs of it, how would you feel if she was killed?'

'The way you do,' Johnny said, 'but I still can't believe it. Petal was a diamond.'

'I know,' said Gust. He groaned. 'And what you've got to understand is the worst thing of all, that she'd be alive now if it wasn't for me. What I'm sure of, someone topped her as a way of getting at me, but I don't know who to get after for it. It could be revenge from whoever sent the men down to Marly's club where this fight was, or it could have been Manny's people, and thinking it over I like Manny for it best.'

'What was this Marly's thing, then?'

'It was two men in Marly's who were sent down there to kill me. They told me that, so I topped one and crippled the other. All right, I did it. I had to; it was them or me. But the law's after me for that as well. Spaulding again.'

'This Spaulding, he get anything out of you?'

'What the law always gets out of me, not even the skin off my shit. But Manny, Manny's different, and if he's had anything to do with Petal he's as dead as a used condom, only I need my back watched.'

'You want to top him?'

'I've nothing to lose.'

'Why do anything tonight?' said Johnny. 'Think it

over. You look terrible, really sick.'

'No, I'm short on time the shit I'm in, it'll have to be tonight. Try and see what I'm going through over Petal; I miss her in a way you wouldn't believe. I thought of her all the time I was banged up and came out to find she was with Connor, but just the same last night it was as if we'd never been apart.'

'All right,' Johnny said. 'No, you can't leave it like that, OK. You made any wages on all this business yet?'

'Yes, talking of that,' said Gust. He got his bankroll out and counted off a thousand. 'Take it. Help me. I'll find the people who killed her, I'll go all over town. There's only one other problem, I might need to hole up. My place is staked out and I've nowhere to stay.'

'There's the house here. Shirley doesn't take up much room even when she's in, so there's only her, me, and the dogs.'

'Would you look after something for me here if I asked you?'

'If it doesn't explode.'

'It's only money. Money's the only thing I've got and you wouldn't believe, it doesn't even buy me a roof over my head.'

'It'll be safe here.'

'I know. Only don't forget the law's interested in me right round the clock, especially now there's blood on the ground.'

'Let's get back to Spaulding for a minute,' Johnny said. 'Does he bend?'

'No, A14 never does. He's like the rest of that little mob, brighter than he looks, and he's got this great fascination with me, it's like a rash. Normally, over this Marly's club thing I'd turn myself in and say it was self defence, which it was, but my record being what it is I don't think any court would swallow it.'

'No,' said Johnny, 'nor do I, and there's another thing. Have you any idea who to go after besides Manny? I only wonder, because Manny's gutless, he's noted; he's a go-between, all he likes is setting up deals and then standing clear. He always did; he doesn't like getting tangled up with murder, he's too yellow. But then if you've got the Hammer in on it as well, that one's capable of anything. He'd smash the devil's own fucking head in. From behind.'

'Yes, there's a great mate of mine,' said Gust, 'and never mind Harry Ford throwing me out of his flat; I'll deal with him too if someone else doesn't get there first.'

'Well you know what it is with rats,' Johnny said. 'What do rats do in a gutter? They fuck each other, then they eat each other, and that's Harry Ford for you.'

'Harry can wait for now. Manny comes first. I've got to start somewhere, and until I know better I'm assuming Manny knows all about Petal's death. So I'm going to see him now, it'll be the second time round today.'

'You know where to find him?'

'He's up in Soho,' said Gust. 'He's out with his mates noshing, they look like east Europeans to me. And Manny only ever eats in one place and that's the Red Wok round the back of the fire station; he fills his great gut out with that Chinese gear.'

'Yes, I know the Wok,' said Johnny. 'It's that fucking great place on two floors. You armed?' Gust nodded. 'Well, I'll just go and get something to weigh my own coat down with then.'

'What have you got?'

'I admit it's on the heavy side for indoors. It's a .765. The slug'll smash a few plates when it comes out the far side of the geezer but I can't help that, it's all I've got handy.'

'If things go sour I know that place inside and out,' said Gust. 'Petal used to work there and I know a few people who'll be sorry she's dead, so don't worry.'

'You mean we're going to do him right in the restaurant? With everyone noshing and having a good look at the free entertainment?'

'If we do it in public it'll cut Manny down to size, and I'm not saying I want to kill him; I want to hurt him, I want to scare him, I want to make him talk.'

'It's the fuzz I'm thinking of. There'll be a huge scream go up.'

'No there won't, I'm not that stupid. We'll be in and out long before the heroes get round, I'll guarantee that.'

'Well it'll be poetic,' said Johnny. 'What, Manny? It'll be all sweet and no sour with me.'

They went out to Johnny's car and started for the West End through the sodden streets. Presently Gust broke the silence: 'I'm in this red fog.'

Johnny overtook three buses waiting at a stop. He didn't say anything.

Gust went on. 'You remember the first drink the three of us had the morning after Petal and I got together? It was over at that pub off Broadwick Street, The Nine Lives, and I'd had a tickle so we drank champagne and I told you in the karzi I love that girl. Remember? Then we went swimming over at Endell Street and you were so pissed you nearly drowned, and after that we carried on boozing all day and in the death we stayed up all night and had a fried chicken in the morning. And then, because of the problems I'd got with the fuzz and getting pissed in the Diadem all the time, the passion slowly kind of wore off, and one day I got home at five in the morning and Petal said, "Listen, Gust, I don't say you're not a man, but what I do say is that you're not my kind of man; to tell you the truth I don't think you're anybody's kind of man. You're a loner, you don't need a woman, so that now when you come back here from pulling a stroke it isn't me you really want, it's just the bed and the roof, so you can stop telling me you love me from now on." And then after that it was just downhill all the way till I went inside, and I'm remembering it all right now of course, and I tell you I'm in despair now she's dead, which she wouldn't be if I'd never gone to her. She died because of that and I should never have done it; I tell you I'm living in this fog, I'm not really here.'

'Look,' said Johnny, 'you may not believe this now, not yet, but you'll keep going, people just do, you'll get over it.'

'No I won't,' said Gust, 'because I've lost the person I need to go on with.' He put his hand on the wheel suddenly. 'All right, stop the car, John, I've changed my mind. We're not going anywhere, just stop here and let me off.'

'What are you talking about? What the fuck's the matter with you now?'

'You're riding with a maniac. So drop me off, turn the car round and go home, do as I say, I'll work this on my own.'

'Ah fuck off, will you? And get your hands off that wheel. Or else throw yourself out if you like but I'm doing fifty, you'll get hurt.'

'All right, then,' said Gust. He forgot about stopping the car and stared through the windscreen. 'I'm trying to work this out,' he said. 'Don't you remember that day we arranged to meet Petal in the French at midday and it got later and later and I was just thinking she wouldn't show when in she stepped from the sunlight looking like a summer leaf, and I am going to start finding out the truth in that restaurant tonight even if my feet have come to the end of the world.'

'I like that,' said Johnny, 'that last bit there, what was that?'

'Something I read in jail. Must be words for when you're going to be taken out and shot, something like that. And then don't you remember me telling you about that weekend just after I got divorced from Cheryl? You couldn't come, it was a Saturday, and Petal and I took that old American banger I had and we drove across the river. It was in the middle of June, and we sat in Battersea Park all day with some beer watching a cricket match and then we went across the common to the Princess of Wales.'

'We were happy then all right,' Johnny said, 'and we will be again; anyway, dreaming never did any harm.'

'No time for dreams now,' said Gust, 'but the other day while I was sleeping out in Soho Square, in the morning I watched the sparrows flying off mob-handed up to Oxford Street, spiralling away over the buses and I thought, the sun shines, the snow falls, we die, but they're still there.'

Johnny drove on without saying anything, but Gust couldn't stop talking. 'Thinking about Petal's like the day I took my old gran to the hospital. She was seventy-eight and the doctor told us she was just going in for a minor op, but I knew better, and so did she. She was lying on her pillows in the back room with her cardigan on and she said, "Get what I need to look decent, then, while I put my teeth in." So I got her clothes, then I got her suitcase out of the cupboard and packed it and she came out dressed and said, "Well, here I am, ready, and where are my reading glasses?" So I made sure she'd got them and when I went back in she was sitting on the edge of the bed, which she had remade all neat. "Is the car there?" she said, and when I told her it was at the door she looked at me and said, "The end's no enemy, you know, son." Later, when I was in jail, I started reading some stuff by Dylan Thomas and I came across a line where he said After the first death there is no other, and it made me think about Gran, so I used to talk to her often in there when I was banged up alone on rule forty-three; she used to slip in to see me. But the day I took her into the hospital I said, "Don't talk about the end like that, Gran," and she just looked at me and said, "My post office book's under the carpet there by the window, and you've done well looking after me, whatever people say."

'Changing the subject,' said Johnny, 'who beat you up like that? Your face looks really terrible.'

'There's no point going into it,' Gust said. 'I just took a hammering, that's all.'

And his face would go on looking like that right the way through; it would never have time to heal.

19

Just after ten Gust and Johnny walked into the Red Wok. Johnny was right, it was a huge great place. There were candles in glass bowls on the tables, which was lucky, because the only other lit feature was the bar way off at the back.

Gust nudged Johnny. 'There's Manny, up at that table at the top there.' He stopped the head waiter; he knew him from before when Petal was working there.

'Hi, Gust,' said the waiter, 'how's things? You want a table?'

'No,' Gust said. 'There's going to be trouble here in a minute and I don't want the wrong people getting hurt. The bother will be over at that big table where those six men are, I'm marking your card.'

'Mr Farb's table?'

'That's the one.'

'What are you going to do?'

'Make a lot of noise.'

'You can't do that,' the waiter said. 'Are you pissed or what? You'd better leave, you're crazy.'

'It'll all be over by the time the law arrives,' Gust told him. 'Just make sure nobody bells them till we leave and keep your own folk dead clear of that table.'

The waiter had his eye on the bulge in Gust's pocket. 'Yes,' Gust said, 'it's real and it's going to have its trigger pulled for it. But don't worry, I'll see you all right after.'

'What's the fuck's the matter with you?' said the waiter.

'Here's what's the matter,' Gust said. 'It's Petal Chang. You remember her.'

'Petal? Sure. You two back together again?'

'No, because she was murdered this afternoon and I've come to see about it.'

'Murdered? Petal? Why would anyone want to do that to a girl like her?'

'That's what I'm here to find out.'

'Look, can't you do it somewhere else? Why does it have to be in here?'

'I don't know why scum like Farb choose your place to eat in,' said Gust, 'but there he is. Now get moving; no one else is going to get hurt.'

'You reckon it was Farb?'

'I wouldn't be here if I didn't.'

'Petal,' the waiter said. 'Yes, OK.' The expression on his face had changed now; it was dreamy and closed. He drifted away, and seconds later the floor space round Manny's table was empty.

'We can start now,' Gust told Johnny.

Manny was sitting surrounded by the Hammer and the four men Gust and Frankie had seen in Marjorie Grove.

Gust went up to Manny. 'Hullo, I'm back.'

The Hammer made a movement and Gust told him, 'Don't move, hell's not a breath away.' He twirled back to Manny. 'This is Johnny Laray, say hullo, Manny. You remember Johnny, don't you, you had him weighed off for three in eighty-six. My brother-in-law,' he explained to the four silent men. He patted his bulging pocket. 'So let's have this talk that got put off, Manny.'

'Talk?' shouted Manny. 'What the fuck is this? Some kind of joke?'

'No,' said Gust, 'it's about that business we started this afternoon and didn't finish, business that's got even more serious since then. So I've come to see how we're going to work it all out, though I've a good idea.'

'You can work it out with your feet,' said Manny. 'Fuck off, you can see I'm eating with friends.' Only he wasn't, because the others had stopped eating. They took the bulges on Johnny and Gust seriously.

'Get this straight, Manny, for you this is the last supper,' Gust told him.

Manny put his spoon and fork down; he never could handle chopsticks. He said to Johnny out of the corner of a mouth full of noodles, 'That eighty-six business, Laray, forget it. It can all be sorted.'

'Yes,' Johnny said, 'sorted all over the ceiling. I'm going to shoot your meal out of you.'

Manny still couldn't believe it. 'Now let's be reasonable about this,' he said. A piece of noodle fell out of his mouth onto the tablecloth.

'I'm not noted for it,' Johnny said.

'There was a death this afternoon, Manny,' Gust said. 'A girl.'

'A death?' said Manny. 'A girl? Tell us about it. Here, what's the matter with your face by the way? Sit down, have a drink. And you too, Johnny. Waiter, bring a couple of chairs up.'

But there were no waiters.

'Fuck the drink,' said Gust. 'Get up, Manny.' He had the thirty-eight in his hand now.

'No,' said Manny, staring at it. 'No.' He tried to push himself back from the table, but he couldn't because he was wedged up between the table and the wall.

Gust leaned over him. 'Now be clever, Manny, it's a big bullet, and your gut'll be in even worse shape if I shoot you sitting down. So stand up, take it like a man, don't make your friends ashamed of you. Standing up, it looks better.'

'How can it look better if I'm dead?'

'He meant better for the undertaker,' said Johnny.

Now anyone could see how all six of them suddenly

wished they were a long way off from the Red Wok; their fear smelled like wet iron. Each man was looking down at his plate where giant prawns swam in a beige sauce at twelve quid a throw, wondering if they would ever get another taste; they were all so close to life and yet so fucking far. And the strange thing was that none of the other diners were taking any notice at all; if they saw anything it was just two men standing up talking to six men sitting down.

'If anything happens to us,' said the Hammer, 'you don't need to be told what'll happen to you. After.'

'There won't be any after,' said Gust. 'I'm a here and now man, but one move out of you and you'll be neither here or now.'

Manny gave up. He was sweating, his lips deflated like purple inner tubes. 'I don't even believe this is happening,' he said. He farted.

'Hot in here, isn't it?' said Johnny. 'What's gluing you to your chair then, your shit? Don't have the shits now, Manny, that's not nice in company. Get up now and don't be embarrassing.'

'I can't,' he whined, 'I'm sick.'

'Stay where you are then,' said Johnny. Manny had a Tsing-Tao in front of him; Johnny picked it up and poured it over Manny's head.

'We'll work out a deal,' Manny said, wiping his face with his sleeve. 'We'll work something out tomorrow.'

'No,' said Gust, 'there's no room for a deal, no room for tomorrow even; I told you this afternoon I wanted it sorted, and that was before what's happened since.'

'We can get it all sorted.'

'No,' said Gust again.

The Hammer moved fractionally and Johnny said, 'Do that once more, and you'll be part of your fried duck.'

One of the foreigners put his cheroot down very carefully, but that was all he did. Gust continued, 'Things have got even worse than they were now,

Manny. Because of the death of this friend. Much
worse.'

'What was the name of this friend?'

'Petal Chang.'

'Who the fuck's she?' said Manny. 'I've never even
heard of her.'

'You'll be meeting her in a minute where you're going.
She'll introduce herself and kill you all over again.'

Manny turned yellow.

'Anyway, you're a liar,' Gust said. 'There's no one in
this town you haven't heard of. It was you who sent
those two heavies down to Marly's to see to me, and
when that went wrong you killed Petal or had her killed.
Now you know she meant a lot to me, you knew we'd
lived together for years, so why did you do that to her,
Manny? Why did you have her head whacked off like
that?'

Manny stretched his hands out imploringly and his
body bobbed up and down. 'It was nothing to do with
me!'

'The law took me up to see her body this afternoon,'
Gust went on implacably, 'and she didn't look pretty at
all. She'd been seen to with a Stanley knife and then
with what might have been a baseball bat. You know a
lot of sadists, Manny. You got friends who like going to
town on a woman with a baseball bat or maybe an iron
bar?'

'I don't even know who this Chinese slut is!' Manny
shouted. 'I keep telling you!'

'You're lying,' said Gust. 'If you didn't do it yourself
you put out a contract on her.'

'Why should I put out contracts on people? And why
should I have anything against you?'

'Because you want me out of the way, Manny, which
at the moment is what everyone seems to want. You
rowed me in on this scam because I'm out on a ticket,
I'm expendable, and I was meant to be fucking expen-
ded. I've got this money that you don't appreciate me

running around with, and those two men who came down to Marly's knew it; their orders were to top me and take their wages out of it, they told me that. And something's going on behind the original deal that you know about and I don't fucking know about. So to get some clarification I'm starting with you, and I can't think of a better place.'

'For me you was paid,' Manny shouted. 'I've got nothing on you, the deal with you was settled, you're paid up, it's over.'

'Not according to the men at Marly's it wasn't,' said Gust. 'According to them it was anything but over, because they told me that certain gear we all know about never ended up where it was meant to.'

'For me it was kosher. Whatever else you're talking about I don't know anything, this Petal Chang and the rest of it, I've never heard of her and I wasn't there.'

'You never are when people die.'

'That's right,' said Johnny, 'you're only around when there's money about.'

'Still, you'll have to show up when you die yourself,' said Gust, 'even you can't miss that treat, and this is it. Get him on his feet, Johnny.'

Johnny leaned over Manny; Manny started to blubber and the foreigner who had put the cheroot down appeared to need something out of his pocket. But Gust wasn't having any of that. 'You're beat on the table, wanker, leave it alone, there's going to be enough mess as it is.'

'You can't do this here!' Manny shouted.

'Who's looking?' said Gust. 'Nobody.'

Johnny heaved Manny up and propped him against the bamboo wall. One or two diners found that interesting enough to turn round, but no one saw anything unusual in a drunk being helped off to the heads.

Just a few tables away a well-known art critic was interviewing an internationally famous painter; they were surrounded by bottles of dry white. A lot of people couldn't understand why the painter had ever made any money out of art at all, and the critic was interviewing him with a view to finding out how it had happened, how he had ever got started.

'Really started, you mean?' said the painter.

'Absolutely!' said the art critic. 'You know. When you knew that the immediacy of your perception had made an irreversible public impact.'

'Why,' the painter cried enthusiastically, 'I've told that story hundreds of times. It was the evening poor Maurice staggered round to my studio after my first major exhibition and squawked, "I hate your lousy paintings, Gerald, they're a cesspool, they are the very cube root of shit." Then he threw the roast beef at the wall, locked me up in the loo and screamed, "Your art runs out of your arse, you pretentious little pouf," and that's where I got the idea for my great triptych, of course, Catharsis In Excreta: Abstract, On the thunderbox!'

'So it's true what they say,' said the critic reverently. 'That, of course, is why your pictures are always brown.'

'Of course!'

'You say you never went to art college,' said the critic, scribbling away.

'Art college?' shouted the painter, slamming the table with the flat of his hand; he was having a terrific time. 'Life is art college!' Just then Gust fired and the bullet, taking a reverse angle off the wall, smashed into his plate, smothering him and various other people with shark's fin soup. Tastefully entwined noodles and pieces of monkfish, painted in soy sauce, drifted upwards till they met a lantern. The painter watched the flying meal open-mouthed. 'The chiaroscuro!' he whispered. 'A revelation!'

People screamed and some of them made for the exit, but Johnny moved across with his gun and herded them back.

'Are you all right?' the critic shouted above the noise.

'All right?' said the painter, wiping soup from his streaming eyes with the tablecloth, 'of course I'm all right! But I see you've taken one near the plimsoll line.'

'A splinter of glass,' the art critic said, dabbing at his chin, 'it's nothing.'

'Of course it isn't!' said the painter. 'You journalists are always in the thick of things.'

The Hammer fired back as Johnny kicked the table at him; the bullet tore through the lining of Gust's jacket and whizzed over the artist's head. He clapped his hands with joy ('More firecrackers!') and began stacking up the broken china on the table, indicating pieces of it with what had been a spoon. 'We were talking about the relationship between line and colour just now,' he shouted at the art critic over the clamour of shots and panic-stricken people running around, 'and as you can now see for yourself, the front line cuts clean through the main course in any painting.' He leaned over and dealt with the blood dribbling down the critic's chin with the latter's tie. 'There,' he said, 'that's better, it's nothing, just a graze. I must remember to come here more often, I don't remember them ever putting on a show like this before.' Over at Manny's table one of the Europeans groaned and doubled up. 'I say,' said the painter, 'I suppose this *is* just cabaret, isn't it?'

'I think perhaps we ought to take cover all the same, whatever it is, don't you?' the critic said.

'Nonsense,' said the painter, 'if it's the real thing, that's what they'd expect us to do.' He picked up the current wine bottle. 'Might as well drink it straight out of this,' he explained. 'It's safer in your stomach, no point wasting time with a glass. Besides,' he added, looking at the remains of his own glass, 'you can't get much of a drink out of just the stem.'

Johnny fired a second time; a packet of condoms erupted from an overcoat on the hanger and fanned out across the room. This time the screaming wasn't so loud because a large number of diners were already under the tables, though there was some background noise from a woman covered with boiled rice and hot chilli sauce who poked her head out from behind a chair to complain that her designer dress was ruined.

'Beautiful,' said the painter, 'quite beautiful.'

'I don't know about you, but I think I honestly would feel happier if we moved on somewhere else,' the art critic said, starting to get up.

'Don't be a fool. I'm surprised to hear that coming from you; I thought the Fourth Estate was used to hot spots. In any case I wouldn't budge if I were you, there's another bottle of wine in the ice bucket and nothing's happened to you yet.'

'Perhaps if we just got down on the floor for a bit.'

'How can we possibly discuss populism in modern art if we're under the table?'

Manny hadn't been hurt yet, but jammed up against the wall by the table he couldn't move either. He said entreatingly, 'Look, stop this, we can still talk about it. What is it you want?'

'I want Petal's killer,' said Gust. He aimed at Manny. 'You going to do anything about this, Hammer?' he said without looking at him. 'Because I'd like you to try.'

'Don't,' one of the Europeans said to the Hammer. 'You only get big trouble.'

The Hammer didn't say or do anything more; he just sat bunched up tight.

'You've got nothing to say about Petal then, Manny?' said Gust.

Manny shook his head: 'How can I when I don't know anything?'

'You're still lying,' Gust said. He fired at Manny and deliberately shot off part of his right hand. Manny shrieked; a detached fragment of the hand knocked sharply on the wall above him and fell back on the table. He bowed and hugged the wound against his balls, crossing his thighs in an effort to make a tourniquet with them. Blood spurted all over the place.

'That's enough,' Gust said. 'Let's go.' He saw the waiter he had talked to and gave him a thousand pounds, told him to spread it around, thanked him.

'We didn't see anything,' said the waiter. 'The telephone seemed not to be working so we hid in the kitchen.'

'I still owe you,' said Gust. 'A big one.'

They reached the door and made their way through the dense crowd there of people weeping and cursing. Nobody tried to stop them or even noticed them; they were too busy worrying about themselves. When they were out in the street Johnny said, 'That was a real grass's wages Farb drew there, only why did you leave his head on?'

'So he can work out why he's a hand short.'

'What happened to your jacket?'

'I don't know,' said Gust, surprised, looking down at it. 'Looks like it must have got a round through it.' He stripped it off and threw it in a waste bin.

In the restaurant the screaming had really started now, coupled with the wailing of ambulance and police sirens; someone must finally have got to a phone. A man covered from head to foot with spicy vegetables pushed past them and shambled out into the street yelling, 'These bastards think they can get away with murder!'

'It's what everybody else gets away with,' said Johnny, as they made way for two squad cars and crossed the street, 'so why not us?'

The avenue swallowed them. A passing 14 bus dropped them off at the Diadem, and they could still hear the shouting and yelling in the distance through the pub's open door. While they were waiting to be served a plausible-looking man wearing a yellow cashmere cap with a gravy-coloured stain on the side came in and leaned over the counter.

'Evening,' he said to the barman. 'The governor about? Upstairs, is he? Good, it doesn't matter, all I wanted to do was cash a cheque.'

'We don't cash cheques,' the barman said.

'What? The governor always cashes my cheques. You must be new here but you needn't worry, everyone in here knows me.'

'Anyone know this geezer?' the barman shouted. Nobody turned round.

'Go on,' said the punter. 'I only need thirty quid, and I'll spend it in here anyway.'

The governor came downstairs just then; when he saw the man in the cashmere cap he cantered up the bar like a giraffe. He pointed a finger at him on the end of an enormously long arm and roared, 'You! Out of my pub! You're barred!' The general conversation, which had scarcely dimmed, continued as before.

Johnny and Gust were ordering their second pint when a woman in designer grunge standing next to Gust turned on him and said sharply, 'If you were going to say any spare change forget it. What happened to your face?'

'I must have cut it on the edge of your tongue,' Gust said.

'She reminds me of Shirl,' said Johnny. Just then police spilled in through the two doors and started looking at all the punters' faces. Gust stood bowed drunkenly over the counter, and when they had done enough looking the coppers left again; they seemed in a hurry.

'Here, Johnny,' said Gust presently, 'you need a piss.'

'No I don't. I was just going to get us another pint.'

'You do need a piss, so get down to the karzy.'

'What's the rush?'

'Don't argue,' said Gust, 'and if there's anyone down there wait till they leave.'

However there were just the two of them downstairs and Gust took most of his money out, which he had put in an old envelope. 'Get home now,' he said. 'Hide that somewhere.'

'What is it?'

'It's money, for the love of Christ. Now do as I say.'

'There's a fucking bundle here,' said Johnny, peering inside the envelope, 'there must be thousands. How much is it?'

'I don't know,' Gust said, 'but don't start counting it in here, and if the heroes come visiting you never heard of it. Take what you need. I'll be back for the rest later, and if by any chance I'm not, spend it on the dogs, not Shirley.'

'Now wait.'

'That's just what I can't do,' Gust said. He patted Johnny on the shoulder. 'My old son, I'll see you.'

He zipped himself up and left quietly, the way shadows fall on a garden.

20

An ageless man whom no one would normally look at twice came to see Draper. He was known as the visitor, but people who worked in the department preferred not to know him at all. He had an office in the building where the lift didn't go up any further, and that was the floor where all the trouble and bad news came from.

'I want a rundown on this Gatov business,' he told Draper, 'every aspect of it, and I want it now, I've got people moaning all over the place.'

'As long as it's not the minister,' said Draper.

'The minister's in Paris, luckily for you, but the police couldn't get away, so let's start with them. I've got a Detective Inspector Spaulding burning my phone out; he tells me you're obstructing the course of justice in a murder inquiry he's on over a killing in a Soho piano bar, so what about it?'

'You mean the Gust thing,' said Draper. 'All right, I know I'm being obstructive, but I can't let Spaulding have him.'

'Why not?'

'Naturally I was coming up to see you about it.'

Sladden coughed and gazed out of the window.

'Why can't Spaulding have him?'

'Because he's working for us, of course.'

'It seems to me you've got almost as many villains

working for you as Gatov has,' the visitor said.

'We've been through a sticky patch, I admit that,' said Draper, 'but things will get easier now that we've really got Gatov going. He looks a bit tired, like the Docklands light railway, but his story's coming along like a Japanese monorail.'

'I don't want to hear about trains,' said the visitor. He played chess with a computer in his spare time and was an expert on en primeur claret. 'I want results. I want to hear about these missiles, what these Russian people are doing with them, and where they are.'

'Gatov's told us all that,' said Sladden.

Ricky muttered, 'He hadn't much choice.'

'I'm waiting,' the visitor said.

'You've got to think of these missiles as if they were ingots on the bullion market,' said Draper. 'The punter hardly ever actually gets to see the goods. The Russian idea is to turn the gear over as often as possible; the generals in charge take all the deposits they can without ever shifting it. But of course if the money was really right then they might just let them go, and the right money is just what Gatov had got fixed up.'

'Stop talking Chinese, will you?' said the visitor. 'Where are these bloody things right now?'

'Where they've always been, in military area 7. They haven't moved as far as Gatov knows. At least not yet.'

'Well, when are they going to be moved? Do you know? What does Gatov have to say about that?'

'We've got a difference of perspective here,' said Draper. 'We've got Gatov's point of view about the missiles and we've got the generals'. Gatov wants to make himself a multi-millionaire as quick as he can; but the generals in charge of them want to keep the missiles where they are and push the price up as high as possible before they sign a movement order, because with things the way they are over there they haven't got a hope of a pension.'

'And transport's another problem even if they wanted

to move them,' said Sladden. 'The trailers that carry them do fifteen gallons to the mile, and it's a hell of a lot of miles to Turkey.'

'Also they've got big overheads,' said Ricky. 'They've got to pay the crews and the technicians off, everyone's got to have his whack.'

'So that's why these people have come to Britain,' said Draper, 'to get the deal funded, get it moving, and make these generals an offer in hard western cash that they can't refuse. But they've got to work out the logistics, which will take time, so it's not for tomorrow.'

'It would be bad enough if it was for the day after,' the visitor said.

'Forget the day after,' said Draper, 'today's more than enough.'

'So here we sit with our arses parked on a hand grenade,' said the visitor, 'whereas what you're for is to make sure they're not.'

'I appreciate that,' said Draper, 'but since we can't destroy the missiles we've got to kill them off at the business end, which we are doing.'

'But how long is it going to take? We can't damp this down for ever. Think of the press; it only needs one leak.'

'I know, but you can't rush it. We'll have to take the time we need.'

'Well, I'll tell you this much,' said the visitor, 'they're not satisfied upstairs. They're beginning to think this whole operation needs closer supervision altogether.'

'Christ,' Draper fumed, 'we don't want the accountants and bureaucrats moving in on it now, it'd be like the Animal Front pulling us off our horses just when we'd nailed the fox.'

'We'll see,' said the visitor. 'Meantime there's another side to it; I don't understand the importance of these stolen passports with reference to Gust and all that part of the operation. As far as I can see you conspired to steal them yourself, using Gust.'

'Look,' said Sladden, 'we all know that if we were going to apply ordinary criminal law to this we'd never get anywhere.'

'Gatov had bought those passports anyway through a villain called Farb,' said Draper. 'It was Farb who used Gust, and we had to intercept them. Besides we used four of those passports as traps. You know all that; you saw my last report.'

'Two of the men who were using those passports are dead.'

'Well there's light and shade in all these things,' said Draper mildly. 'Besides, there's no final solution to this missile problem; all we can do is try and contain it, you know.'

Draper's soothing tone irritated the visitor. 'Don't flannel me,' he said. 'And I'll tell you what I know. From where I'm sitting in this pantomime it's all shade and no light, and when it gets dark enough there's going to be an internal inquiry which will make your balls squeak.'

'A little more patience,' said Draper, 'that's all I'm asking, there's no need to panic. And there's another spin-off. When this is over there'll be a lot fewer of our own homegrown villains around, never mind Gatov.'

'Well that'll be one good thing at least,' the visitor said, 'because I don't want anyone getting away now.'

'Nobody's going to get away with anything on this one,' said Draper. 'Not while I'm in charge.'

'And these missiles?'

'The best we can do, is make sure they stay where they are until things in Russia have sorted themselves out.'

'That'll be in a couple of hundred years,' said the visitor. He stood up. 'But you've only got a week.'

'What?' said Sladden. 'A week?'

'One week. Seven days. And all of them working days.'

'It might be over sooner than that,' said Draper.

'It had better be,' said the visitor. 'Anyway, you heard me, I said a week. So clear this up before it blows up; meantime we'll be upstairs watching you the whole time.'

21

The two men ran after Gust through the rain when he left the Diadem and jumped him outside the Prince Edward cinema. The fat one said, 'Don't be deliberate, every time you move means a month in hospital.'

They were experts; they handled him with the careless aplomb of tennis stars bouncing a ball on centre court. They ran him down the street and bundled him into a weather-beaten XJ6 which crept out of Greek Street; right through, the driver never spoke or even turned round.

Gust was no dwarf, but the fat man was nearly twice his size. His face was the same colour as his tussore suit – pink; the suit was a size too small for him and it steamed with rain on body heat.

'You ought to wear corsets,' Gust said.

'I do on my time off,' said the pink man. 'Black ones.'

'Are you the two who've been watching my place at Allison Road?'

'We watch a lot of places.'

'Who do you work for?'

They didn't answer that.

'Where are we going?'

'Depends on you,' said the pink man. 'You mightn't be going anywhere, or alternatively you might be going somewhere and then not come back.'

'What I want to know about, is Petal.'

'Petal?' the pink man said to his partner. 'What's he talking about now?'

'She was a Chinese girl,' said Gust. 'She was beaten to death this afternoon. You look as if you were handy with a baseball bat, did you have anything to do with it? Because if you did you'd better send off for a correspondence course on prayer.'

The pink man roared with laughter. 'I like this one,' he said to his mate, 'he's got a funny side to him.'

Gust tried to move away from the suffocating heat of the pink man, but half a ton of sodden flesh rammed him back in his seat.

'You're in a hurry to leave but you can't really, can you?' the pink man said.

His oppo hadn't said anything yet, but now he piped up. He was thin and wore a dirty white suit with black pinstripes. He looked Italian; but what he resembled even more closely was evil in a bad light. 'My nails are long, aren't they?' he said to Gust. 'Have you seen my nails? Aren't they sharp? Really long and pointed.' He held them out.

'I should think they must cut right through the mandolin strings,' Gust said.

'There's dirt under them too. Look at all the dirt.'

'Hard to miss it.'

'I keep my nails dirty like that all the time,' said the pinstriped man proudly.

'Why's that?' said Gust. He yawned.

'Because I like leaving dirt deep in a man's face.' His hands flashed and his nails sank into Gust's cheek. 'That way I get still more dirt in them, including yours. That gives me a rush.'

Gust wiped some of the blood off himself with his sleeve.

'Last time I had these nails of mine seriously into someone's face,' the pinstriped man boasted, 'it took three men to get me off him.'

'I see enough sick crap as it is without having it sit next to me,' said Gust, 'and what I'm wondering is, if you went up to see Petal today by any chance with this moron here. Did that get you a rush too, beating a woman to death? That's what I want to know.'

'Well even if I had've done,' said the pinstriped man, 'what could you have fucking done about it?'

The pink man wiped away tears of laughter from his immense features and wheezed, 'Sod all.' He added, 'By the way, meet Dingo. I'm Stuart.'

'Yeah,' said Gust. 'I'm overwhelmed.'

'This could be the beginning of a love nest,' the pink man said, putting a hand on Gust's knee. 'Something lasting and intimate.'

The pinstriped man was patting Gust down. 'Hey, you wouldn't believe it, Stuart, but this cunt's got a gun.' He slipped the Beretta out of Gust's waistband and smelled the barrel. 'Been fired too.'

The pink man turned to Gust. 'Oh yes? Who was that at, then?'

'That was some target practice I did in the back yard,' said Gust. 'Rats. But of course if rats always came your size I wouldn't need to bother practising, would I, I couldn't miss.'

The pink man hit him across the side of the mouth. Gust felt his face swelling up again; it was the side Connor had walked over.

'What was that you hit me with?' he said. 'It wasn't just your fist.'

'I hit you with money!' snorted the pink man. 'See? Just the evening paper with some change in it, that's all it takes, now fucking behave.'

Gust spat out some blood. 'I'm learning to love you two.'

'All right then,' said the pink man, 'let's get down to it. We know you're hard, we heard about the gig with the cocktail stick at Marly's, that's why we're taking you seriously. Now, what we're after, we know you're running about with a load of money on you.'

'Who told you that?'

'Don't you fucking worry who it was, you've got enough worries as it is.'

'He hasn't got any money on him now,' said Dingo.

'Pity,' said the pink man, 'because my boyfriend fancied a squash court. Never mind,' he said to Gust, 'we'll find it, won't we? The other thing we're interested in is a lot of passports that have gone missing, a thousand of them. Now come on, we know you nicked them, where did they go?'

'Why's everyone so excited about these passports?' Gust asked. 'Or were you two psychopaths in on that too? Because I'd never have touched it if I'd known.'

'You don't know who's in or out of what,' said Dingo. 'In fact you're one of those people, you don't know anything much.'

'Except that it's us asking the questions,' the pink man chuckled.

'You ask them, I don't answer them,' said Gust. 'Even you must have noticed that.'

'How friendly are you with a man called Johnny?'

'I'm friendly with a lot of men called Johnny, and then there again, there must be another couple of hundred of them, I hate their guts. Why?'

'I mean Johnny Laray, used to be your brother-in-law. Seen him lately?'

'Well, he wasn't in Maidstone with me, which is where I just got out of.'

'You've been out long enough to pull the passport stroke, and long enough to see Laray, so don't be inventive or you'll get a smack in the heirlooms.'

'It wouldn't make any difference,' said Gust. 'I can't tell you what I don't know. All I'd like to know is, who sent you?'

'You don't care about that,' said Dingo. 'Just talk.'

'You'll have a long wait,' Gust told him. 'I can't help you over money, I can't help you over passports, what

else can't I help you with? You're not working for
yourselves, that's for sure; you're too stupid. You're so
stupid you'd have killed me by now if you had been.'

'Why don't we just kill him at that?' said Dingo. 'I
wouldn't mind.'

'Well, it's true I had less aggro in Maidstone than I've
had since I've been out.' Gust had a thought. 'You do
any grassing at all? Either of you deal with the law ever?
You ever come across a man called Spaulding?'

'Who's he?'

'Never heard of a Detective Inspector Spaulding from
Poland Street? Because I wouldn't put it past you, a rat'll
work for anyone if there's a couple of quid in it. Yes, I
reckon you're grasses, you stick out like two old baldies
at a wig show.'

The pink man warned, 'You're going very near the
edge, Gust, but I'm being patient with you.'

'Only so you can draw your wages,' said Gust. 'I tell
you, you'd have topped me by now if you hadn't been
told not to.'

'I don't deny it would be a pleasure,' said the pink
man. He thought for a minute. 'What did you do with
all this cash you had from Farb, then? Did you slip it to
Laray?'

'Empty your pockets again,' said the pinstriped man,
'all of them, come on, or I'll do it for you.'

'You do it,' Gust said, 'only don't tickle.'

'Just a couple of ton in fifties,' said the pinstriped man
in disgust when he had finished, throwing the money
back at him, 'Jesus Christ, a frog couldn't fart its way
across a pond on that.'

'It's people who don't look after their friends who
make serious enemies, Gust,' said the pink man. 'That's
the state of the planet these days.'

'Who are my friends supposed to be?' said Gust. 'And
drop the planet talk, anyone'd think you'd just dropped
in for a visit.'

'He's cheeky, this one,' said Dingo. 'Don't you think

he's cheeky, Stuart? Don't you think he needs another spanking?'

'If I were him,' the pink man said, "I wouldn't let my thoughts stray any further than making my will.'

Gust sat back. 'It was nice weather today, or it was till you got into it.' He stared out at the rain. 'Did you notice the wind coming down Green Park? Must have crossed Piccadilly and finished up round Victoria, cleaned the place up a bit, pity it missed you. Talking of that, you been round to see your two flowerpot men in hospital?'

'They should have sent us down to that club,' Dingo said.

'You'd never have got in, that's the problem,' said Gust. 'Even Marly'd draw the line at you two.'

'There's been a lot of bother over that fight,' said the pink man, 'some important people have got very upset. Especially as one of the geezers died. What did you do that for?'

'I was stupid,' said Gust. 'I wanted to stay alive.'

'Did you really? Whatever for?'

'Is that what you asked Petal Chang when you whacked her head off?'

'We've finished talking about that.'

'I haven't,' said Gust. 'And nor will I till I find out who killed her. I'm telling everyone, until then I'm in a red fog.'

'Fog?' said the pink man. 'You want to get glasses for that.' They roared with laughter. 'Except you've got other things to worry about right now.'

'You're the worried people,' said Gust. 'You think I've got information, and that's what's keeping me alive.'

'Well it's true enough that until everybody's got what they want, that money and those passports, we're just letting you live to see where you lead,' said Dingo. 'But anything could happen to you after that, maybe even before.'

'I know, that's why I'm not saying anything.'

'Really?' the pink man said. He turned to the pin-striped man. 'I don't think we've heard anything as bold as that for some time, have we Dingo?'

'Then let's talk about something else,' said Gust. 'There was a man shot in a Chinese restaurant about an hour ago, you mightn't have heard. In the middle of noshing with his mates too, the place was packed.'

'Shot dead?' said Dingo.

'No, he just lost his right hand, it ended up in his soup.'

'Whose hand was that, then?' said the pink man.

'Manny Farb's.'

There was silence in the car for a while.

'Manny Farb?' said the pinstriped man in the end. 'Somebody took a shot at Manny? The geezer's joking.'

'Might as well hear the rest,' the pink man said. 'Who did it then?'

'I did,' said Gust. 'You want to get an update. Give him a bell in hospital, why don't you? Ask him about it.' He quoted Dingo: '"This gun's just been fired." Oh dear.' He started laughing.

'I hope that's not true, what you're saying,' said the pink man, 'for your sake.'

'It's true all right,' said Gust, 'and that was down to Petal Chang too, same as you two will be if your faces fit.'

'What you're saying there really is fighting talk.'

'I know it is, my farty old friend.'

'Well, if the people in Marly's didn't manage to top you,' the pinstriped man said, 'maybe we could do it. Anyway, remind me to have a go next time we meet just for the fun of it, and it will be fun.'

'You're not up to it,' Gust told him. He didn't look into the pinstriped man's eyes but through them. 'It takes a man with bottle to do that, not something that crept out of a takeaway bag.'

'Just for the record,' said the pinstriped man, 'we have killed people.'

'I know,' said Gust, 'I can smell it on you. But only from behind.'

'Well, believe it or not,' said the pink man, 'if we had a go at you you'd be a dead rabbit.'

Gust nudged him. 'Yes, though don't forget one thing, sweetheart – so would you.'

'All right,' said the pink man, 'that's not what this is about, at least not tonight. We just wanted to make contact with you, have a chat.'

But they looked thoughtful. They gave him his gun back unloaded, and let him out at Old Street station.

They said people would be in touch. The pink man said as an afterthought, 'You ever come across a man called Hawley?'

'I've heard of him. I heard he was shot. I've never met him.'

'Then just hope your luck holds.'

'I don't think it will hold,' said the pinstriped man.

They slammed the car door in his face and drove off.

22

Christine jerked up in her bed as she heard someone coming through the window, and shouted, 'Fuck off you maniac, whoever you are!' Then she saw Gust's head between the curtains.

'Can I come all the way in?' he said. 'It's a long drop out here.'

'What the Christ?' she said. 'it's four in the morning. All right, come in, but watch my china cats on the sill.'

Christine had been born in Meard Street of parents she hardly remembered back in the days when its eighteenth-century houses were packed with whores, and she had spent all her life in Soho. She and Gust had known each other a long time. Her name wasn't really Christine at all; that was just what people called her. She was always in and out of the Diadem, the Mutineer and the Nine Lives where the villains, busted solicitors, writers, journalists and racing folk all hung out. She was always on the tap ('just to keep my hand in,') and she might even let a punter have a slice on the mat when money was short. One night a man she had asked for a light pulled a gun on her and Christine held her hand out for it saying, 'Don't fiddle with that, sonny, you don't look as if you knew how it works.' The man dropped the gun and fled. She was terrified afterwards, telling people, 'I wouldn't have dared say it if I hadn't been pissed.'

But whatever she was she wasn't a grass and she still hadn't many enemies, which was remarkable in Soho, considering she was thirty-six and had had plenty of time to make some.

'What's the matter with your face?' she asked. 'Did you throw it at a train?'

Gust stared at her across the sheet she had pulled up to her chin; he knew what his face looked like. 'Can I talk to you?'

'All right,' she said, 'only don't come near me, that's all; I haven't a wriggle in me.' She reached for her Casterbridge filters. 'What is it?'

'I'm on the run.'

'Again? On second thoughts, I don't really like the look of you.'

'Come on,' he said. 'We're old mates, don't pull the plug on me.'

'All right. You'd better sit down anyway. You look whacked.'

'Five floors up the fire escape doesn't help.' He sat down on the bed.

'I meant the armchair,' she said, 'but never mind, you can sit on the bed, only don't try getting into it. All right then, what's the matter? Looks as if something was.'

'Petal's dead.'

'Petal?' she said, bemused. 'She can't be. I saw her yesterday morning in the supermarket.'

'It happened yesterday afternoon. She was beaten to death.'

'There's been nothing in the linens or TV, how do you know about it?'

'I can see what you're thinking,' he said. 'You think I was jealous of her and Connor so I killed her. You're wrong. It was the law told me about it. Not only told me, they took me up to see her.'

'I don't believe you,' she said. She set her back up

against the head of the bed and stared at him.

'I'd stayed the night there, I'd nowhere to go and she took me to her place. I was out when it happened. Listen, I'm not lying to you.'

'Did you have anything to do with her being killed?'

'No. Not even the law thinks that. The trouble was, she was putting me up.'

'What difference does that make, if she was putting you up or not?'

'I'm mixed up in something.'

'I don't want to know about it,' she said immediately. 'Isn't there anywhere else you can go?'

'Being just out of the nick it's not easy,' he said. 'I was going to stay with a friend of mine, but he's done enough for me as it is. Except for one or two people like you I'm out of friends, Christine; I usen't to have to run five floors up the outside of a building to find my mates.'

'Christ you really do look like a garbage strike.' She wrinkled her nose. 'And you stink.'

'I've had to wash up in pubs.'

'And look at your face. You ought to have something done about that.'

'It'll go down.'

'You'd better have a drink at least.'

'Christ, have you got one? I could murder a scotch.'

She reached under the bed for the bottle of Bell's; she liked a nightcap herself. She poured him a triple. He drank half of it and put his head in his hands; she had never seen him do that before.

'I ran straight into this nightmare,' he said, 'and all I did was get out of jail.'

'I think life was safer with you inside,' she said unsympathetically, 'and anyway, there's more to it than that, you just said so.'

'Well I know this much, there are people I've got to get out of the shit.'

'You seem to have mostly got them into it,' she said, 'the way you're telling it.'

'I've got to find out who killed Petal. The people who did it were sent in to do it. I want them; but I also want the individual who put out the contract.'

'Well, get on with it then, what are you waiting for?'

'I've put the frighteners on some people already, but things have happened since and I don't know if they were the right ones.'

'As if I knew what you're talking about.'

He finished his drink. 'Everything should have been simple but it wasn't. You got another drink like that?'

'What do you think I am? A piano bar?'

He gave her a twenty pound note.

'Where did this come from?'

'Don't worry, it'll spend. Just fill it up, Christine.'

She filled his glass. 'Don't steer me into any of this.'

He shook his head. 'I'm only here because I need some sleep. It's just for tonight.'

'The way you chat a woman up,' she said bitterly. 'Is that what you used to tell Petal?'

His face went as cold and flat as a wall. 'Be careful,' he said, 'my mind's in a bad way.'

'Yes, I'm sorry, I take that back. You'd better get into bed, but not till you've had a shower.' She gave him a drink to take with him. She lay thinking while he was gone; she couldn't believe Petal was dead. When he got back Gust thought the bed looked good till he hit the springs, which had suffered under the weight of many a porn dealer and even an MP or two in the good times.

Presently she turned the light off, but tired though he was, he lay awake, staring at the ceiling blinking with the neons from the buildings opposite; on, off, red, blue and green.

She had fallen asleep and he turned on his side so as not to disturb her. *You're gone, Petal*, he thought. *I had something with you that I never had with anyone else; we talk differently now that we're alone in my head. We were as happy as people like us ever can be; but now everything we did, it's like watching an old film, you and me in the Eclipse,*

*out drinking with Johnny and the Irishman, and then next,
there's your body on the floor.*

Later on Christine woke and found the bedding wet
through on his side and thought he must have pissed in
it; then she realised that the damp was too high up the
bed and felt the pillow. It was soaking, so then she
passed her hand over his face and found that sweat was
pouring off him; his face was red hot, his feet icy.

23

Spaulding was at his desk in the detectives' room at the Factory fighting a tide of paperwork when DCI Bowman came bombing through like an ape that had been let loose on a Regent Street sale. He was wearing his usual bygone age gear – trilby hat, blinding yellow tie, the lot, right down to the polished brogues. Spaulding reckoned he had put on another pound every time he saw him, which luckily wasn't that often.

'All right then,' Bowman shouted, 'any of you shower got your brains in straight this sunny morning, or are we all skiving?' One detective dropped his ballpoint on the table, somebody else sighed; it was impossible to concentrate on anything with him around.

'Trouble already and it's only nine o'clock,' Bowman said, perching a buttock on the edge of a desk. 'PC fucking Wildbore again, that mate of Rupt and Drucker's. He gets fed up sitting in the patrol car, sees a pregnant woman and only lobs a firework he happens to have handy; lands right in front of her. She's filed a complaint of course, lost her baby.' He spotted Spaulding. 'Hullo, Dicky, you're just the man I want to see. Still picking your nose with your gloves on, are you? Come through to my office.'

Bowman swept off, with Spaulding in his wake. 'Sit down, Dicky.' Bowman squared off everything on his

172

desk that was already squared off, to wit, a photograph
of Mrs Bowman and Miss Bowman, who was squinting
into the sun sulking, also a pen set, aimed over his
shoulder at the window behind him like a row of
Katyusha rockets. 'Clean desk,' said Bowman, 'means
you're on top of the job, son.' He leaned back in his
chair and farted. 'Well speak up, Dicky, how's things?'

'What things?'

'All right, then. Gust.'

'I thought that was the thing you meant.'

'Any leads?'

'No,' said Spaulding, 'but I've hardly started yet.'

'I know that,' said Bowman, 'and I know you. Your
clothes are a mess, you look like a bag of shit tied up with
string. Look at you – and your face is nothing to write
home about. You're about as sexy as a box of wet
matches, and I couldn't send you round to any of the
embassies. Still, you're stubborn. You stick to a case like
a cockroach to a pile of garbage and you've got imagination, which is why I took you off the beat and which is
why you're one of my inspectors. Remember I backed
you all the way, son.'

That was his version. In fact Bowman had tried to block
Spaulding's promotion at every turn because he hated
competition, so Spaulding said nothing, allowing his
silence to continue just as he would have with a suspect,
knowing that Bowman would have to break it since, unlike
Spaulding, he obviously had something to say.

'All right,' Bowman said in the end, 'this battle at
Marly's Club, the Chang girl's death, the whole of this
Gust business – I don't think you'll get a conviction
anywhere there even if you get the evidence.'

'Why won't I?'

'Because no one from Marlys'll go to court.'

'Not until they've been properly leaned on, of course
they won't, no. It's like every other case, it's a matter of
time. Patience, digging out witnesses, spadework.'

Bowman shook his head; he liked sitting on

opinionated juniors. 'Rawlings has been down there with one of his sergeants. He started asking questions but upstairs hauled him straight off it.'

'Well, nobody's hauled me off it,' said Spaulding. 'Besides, Rawlings is bent. Marly gives him the old dropsy at the end of the month, everyone knows that.'

'You want to be very careful passing remarks like that,' said Bowman, 'but in any case my view is that the Crown Prosecution Service won't take it on, I'm ninety per cent sure of that.' He lit a cheroot.

'Then I'll bet on the other ten per cent.'

This time there was an even longer silence. Bowman tried to blow a smoke ring, failed, gazed up at the ceiling and didn't look at Spaulding. Spaulding rode that silence out too.

'You're wasting your time,' Bowman said in the end.

'I'm wasting it in here, that's for certain. I've got a stack of work waiting outside there, a lot of it to do with Gust.'

Bowman put his cheroot down. 'All right then,' he said reluctantly, 'to come right down to it, I'm getting flak about Gust from on high.'

'Flak?'

'There are complications.'

'What complications?' said Spaulding. 'And where's the flak coming from? Nobody's told me anything.'

'I'm telling you now.'

'What are you getting at? Are you feeling your way into taking me off this?'

'I didn't exactly say that,' said Bowman. 'What I'm saying is, just back-pedal on it. Go easy.'

'But why? We're talking about two murders here.'

Bowman ran out of oratory. 'I know,' he said lamely, 'it's just that there are what I've been told are other factors.'

'You still haven't said what factors.'

'That's because I don't know what they are,' said Bowman.

Spaulding couldn't believe it. It was the first time he had ever heard Bowman admit that there was something he didn't know; it was one for the Poland Street book of records.

'This flak,' he said, 'who fired it? The Voice?'

'I've told you not to refer to the Commander like that.'

'Why not?' said Spaulding. 'Everyone else does.'

'That's no excuse. As for this memo, I'm not saying who sent it, all I can tell you is what I've been instructed to say.' Bowman relit his cheroot.

'I'll need something more specific than that.'

'You'll get it in due course,' said Bowman. 'That's to say, when I've got it myself.' His phone rang. 'All right,' he said, 'carry on.' He jerked Spaulding out of the door with his head.

'Well, how was the best dressed man in the street then?' said one of the DCs when Spaulding got back outside. 'Chipper?'

'Chipper, yes,' said Spaulding, feeling for a Westminster, 'and unintelligible as usual. Like politically correct art. You know.'

They knew all right.

After finishing some of his paperwork Spaulding found he had to go to another police station about a suicide that the forensic people thought might be a murder. While he was driving there he tuned his car radio to a station called People Now, a bandit signal that transmitted from somewhere in north London.

'What we need in this country,' the speaker was saying unemotionally, 'is firm government. But what we've got is a bunch of weak-kneed old frauds lashing out panic-stricken at targets which they're too far removed from reality to identify. Or else, equally catastrophic, whatever the problem, they've got a million excuses for doing nothing about it. Efficient rule isn't based on excuses, and unless we can quickly produce some form of government qualified to act for the people instead of against it we are in for a colossal amount of trouble, and it will be no good TV pundits, ex-cabinet ministers, journalists or anybody else explaining what we ought to have done once the outsider has won the race. Turning to the current situation in Russia . . .'

Spaulding switched the radio off and made a mental note: *Body armour, three hundred quid.*

He had considered buying it for some time, but he would have to pay for it himself; no wonder he was always broke.

24

Gust went into the Diadem; it was early afternoon. An abandoned copy of the *Standard* lay on the bar and he flattened it out at page one. The headline was 'Gangland Slaughter: 3 Dead.' The story ran: 'Police were called to a flat in Marjorie Grove, Clapham late last night after neighbours in Darby Mansions reported sounds of the entrance door to a second-floor flat being smashed in, followed by the sound of gunfire. Mr Andy Simms, 62, who occupies the flat opposite with his son and grand-daughter, said, "I heard shots and looked out of my door across the passageway and I could see straight into Mr Farb's flat because the door was open and hanging off its hinges. It was mayhem, wounded men screaming, total chaos. There was one man by the entrance with a sledgehammer, and another by the sitting room with his back to me who was holding a pistol. Then there were three more shots from further inside the flat, but I didn't see who fired those." Asked if he could describe the attackers Mr Simms said: "I never got a proper look at them; I just noticed that the man with his back to me swearing in the hallway was tall, sweating heavily and thickset. But I didn't see any more because my son pulled me back inside our flat and rang the police.'

'Police confirmed that on their arrival they found the bodies of three men in the flat with gunshot wounds to the head and chest. Detective Inspector Dick Spaulding, leading the inquiry, said, "It looked as if a bomb had gone off in there. We believe it was definitely an underworld settlement of accounts; all three victims had criminal records ranging from extortion, demanding money with menaces and armed robbery to aggravated bodily harm. There were at least two attackers, possibly three." He added, "One intriguing fact is that the place was ransacked while the raid was in progress."

'The dead have been identified as Emmanuel Farb, 48, of Clapham, SW4; Farb had been discharged from hospital the previous day after being wounded during another shooting incident at a West End restaurant. The other victims were Leonard Williams, 39, known as "The Hammer", of Walthamstow, and Henry James Ford, 51, of Frith Street, west London.

'Asked to comment further, Inspector Spaulding said that inquiries were under way, but appealed for any witnesses besides the Simms family who might have seen the attackers leaving the building to ring the crime helpline, or contact their local police. "These men are dangerous," he said, "and should not be approached."'

The phone on the bar was ringing. The barmaid listened, then came over and said to Gust, 'Message for you.' She handed him the piece of paper she had been scribbling on. Gust picked it up, read it, and bought a Carlsberg. All the message said was: 'Money gone to the dogs.' Gust didn't like that. He put the paper in his mouth, chewed it and swallowed it with some beer.

The girl said, 'What *are* you doing with that paper?'

'I'm eating it,' said Gust, 'can't you see?' He went upstairs and made a call to Johnny's place. There was no answer, and he didn't like that either. When he got back the phone behind the bar was ringing again. This time the girl simply held the receiver out and said: 'It's for you again.'

Gust picked the phone up. 'Yes?'

A man's voice he didn't recognise told him to stay

where he was for half an hour, then rang off.

'Have I got measles or something?' the girl said angrily. She didn't dislike him or anything, rather the contrary, but she felt she ought to be smart with the customers because she was new in the place and didn't share their perverted sense of humour; perhaps humour would grow quickly, she thought, like her hair did. 'Why do corpses like you get all the calls?'

'Because some of our friends like to remind us we're still alive,' said Gust.

'I don't see why you don't just turn this pub into your office and have done with it.

'Because the devil's always on the move.' Gust wasn't really listening to her. He didn't like the phone message any better than the one from Johnny, but he decided to wait and see what happened anyway.

Quite soon a dark-haired man smartly dressed in black walked into the bar. He looked around, taking his time, then came over and sat on a stool beside Gust. He ordered a Campari. 'What are you having, Gust?'

'Nothing. Who are you?'

'No one you'd really want to know very well,' the man said.

Gust could see that. Under his black raincoat he wore a black suit and a black shirt buttoned to the top with no tie; he was thin, with black marksman's eyes that sat unblinking in his face like olives on a white dish.

'What's this about?'

'We'd just like you to come over for a talk. Don't worry, you'll get out all right.'

'Out upright, you mean?' said Gust. 'With the heart still pumping?'

The thin man shrugged. 'If you behave.'

'I never behave.'

'Make an effort this time and stay alive, because that's the way we want you.'

'That's nice to know, because it's not the way everybody wants me just now.'

'So I've heard,' said the thin man. 'Sounds tough.' He finished his drink and stood up. 'Shall we go?'

'Why not?' Gust said. He left the the Diadem with regret.

The thin man had a new Saab outside with a driver, who opened the back door for them with a whiplash action.

'Going for a ride, are we?'

'What do you think?' said the thin man. After a while he spoke again. 'You've been away a long time.'

'Everyone knows where I've been.'

The driver turned the car round in the thick traffic and headed west.

'You got any old iron on you by the way?' the thin man said.

'Not any more,' Gust said. 'I hocked it, I was broke.'

'Let's check just the same. The thin man was as tiresome as a customs man. He found Gust's Beretta straight away and put it in his pocket.

'I didn't think you were that broke,' the man said. 'By the way, you eaten today yet?'

'No. Why? You going to ask me to lunch?'

'No. People aren't keen to go to a restaurant with you these days.'

'Then why the question?'

'Just that it's bad to get shot on a full gut.'

'You said I was coming out the way I went in.'

'That's right,' said the man, 'but only as long as you don't step out of line. There's someone called George where we're going; he's quick-tempered, he often doesn't stop to think.'

'More likely he just can't think,' Gust said.

The thin man shrugged. 'Makes no difference to the folk he puts down whether he can or not.'

'That's nice to know.'

The thin man said politely, 'It's your skin.'

They got to Shepherd's Bush, turned off Goldhawk Road into a street with no name on it and stopped at a house where the number had been removed from the door. The driver let them out smartly and the thin man smacked him in the face hard. 'Quicker next time,' he said. 'Give respect, you've a lot to learn. I'll give you a real spanking next time.'

'You throw your weight about for a little feller, don't you?' Gust said.

'I teach respect,' said the thin man, 'you know how it works. And take my advice; be extra polite to Mr Hawley.'

'Hawley?' said Gust. 'You mean the man they used to call the paymaster? I thought the Morrows shot him in a south London deli. I heard he died.'

'He recovered,' the thin man said. 'He's very resilient is Mr Hawley, so be respectful and polite. And another thing. Remember Mr Hawley doesn't smoke; he can't even stand the smell of tobacco, so don't light up whatever you do.' He knocked on the door and a giant with the face of a very stupid child opened it.

'What's this then?' Gust said. 'Girl or boy?'

'Mr Hawley likes to have big men around. Big is beautiful, he says.'

'I like that,' Gust said. 'Very original.'

'Everything Mr Hawley says is original,' said the thin man.

Gust followed them along the ground-floor passage that led to the back of the building. There was food cooking somewhere; it smelled good. 'My cooking,' the giant said proudly.

'I'll borrow your apron sometime,' Gust said.

'I like to hear you crack jokes the way you do,' the thin man said. 'For a man in your position it can't be easy.'

'How would someone like you know what's easy?' said Gust.

While the thin man thought about that they walked on to a door that led down a narrow flight of steps.

'Watch your head,' the thin man warned him. 'It's low, you could knock it badly if you weren't careful.

Mind, I can already see looking at your face where you haven't been careful.'

The giant opened the door into a cellar. There were three men sitting in it; one of them was Johnny, bound to a metal chair.

'Gust's here, Mr Hawley,' said the thin man. He nudged Gust and whispered, 'Remember the respect. Respect with Mr Hawley pays dividends, lay it on thick, it can buy time.'

Gust wasn't listening. He was looking at Johnny, and Hawley watched him doing it. He was a big man who had shrunk; he wore a designer suit and dark glasses. He spoke in a low voice and fiddled from time to time with the tube of a colostomy bag that looped out of his waistband.

'Forget Johnny,' he said.

'What happened to his nose?' Gust asked.

'George stuck some lighted matches up it.'

'George?' said Gust, turning to the squat man on Hawley's right. 'That's a pretty name.'

George didn't look up; he didn't look like the kind who ever did unless he was going to kill someone. He sat chewing on the end of a cigar with a big pistol out in front of him on the table; sometimes he picked it up, loading and unloading it.

'Johnny wound him up,' said Hawley. 'You know.'

'I know a heap of shit when I see it,' Gust said.

'The respect, the respect!' muttered the thin man.

'Didn't you expect to find Johnny here?' Hawley said.

'Except that I'd get out of here alive I wasn't told what to expect,' Gust said.

'No you weren't,' said Hawley. 'You don't know half what's going on anyway.'

The thin man prompted Gust in a loud whisper: 'Answer Mr Hawley.'

'Anyway,' said Gust. 'I know some of the things you've done like I know what you're doing to Johnny now, and I'm glad they shot you in the stomach, Hawley;

a bullet wound in the stomach never really heals.'

The thin man shook his head, sighed and gave up.

Gust pointed at Hawley's colostomy bag. 'I see the Morrows blew most of your guts away. Pity they didn't take the lot.'

'I know you were told I'd keep you alive,' said Hawley, 'but don't push it, because while you're in a state to walk I want to talk to you about an investment of mine and I haven't much time; I'm not in Britain much these days.'

'I'm not surprised, not after what you stopped in the slop bucket last time.' Gust lit a cigarette.

'That's right,' said Hawley. 'Don't wait to be told if you can smoke, just do it, just light up. Don't ask if I mind or not, smoke your head off, feel free. I'm a non-smoker, didn't anyone tell you?'

'I told him, Mr Hawley, I told him,' the thin man said anxiously.

Hawley looked at the thin man once, without expression. 'You need voice training,' he said. 'Remind me.'

Gust smoked, ignoring them. He looked at Johnny. His shirt had been torn open to the waist and he had burns on his chest; his nose was swollen and suppurating. He appeared to be half asleep; his face was a bad colour, bluish, and he sat lolling in his chair squinting upwards.

'He's not very fit, is he?' Gust said.

'No,' said Hawley. 'He's taken some heavy punishment.'

'Have him looked at,' said Gust. 'He's seriously ill.'

'Looked at?' said Hawley. 'Whatever for?'

'He's my brother-in-law.'

'I know that, and I don't give a shit.'

Gust dropped his cigarette on the floor, trod on it and lit another.

'Meantime I've got a problem,' said Hawley, 'apart from you smoking like that. In fact I've got several problems.'

'Me too,' said Gust.

'You?' said Hawley. 'Yes, you've certainly got problems. In fact if I was in your place I don't think I'd know
what to do if I'd got as many problems as you've got.'

'Well, I wouldn't go snivelling to other people with
them the way you're doing.'

'Let's keep this meeting polite if we can. Let's keep a
show of respect.'

'Do something about Laray then.'

'I'm going to in a minute,' said Hawley, 'but let's talk
about your problems and ours first, because they co-
incide. That's very bad news for you, Gust, and it's even
worse news for Johnny.'

Johnny shut his eyes and Hawley noticed it. 'Wake
him up.' George reached out with his cigar and ground
it out in Johnny's cheek; Johnny screamed and tried to
throw himself out of his chair.

'He could have got him in the eye with that,' said
Gust.

'Wouldn't have mattered if he had,' Hawley said. He
started ticking items off on his fingers like a granny
going round the supermarket. 'First, these passports.'

'You mean the stolen passports? Those were Manny
Farb's.'

'Fuck Manny Farb. You ripped those passports off.
Harry Ford had them, that's when you got your money,
and then where did they go? Next we have what you and
Johnny did to Manny in the Red Wok. Now I don't give
a fuck what there was between you and Manny, that isn't
the point. The point is that *we* look after the heavy side;
we can't have cowboys like you playing darts on people
in public. Nothing but what you did there's worth a
good spanking.'

'Did you send those two men down to Marly's Club?'
Gust asked.

Hawley didn't seem to hear that. 'Why did you and
Johnny go in and shoot Manny?'

'Because of what happened to Petal Chang. At the
time I reckoned it was Manny did that but now, more

and more, talking to you, I'm beginning to think you know far more about it than he did. In fact I think you know all about it. I even think you very likely know who it was.'

'I don't answer questions,' said Hawley, 'I put them. And Manny's dead now anyway, his mates too.'

'I know, I read about it. So who killed Petal Chang?'

'You're nothing but a small-time robber and you're not even good at it, that's why you've done all that porridge; I don't have to tell you anything.'

Gust lit another cigarette, striking the match on the table. Then he spat on the floor.

'Why did you spit on the floor?' said Hawley.

'Because I was aiming at you,' Gust said.

'You were way off; here I am sitting at the table.'

'I know, but you should be where the shit is, on the floor.'

Hawley didn't smile at that. The thin man drew a breath in with a hiss of disbelief and there was silence in the room for what seemed a long time, until Hawley spoke again. 'I never met a man so fed up with living, it's like talking to a corpse talking to you. Still, a thousand blank passports at two and a half long ones a shot resale to my particular customers, that's two and a half million quid. That's a lot of bread, Gust, you do realise.'

'You mean it would have been a lot of bread if you'd copped for it.'

'I don't know how I manage to control myself with you,' Hawley said, 'it's really hard going. So how about these passports?'

'I delivered them to Ford,' said Gust. 'I took my whack and that was me finished.'

'I like the word finished,' said Hawley. 'That's very appropriate.'

'You're fiddling with the wrong motor,' Gust told him. 'The bonnet you should be looking under is Harry Ford's, that's where the bent wiring is.'

'Harry's dead.'

'Was that you?'

'He had to go.'

'You'll be opening a morgue soon the way you're going.'

'We'd squeezed him dry,' said Hawley, 'but here's something interesting. After Harry died we pulled that Clarice woman of his in for treatment on her teeth which we decided were in a bad state, and when we'd pulled three of her front ones she came up with the name Sladden. But no description. The name was all she knew and we can't find any trace of this individual. Maybe you can help.'

'No I can't,' said Gust, 'and you probably hurt the woman so bad that she invented any old name just to get away from the pliers; he probably doesn't even exist. Still, if he doesn't exist he can't have got the passports, can he?'

'Well, it's a pity Harry and Clarice unfortunately died before he said anything about this Sladden, whoever he is. George was over-hasty there. We'd already flagged Harry in for running repairs, but even under really diabolical pressure he still told us he'd delivered the gear to Manny. It's too late to ask either of them now, of course, but whether Manny got it or not my punter definitely didn't, so that although we've straightened the books out on the body-count side we're still seriously out on the books, and it's the loss of a lot of money we're talking about here, Gust, a lot of money and a lot of respect.'

'You know Manny was a grass,' said Gust. 'That's why Johnny came to see him in the restaurant with me; Manny got him weighed off for three in eighty-six.'

'I don't discuss who's a grass or anything else with a slag like you,' Hawley said. 'All I'm saying is that if Ford didn't have those passports, which he hadn't, and Manny didn't have them when we turned his place over the night we wasted him, and this Sladden doesn't exist, then the only person who can have the passports must be you. Or else you must know who's got them, or where they are, because there isn't anyone else.'

'Haven't you found any trace of them at all?'

'I know four of them have been used. Snag is, though, that two of the holders are dead, the third's missing, and we don't know who the fourth is.'

'It's certainly raining right in on you, I can see that.'

'Don't be funny,' said Hawley. 'We are not only right losers in this game so far but we are also a laughing-stock on the manor, so this is what I'm going to do. I'm going to give you two days to get hold of every one of those passports and bring them back. If you don't find them you're in the deep end of shit, and you know what that means.'

'I do,' said Gust, 'and I'll no doubt see you there.'

'Anyway,' Hawley said, 'that's the score.'

George was getting bored. 'Are we going to go on talking like this all day?'

'No we're not,' said Hawley, 'this'll be over in a flash.' He looked at Gust. 'And I mean a flash. I've been over Johnny, my friends here have been over him, but we got nothing, which is a terrible thing for him.'

'He doesn't know anything,' said Gust, 'that's why you got nothing out of him. Why should he know anything? He wasn't on the passport caper.'

'No, but you could have talked to him, and I reckon you must have. After all, the two of you shot Farb up in the Red Wok. You could have told Johnny things. You probably did; you haven't that many mates you can talk to these days.'

'No, I haven't. Particularly now Petal's gone.'

'Fuck her. What you're going to see next will make your brain turn over very fucking fast while it's still in your head.'

'Don't touch Johnny. I didn't tell him anything about those passports.'

Hawley looked across at George. 'Get him into the

corner there, I don't want bits of him all over my new suit.'

They picked Johnny up, chair and all, and carried him over to the far wall; then George went back to the table and picked up the pistol.

'I tell you, you just can't do that,' Gust said urgently.

'Why?' said Hawley. 'Do you want to talk? You want to tell us about Sladden? You want to tell us where the passports are? Get them for us?'

Gust didn't say anything. He remembered vaguely reading about someone called Judas.

'It's your last chance,' said Hawley.

'You might as well do it to me,' Gust said.

'I want you alive, you cunt,' Hawley said. He angled his watch towards the light and said to George, 'Get on with it, will you? My plane leaves in three hours.'

George didn't get up; he didn't even bother to take a bead on Johnny. Hawley told Gust, 'You want to watch this, George is good. Lucky you don't mind loud noises, that iron of his really goes off.'

Johnny mumbled, 'The dogs.' It was all he said throughout.

Hawley sat forward and was about to say something, but George fired. The gun roared like an angry copper and the bullet hit Johnny in the face, striking him above the nose; something unintelligible immediately scribbled itself in red on the wall behind him. His stomach let go with whatever it had in it; he crashed over in the chair, a bundle of rags, and that was that.

'The dogs,' said Hawley. He looked thoughtful. He said to Gust, 'Not going to spew up, are you? You OK?' The giant had come in with brooms and a pail of disinfectant at the sound of the shot. George had already started clearing up. The giant and the thin man gave him a hand.

'OK?' said Gust. 'Why shouldn't I be OK? You're not the only man who's seen bodies around.'

'I meant seeing that it was almost family.'

'I'm getting used to that, but there are one or two other things.'

'I can't go into them, I haven't time.'

'I know you haven't, they took it away with your stomach.'

Gust walked over to Johnny's corpse; tied to the chair he looked like a scarecrow knocked down in the wind. He shoved George and the giant aside. 'He looks much smaller suddenly, doesn't he?' he said to Hawley in a conversational tone. 'It's true what they say, isn't it, straight off death empties a man.' He pulled his T-shirt off and cleaned Johmmy's face; when he had finished he threw the T-shirt in the giant's waste bucket and put his sweater back on. 'You missed his eyes, George,' he called across, 'that was thoughtful of you.' He looked at Hawley. 'Am I going to close them or are you? It's you they're looking at; they'll be the first thing you see when you get to hell.'

'I have to go,' Hawley said.

'Seeing you're squeamish I'll do it,' said Gust. 'Must show respect for the other world.' He closed Johnny's eyes and stood for a while looking down at him. 'There. Plenty of respect.' He turned to Hawley. 'Did you kill Petal Chang?'

'The Chinese girl? She had to go because you had to be taught a serious lesson after what you did at Marly's. That story went right round the West End and we lost respect; besides, she was sheltering you, so yes, she was visited.'

'With a baseball bat,' said Gust, 'go on, say it after me: "She was visited with a baseball bat."'

'She was the nearest to you we could get.'

'She paid for that all right,' said Gust.

'She should have picked a different boyfriend.'

'Who did it?'

'I don't know who it was,' said Hawley, 'I just put a contract out on her.'

'I wonder if it was a little man in a pinstripe with filthy

nails,' said Gust, 'and maybe a fat man in a pink tussore suit as well, the man with a gun in his hand seen over at Manny's place the night he died. It could easily have been them.'

'Well, whoever it was, there it is. It's too late to do anything about it. Coming back to now, find us those passports, Gust.'

'Otherwise what?'

'Otherwise you can leave your bollocks to science, not that many people think with them.' Hawley turned to the thin man. 'Take him back where you found him, buy him a drink – why not? I reckon he needs one.' He returned to Gust. 'Remember I can pull you in any time. Two days you've got, now piss off and feel happy you're walking.'

When Gust got out into the street he said to the thin man, 'I sincerely want to thank you for the way you helped carry John into that corner the way you did and set him up for the kill. Do you know that nearly brought tears to my eyes?'

'That was respect,' said the thin man, 'it was natural. And I'm glad you take it that way. I appreciate it, you're a mensch.'

'You're as full of respect as Rampton is with nuts, you are,' Gust said. 'I've had about enough respect for one day.'

'Anyhow,' said the thin man, 'at least Mr Hawley's given you time. And I nearly forgot.' He took Gust's .38 out of his pocket and handed it back to him unloaded. 'Get into the car. I'll take you wherever you're going.'

'No thanks,' said Gust, 'you take the hearse.' While the thin man was settling into the car he leaned in and said, 'Don't forget you owe me a tooth, by the way, and you've probably read what it says about an eye.'

The thin man shrugged; he didn't get it. 'You should have been more polite to Mr Hawley. He commands respect wherever he goes, Mr Hawley does.'

'He scored zero with me,' said Gust. 'Funny.'

He walked down to Hammersmith and along King
Street towards a pub called the Top Of The Morning.
I'm burned out, nothing matters, he thought. People got
out of his way; they thought he was drunk.

When he got to the pub he found that the Irish fiddler
who played there had packed up and gone. He stood at
the end of the bar with a pint; when he had drunk six he
smashed his glass on the bar and walked out. No one but
a local off-duty copper turned round, and that was only
because he was new on the street and didn't know who
anybody was.

Gust wandered around for the rest of the day and
wound up spending the night at Allison Road. The Jag
wasn't outside any more and he hadn't anywhere else to
go anyhow; he couldn't face Christine or any other
company.

He went to bed. For a long time he couldn't sleep,
and when he did he woke again almost at once to find
he was sitting bolt upright. In his sleep a hooded man
had attacked him and left blood on him; the sensation
was so vivid that he even found himself trying to wipe
it off.

When it got light he got up and took the gun out of his
coat. He tore off a piece of blanket and cleaned it; then
he checked and loaded it with a clip he had hidden in his
mattress. He went over to the uncurtained window and
stared down at the street. He watched mothers wheeling
their kids to the shops; there was some weak sunshine
about, a lot of shadow. There was still no Jaguar parked
outside; no sound in the house but a cat mewing
downstairs. He thought of Petal and of what he had told
Johnny about her the night they went up to the Red Wok
to see Manny. 'I'm in this fog,' he said aloud. 'I can't
think straight.'

The dream went on troubling him while he dressed
even though he was left with just that one detail, the
hooded man leaving blood on him.

'Dreams don't foretell the future,' he said. 'It's

chance that's against me; it always fucks you up if it can.'

He felt ready to let everything drop. He had plunged into a lake to find it had no bottom, but it was no use telling his body that; it would keep going of its own accord. The trouble was with his mind; it was his mind that kept telling him that there were too many people against him. But what body had ever been overruled by a mind? Bodies often lasted longer than a mind did; he remembered going to see his mother in the old people's home, her toothless mouth open as she crept along the corridors with no memory, forever searching and never finding anything, her hands twisted into each other. 'She's looking for her teeth,' the Irish nurse on the ward had told him one day. 'We keep them for her and give her them back at mealtimes, if not she just takes them out and loses them; she's a holy terror is Mrs Gust.'

When he had finished remembering his mother, whom he hadn't thought about for years, he found a lassitude had opened up in him the way that half-healed wounds do. It wasn't just a momentary depression; it was a void which, once created, immediately spread like the blood in the dream. He knew that such feelings were dangerous, indeed the ultimate danger; they sapped a man's force. Alone with them in that sad room at Allison Road, in that dirty old house filled with unemployed ex-cons, he experienced what he was undergoing through the cold eyes of a stranger.

With this difference, that the stare came from himself. *If Petal were here*, he thought, *or Johnny, any of my friends. If we had drink, clubs, music* . . .

But there was no music, nor would it have helped him if there had been, because music can only recall the past, not recreate it, and his friends were either dead, like the Irishman, taking their warmth into the ground with them, or else they were in jail serving long sentences; sentences so long that even when the inmate finally emerged, blinking at the outside world, they would hardly know each other; it would be embarrassing, because so much time had elapsed that there would be nothing to say.

He had never in his life imagined that he would get involved in a situation this bad. That was what he told the blank window, and when he had finished telling the window he told the walls.

In the end hunger got the better of him. He went down to a pizzeria for a takeaway Margherita and a coffee, then sat down on a public bench near the traffic lights to eat.

He found himself missing the Irishman still; the Irishman was always so bloody cheerful. He remembered the things they had been through together and suddenly he knew how death would feel: his strength ebbing away as an underfed man's does in cold weather, the way he remembered telling Frankie it felt in the car going down to Manny's in Clapham: a freezing wind. That day seemed years ago now.

He flattened his plastic coffee-cup with his foot, threw it in the hedge and stood up.

25

Spaulding got a call to go to Engels Park in north London, far out towards Barnet; he arrived to find men standing round a tree between the park railings and a rusted play-swing. The ground was soaked with dew, and dead chestnut leaves floated down through the still autumn air.

Someone in his fifties with a red face and a scarf on came over. He said hoarsely, 'Cumbernauld, DS,' and pointed at a bright red bag at the foot of the tree.

'Who found him?'

'Man going to work.'

'Seven-thirty in the morning,' said Spaulding, 'and here I am a million miles from the Bar Italia and a decent cup of coffee.' He went over to the bag, unzipped it and looked at the face. 'That's Laray all right,' he said, 'ready for a funeral if ever I saw one.' He added, 'The bastard would be.'

'With a bullet through the head,' said Cumbernauld, 'what else can you expect? What did you want him for anyway?'

'A lot of things,' said Spaulding, 'a long talk first. I wanted to ask him about an incident in a Chinese restaurant off Shaftesbury Avenue, a nasty little villains' spat with shooters; he fits the description of one of them. He's also the brother-in-law of someone else I want to see badly, an ex-con called Gust, and that's another case I'm having no joy with. I tell you, I've had it up to here; every time I get anywhere near anyone to do with this man Gust they go pop. This man here, Laray, he's a robber, he hired out as a heavy, he had plenty of form, lived in Brockley, keen on greyhound racing, kept dogs. Christ, he's way off his manor, what the fuck does he think he's doing dying right out here? I don't suppose they left anything? Empty shells? Prints?'

Cumbernauld shook his head.

Spaulding said gloomily, 'The cases I get they never do.'

'He wasn't killed here anyway,' said Cumbernauld, 'he was dumped.' He turned the stiffening body over. 'Look at that exit wound, it's taken the whole back of his head off.'

'Thanks very much,' said Spaulding bitterly, 'I can see it has.' He zipped the bag up again. 'Have they worked out how long he's been dead?'

'His temperature puts it late last night, early this morning, but they won't know any more till he's on the slab.'

'How did he wind up here in the park do you reckon? They throw him over the railings?'

'No need,' said a local sergeant, 'the lock on the gate's been broken for years, all they had to do was drag him in.'

'You can see the heel marks,' said Cumbernauld. He coughed, leaving a tangle of steam in the air. 'Anything more we can do, then?'

'Nothing except get your breakfast,' said Spaulding. 'Some people have all the luck. Me, it's back to the office, and bang goes another lead.'

'Yes,' said Cumbernauld, 'and I should think it must have been a big bang for Laray.'

26

'I wouldn't put a penny of my money on Gust,' said Sladden. 'I wouldn't put the price of a ghost's dinner on him.'

'Unfortunately we have to trust him,' said Draper.'We're working with him.'

'Working with him?' Sladden said. 'How do we know we're working with him? He could be working for anybody. Everyone seems to have got shares in Gust, even this copper Spaulding.'

'It's Spaulding I'm bothered about,' said Ricky. 'Gust, I can take Gust. But Spaulding, what are we going to do about that interfering dickhead?'

'Spaulding's just a copper working on what he thinks is a straightforward killing in a piano bar,' Draper said, 'and we can't tell him anything different. I can hardly tell him to drop Gust because he's our mole in a case that's got red stickers on it, can I? That's why Spaulding's got no idea what the real strength is.'

'You're going to have to tell him though,' said Ricky. 'Your problem's going to be to get clearance to straighten him out.'

'But the real problem's not Spaulding,' said Draper, 'though Christ knows we could do without him. My main worry is that Gust's bird's been topped and what is Gust going to do about that, because if he goes AWOL he could york the ball right over the bloody pavilion.'

'Terrific,' said Sladden. 'Just where there's no one to catch it. And he's started; look what happened at the Red Wok.'

'Yes,' said Ricky, 'that was a naughty one.'

'I never expected that to happen to the Chang girl,' Draper said.

'Well, why didn't you?' said Ricky. 'Gust delivers the gear to Ford and then it disappears; did you think villains like Farb were just going to sit back and swallow that? Where did you go last time you moved? The moon?'

'Well, *you* didn't expect it,' said Sladden. 'I thought you were going to shit your knickers when you heard.'

'Anyway, Ford's dead now,' Draper said.

'No wonder,' said Ricky. 'The way this has been played what else could he be?'

'All right,' Draper conceded, 'it's true the planning went a bit doolally there.'

'Doolally?' said Ricky. 'I can think of a stronger word for it than that. The heat's full blast on Gust, plus his bird's been topped; no one's going to behave normally under that kind of pressure, and he didn't. He did the Red Wok.'

'Well, it's no use moaning about it,' Draper said. 'We'll have to play it the way the cards are now.'

'Well, the cards are a shambles,' said Ricky. 'There's been too much brown bread on this one altogether. We've got ourselves into an almighty fucking jam, we've got just the rest of the week to get out of it, and my guess is we'll be getting another visit from upstairs any minute. Eight fish fingers so far, and it isn't finished yet.'

'I can count,' Draper said irritably, 'but think what's at stake. Anyway, the main thing is, we've got Gatov, and Gatov's talking. As for the villains, Gust's concentrated them all on himself. But that's what we wanted; that's how we set him up.'

'I'm still against it,' said Sladden. 'I repeat what I've said all along, Gust's a fucking menace, especially now Chang's been wasted. We could have another Red Wok on our hands any minute; he doesn't know which tree he's in and what's much worse, nor do we.'

'I don't think it's that bad,' said Draper. 'We've broken Gatov, we've got the passports; all we have to do now is make sure none of these people fuck off somewhere ten thousand miles away at the last minute so that the whole thing's got to be done again. On the other hand, if things work out, we clean up, make our report, upstairs squares it off with some junior minister and a few arseholes at Whitehall and that's us finished.'

'Don't even mention any of them getting away,' said Sladden. 'That reminds me of when I was a copper – you catch the bastards and then some nerd says you've got to let them go. I wish I could just do it my way.'

'We know all about your way,' said Draper. 'Do it your way and there'll be more blood all over the scenario, which is a double dose of what I don't want.'

'Particularly with the visitor taking an interest,' said Ricky.

'OK, OK,' said Sladden. 'But it's a pity.'

'We've got to make sure they never flog any of that gear,' said Draper, 'whether from here or anywhere else. What still amazes me is that these people thought the UK was the place to trade it from, though mind you, with this inept government it's little wonder.'

'Frankly,' said Ricky, 'if I were Joe Soap and didn't really understand how bad things were, if I was never given the correct figures on anything, paid my council tax, voted Tory every five years – if I weren't being paid to dig into all this shit, would I really care?'

'Of course you wouldn't,' said Sladden. 'You'd read about it when it was over, have a bleat down at the pub and forget about it. You'd prove the clerks right, the punter'll swallow anything, least said soonest mended. If there's a balls-up deny it like Reg Christie propping the garden fence up with a human thigh, stand in front of it while the law's asking you about it, see them off, go indoors, have a cup of tea and on to the next shambles, why not?'

'All right,' said Draper, 'that'll do.'

'If it wasn't for Gust it might,' Sladden said, 'but Gust, I still say I'd like him out of the way now before he has a chance to fuck this up. His girl's dead, he's unstable anyway because villains always are, and he also knows we've got the passports. In fact apart from ourselves, now that Ford's dead, he's the only one who does know, and what's he going to do about it?'

'There's not much he can do about it,' said Ricky.

'He could open his yap,' said Sladden, 'so why take a chance? Clobber him. Put him down now is what I say, it'd be safer. You're working on the theory the man's sane, I'm not. Madmen don't work on the principle of what's possible, they just go ahead and do it.'

'You should know,' said Ricky.

'That's enough,' Draper interrupted. 'We'll work Gust my way and that's the end of it. It won't be a pretty solution whatever happens, but I can't help that.'

'All right then,' said Ricky, 'if that's settled let's get back to Spaulding.'

'I'll look after Spaulding,' Draper said.

'Good,' said Sladden. 'Because that's what you draw all that money for.'

'Thanks,' said Draper, 'I'll make a note of that, Sladden, thanks a lot.'

'You're not going to tell Spaulding things he oughtn't to know, are you?' said Sladden. 'Not the classified stuff?'

'Classified, is it?' said Ricky. 'I like your sense of humour; except for the missiles Gust knows almost as much about this as we do, so why not tell Spaulding the whole story too? You might as well spew the lot up.'

'I'll have to tell Spaulding something,' said Draper, 'he's a police officer. I'll have to get clearance for at least some of it; it's the only way to get him off our backs.'

'Have fun,' said Sladden. 'Spaulding's an obstinate bastard, wait till you have a go.'

27

'Thank you very much for coming round so promptly, Mr Spaulding,' Draper said.

'It wasn't my idea.'

'I know it wasn't,' said Draper, 'but never mind, sit down, have a drink.'

'I don't drink on duty.'

'It's a matter of different lifestyles,' said Draper, pouring himself a large scotch. 'So how are you getting on with Darby Mansions then? Any progress?'

'No, none so far.'

'What, no progress at all?' said Draper. 'Three villains shot dead in a block of flats and not a single lead? I'd have thought there'd have been at least a whisper.'

'There might have been if I could have found anyone alive to do the whispering,' said Spaulding, 'but they keep dying, including a man called Johnny Laray, he's the latest; I just went and looked at his body this morning.'

'Name means nothing to me. What happened to him?'

'A nine-millimetre bullet through the head happened to him,' said Spaulding, 'and he'd been tortured as well.'

'There must be someone around who knows something, though.'

'Yes there is,' said Spaulding. 'There's Gust.'

'Gust? I can't understand why you're so interested in Gust. And what makes you think I can help you over him, anyway? All I know about Gust is that he's an armed robber; I remember him from way back when I was still with the Met.'

'Well, he's still in the news,' said Spaulding. 'Look at these cases I'm on – all down to him, I know it. First there's the fight down at Marly's, then the Chang girl, next it's the shooting incident in the Red Wok followed by this business in Darby Mansions, where I'm dead sure there's a connection with Gust, now it's Johnny Laray, who was his brother-in-law; one way or another Gust's mixed up in this whole load of shit, and nearly everybody in it is either seriously damaged, or dead.'

'Where's the evidence? It's all very tenuous.'

'Is it?' said Spaulding. 'How do you know it's tenuous? How much do you know about Gust yourself, anyway?'

'Only what I've just told you.'

'I'm really fed up with this,' said Spaulding. 'All I have to do is mention Gust to anybody and straight away I'm up against a brick wall.'

'He's not connected to your inquiries,' said Draper, 'that's why.' He lit a cigarette.

'Maybe he's involved in something you're up to though,' said Spaulding, 'and maybe the others are too. In fact to me it's becoming obvious.'

'Nothing's obvious.'

'Not if you can help it it isn't, no. The obvious melts away like snowflakes in spring when you get your hands on it.'

'Mind your language, Inspector.'

'I'll put it this way, then,' said Spaulding. 'Why would I have been told to come and see you if it wasn't to do with Gust? We haven't anything else in common.'

'It's only you who says we have got Gust in common. I'd like to hear some more of your views on that.'

'Well, I've got some,' said Spaulding, 'but they'll have to wait till I've interviewed the man, so my view at the moment is that I'd like to have a session with him over at Poland Street, it could take all day and night. Or even longer.'

'I might as well tell you this,' Draper said. 'However long it took you'd get nowhere.'

'That's what they all say, and that must be because I'm not meant to get anywhere even if I did get hold of Gust, whether or not I question him about the death of his brother-in-law, or Marly's club, or Manny Farb and the shoot-out at the Red Wok, where no one seems to know anything either. All we've got there is vague descriptions of two men from various staff and customers, that's all, and it's not a lot.'

'Well, even if it was a lot you'd still be wasting your time.'

'I'll be the judge of that.'

'Look,' said Draper, 'why do you really think you're here?'

'That's what I want to know.'

'I'll tell you then, and this is the plain truth: it's because you won't be seeing Gust at all. Not ever. It's as simple as that.'

'I'll just remind you at this point, that we could get onto dangerous ground here. I'm in charge of these inquiries because I've good reason to think they're connected. As for you, I know what you do for a living all right, but I wouldn't like to think you were withholding evidence from a murder inquiry either.'

'What it comes to,' said Draper, 'is that we've each got our own brief.'

'So it's the brick wall again.'

'It is,' said Draper. 'It's the Home Office versus the MOD.'

'Well, I'm not satisfied with that. It's obvious to me that you know what was behind that club battle and the one at the Red Wok. Also the reason for Laray's death, even, and the shoot-out at Darby Mansions.'

'Well, it's our business to know what's going on,' Draper said mildly, 'the same as it is yours, only of course we see things from a totally different angle.'

'Not so different as to leave a suspected killer running about loose, I hope.'

'No of course not, we do exercise some control.'

'I'm fucked if I can spot it. Anyway, whether you exercise any or not isn't my business, my business is to follow up any lead I get.'

'I've just told you why you can't do that. It's conflicting interests.'

'No. None of this is good enough for me, I'm not satisfied.'

'All right,' said Draper. 'I wanted to sidestep this because it's my head on a platter, but I can see I'm going to have to explain my views further.'

'I think you'd better,' said Spaulding, 'because my own view's simple. If Gust's responsible for the deaths I'm investigating I want to put him away for a long time; he's dangerous, he's barely sane and he should probably never have been released in the first place. He's an armed robber; a man was killed in the raid he went down for. Now he's out on licence, and I know even if I can't prove it that he murdered one man in Soho the other night and crippled another. And what happens immediately after that? His Chinese ex-girlfriend gets the chop in her flat. I'm not saying it was him, I happen to know it wasn't, but the man's a mobile death sentence just the same; people die wherever he happens to be.'

'I hear you took him up to see the Chang girl's body,' Draper said. 'That was an original touch.'

'I wanted to get him talking.'

'It's not in the book, though. And did it work?'

'No.'

'Well, what do you expect from a villain?' said Draper. 'Full and frank cooperation? As for this piano bar thing, those two men were contract killers put onto him by grade A villains, did you know that?'

'No,' said Spaulding, 'all I know is that they weren't in his league. I also realise that you know a great deal more about Gust than you just said you did. This contract, for instance, how did you get to know about that?'

'Never mind. By the way, did you know there are a lot of people after Gust?'

'No.'

'And the Chang girl, what do you know about her?'

'Only that she used to be Gust's girlfriend before he went inside.'

'Yes,' said Draper, 'well, the mistake she made this time was to put him up, and as the people who are after Gust couldn't find anyone keen to top him after the Marly's incident they topped her instead so as to give him a bloody good fright; and if you ask me he'll catch whoever killed her quicker than you will because he's really motivated.'

'Who are these people after Gust?'

'I'm trying to decide if you really need to know that,' said Draper. 'On the one hand you might stop fucking us about if you knew what we were doing; on the other hand you might go on trampling all over it and do even more damage.'

'I'm only interested in Gust.'

'I know,' Draper said, 'and that's tough, because there's a lot more to this than just him.' He lit another Westminster. 'In any case, what this meeting is for is to tell you that up to now, for reasons which I admit you know nothing about, you have been getting seriously up our nose over this Gust business; you've been muddying waters that are already jet black and your efforts are totally counter-productive to ours. So here's the message, Spaulding, and it's final: lay off Gust.'

'I can't do that. That would have to go the distance on my side, all the way up to the top.'

'It's already been there and back, and that's why you

were told to come and see me.'

'As far as I know I'm still on the Gust case, I've heard nothing different.'

'That's because your people are waiting to see what you and I can sort out,' said Draper. 'I should know, I've just had them on the phone. But there's no time for a lot of bullshit, things over here are moving too fast.'

'That doesn't give me the authority to drop my end of it,' said Spaulding, 'and I wouldn't drop it if I had. Anyway, what does it matter to you if Gust's in jail or not? It's where he belongs.'

'That's what I'm trying to explain within the limits of what I can tell you,' Draper said. 'Gust's mixed up in something that goes far beyond the scope of a gangland murder inquiry, so stop dealing with it as if it was one. In fact,' he added, 'I just told you, stop dealing with it altogether and leave it to us.'

'Is that all you've got to say?'

'It's all there is to say. We're talking about national security and that's that.'

'Well, it won't do,' said Spaulding, 'so I'll carry on the way I'm going; I don't see it your way.'

'Then I'll tell you how I see it my way. Have you thought about looking for another job at all, such as a security guard in a supermarket, or a bus conductor? Because with the attitude you're taking now's the time.'

'I've got my senior officers behind me.'

'You don't know what your senior officers are behind, because to put it bluntly you're in no position to know.'

'All I want is Gust for these deaths,' said Spaulding, 'and I'm going to go on wanting him till I get him. There's nothing more to discuss.'

'And that's what we don't want,' said Draper, 'so there's a direct clash of interests. *That's* what there is to discuss.'

'Don't get the idea that you can make me drop this case. I've never done that yet.'

Draper leaned wearily back in his chair. 'All right, I

thought it would come to this. Contain your zeal till you hear some of this from my side, then perhaps you'll cooperate.'

'I'm listening.'

'Let's talk about passports,' said Draper. 'British passports. A thousand of them. Clean, brand new, blank and hijacked.'

'Stolen passports aren't my kind of work.'

'I know they're not. They're ours.'

'What about them?'

'Gust hijacked them.'

'I'll have him for that as well then.'

'No you won't,' said Draper, 'you won't have him for anything, because the fact is that he's working for us; we set the whole thing up. Originally Gust was going to nick those passports for a villain called Manny Farb. Yes, Darby Mansions, you're getting there. Only we turned the operation round; that's what you've got to get through your head. It's all right, absorb it, take your time.'

'I still want him, though,' Spaulding said after a while.

'Well, learn to live with the fact that you're not going to get him,' said Draper, 'because everything he does is covered by us. We know those two men went down to that bar to kill him, we know who sent them, we know why, and it was lucky for us Gust came out sunny side. We'd have been in right shtuck if they'd killed him because he's in the middle of this pool of sharks, in fact he's the bait.'

'Where are these passports now?'

'We've got them, of course, except for four.'

'What happened to the four you haven't got?'

'We let them through to the people they were intended for, of course. Russians.'

'Just a minute,' said Spaulding, 'I heard about two Russians dying in the space of a week the other day; one shot himself, the other turned up on a rubbish tip minus a leg.'

'That's two of them, yes.'

'Were they murdered?'

'Well, yes, they had to go,' said Draper. 'These things happen. One of our folk, Gutteridge – they killed him – warned us they were going to tell their people in Moscow that the UK operation wasn't safe, and we couldn't let that happen. They'd have cancelled, and then Gatov wouldn't have come over. He was the man we wanted, and we got him.'

'Why did Gust agree to rip these passports off for you in the first place?'

'Try and think straight. We told him we'd wipe out the five years he's got hanging over him if he cooperated. He was reluctant to start with, but he ended up facing facts.'

'It still doesn't make any difference,' said Spaulding. 'I'm a police officer, and my legal duty once I've got proof is to arrest Gust for that club death and charge him.'

Draper shook his head. 'It'll never go to court. If it did, everything we're doing would come out, and that's the last thing anybody wants, so that even if your people sent it to the CPS the file would come back not in the public interest; they'd tell you to drop it, and I'm not joking.'

Spaulding was beginning to realise that. 'Still,' he said, 'these Russians, what's in it after all? They were only dealing in stolen passports. It's immigration stuff; it's not the end of the world.'

'You're so wrong,' said Draper. 'The end of the world is just what it could be, but I'm not in a position to give you any information about that.'

'I should think that over again, because we're not going to get any further if you don't.'

'All right then, but it'll be off the record.'

'I understand that.'

Draper sighed. 'Well, that means I've got to talk about Yuri Gatov. I'm not supposed to, but I'll just have to take a chance. Until 1990 Gatov was with the KGB, second directorate, fourth bureau, that's disinformation. But then he woke up one morning and there was no more Soviet Union, so he privatised himself; he'd been preparing for that. Some of his ex-colleagues were murdered or killed themselves, but Gatov wasn't like that. He wanted western partners, and he had files on anyone likely to get in his way. You know how they work. Any refusal to cooperate, say from a senior officer with a position to protect, and out comes a video of him sucking a prostitute's toes in some dive off the Arbat; and Gatov would see to it that he was sweeping the streets next if he was lucky.'

'But why did he want the passports? And why British ones?'

'Blank British passports east of Berlin?' said Draper. 'Use your brains. Not least because if you fill it in with a dead name and details you can get a British birth certificate to go with it. They trade at around two thousand each sterling, and for Gatov they were going to serve various purposes. One, install him and his friends as bona fide UK citizens; two, sell off the rest, because the information you can buy in Russia with the offer of a new British identity is worth far more to a man like Gatov than any two thousand quid.'

'What kind of information?'

'These people aren't just ordinary Russians,' said Draper. 'They call themselves irredentists; they don't want to know about the CIS. They want to set up their own republic, and you've got to think of the massive returns if you strip the assets of an area and sell them off.'

'What assets? What have they got to sell?'

'What they've got,' said Draper, 'is the seventh military district of the Soviet army, if you know what that means.'

'No I don't. All I know about is investigating deaths in bed-sitters.'

'Seventh district contains a stockpile of nuclear warheads. It's the biggest in the country, and to our
knowledge two of the bloody things have gone missing
already.'

'You're not going to tell me they're in Britain.'

'How the hell you ever made detective inspector I
don't know,' said Draper, 'you'd be no use to us here.
No, they're not in Britain, but they could just as well be
aimed at it for all we know – what do you think we're all
scrambling about for?'

'I'd be interested to meet Gatov.'

'Well, I'm afraid you can't,' said Draper. 'He's not
very fit at the moment, he's tired, he's not making much
sense. It's all right, he's not dying or anything, but in the
process of giving us all his information we had him going
through the hoop rather, running and jumping about a
good deal. I think the exercise was too much for him;
after all, he's well into his fifties. Still, we got all manner
of things out of him, names, all the bank accounts. I said
to him: "Now look, Yuri, you're not going anywhere and
it works like this, I want the lot out of you. It doesn't
have to be difficult, but it could be if you weren't helpful,
because I'm in a hurry." Well, he'd got more bottle than
I thought he had, and of course he was choked to see all
his plans come unstuck. "You shouldn't have worked
with villains, Yuri," I said, "particularly in a city you
don't know, it always goes wrong." "Where do you want
to start, then?" he said in the end (we didn't get there all
in one go, of course, there was a good deal of the old
how's-your-father on the way). "We want all the names,"
I told him, "then we'll check your list against the
Dziadek woman's when we're ready to pick her up, also
Gates' list." "I don't know anyone called Dziadek or
Gates," he said, and I said: "It's quite amazing the things
people know and think they've forgotten, Yuri; we'll
rope you up to the beam again by your thumbs for as
long as it takes with an hour extra if you piss or shit
yourself and you'll find your memory'll come flooding

back." Meanwhile I said to my team, "Just move the general over to this light socket here, will you, he knows this old game, you've used it yourself in your time haven't you, Yuri?" "I'll appeal to Amnesty!" he shouted. "Don't be a fool," I said, "how can you do that, Yuri, you don't exist.'"

He looked up from his desk and said to Spaulding, 'Of course, you and I don't quite use the same rule-book.'

'So I'd noticed.'

'You can take the moral high ground as much as you like,' said Draper, 'but I'll say this much for our methods: they work.'

28

Gust went into the Diadem as dark fell, but he had hardly found a place at the bar when the governor yelled at him, 'Gust! Phone!'

The man on the phone said, 'Gust? My name's Richard Gates, we haven't met. But that doesn't matter, we've got things in common.'

'What things?'

'Listen, it's short notice, but could you have dinner with me now? I'll have you picked up.'

'OK,' said Gust.

Well, why not? Something had to happen anyway. He went out into the street; he wanted to see if there were any of Hawley's men out there. But he knew it was pointless; how could he know who they were using? He leaned against the wall by the pub door, drinking scotch; he hadn't finished it when a Mercedes pulled up. The driver reached back and opened the rear door; the first thing Gust noticed was that the interior smelled of expensive scent.

'I don't want to be followed,' said Gust.

'Nothing follows this car,' the driver said.

They sped down the Mall to Hyde Park Corner and into Knightsbridge. Gust lit a filter and opened the window; Casterbridges weren't everybody's taste and they certainly didn't mix with the scent. The car slowed opposite the barracks, turned into Trevor Square and stopped at a place called Oblomov's.

Gust got out of the car. There was no porter on the restaurant door, but he noticed professionally that there were alarms, video cameras at the entrance, and that both door and windows were made of armoured glass; you could have fun trying to break in there. A man in a dinner jacket appeared and led him through, and if he thought Gust's jeans and sweater were on the casual side he didn't say anything about it.

It was certainly a remarkable restaurant. Everything except the tables, which were yards apart, seemed to be made of black leather, and it was three-quarters dark except over the piano, which was being played by a blond man with a red tuxedo. The rest was lit by dimmed candelabra which would have looked happier in a palace, and Gust knew without even looking at the menu that nothing on it would cost under twenty quid.

In the distance at the back a man in the kind of blazer that made its wearer look like a member of the Yacht Club was getting to his feet. A dark-haired woman sat beside him. One gold-slippered foot showed from under the table and she could have been any age except twenty, any nationality but British.

'Sit down,' the man said. 'I'm Richard Gates. This lady's an associate of mine, Lena Dziadek.'

Neither name meant anything to Gust.

'Drink?'

'Scotch and ice.'

'Nice in here, isn't it?' said Gates. 'Must be a change for you after Maidstone.'

'Don't let's bother with the CV,' said Gust.

'All right. How's freedom?'

'Busy,' said Gust. He leaned towards the woman and recognised the perfume she was wearing from the car. 'Are you German?'

'No,' she said, 'I'm a professional refugee and what's your problem in life?'

'Leading a normal one,' said Gust. 'So where are you from tonight?'

'I was being a Finn till you arrived, but now I'll drop that and be a Czech, which is what I really am.'

Gust didn't believe a word she said.

'Hungry?' said Gates.

'Ten years on slops spoils you for good food,' said Gust. He ordered a dozen oysters.

'We've finished,' said Gates, 'we can talk while you eat.'

'Who are you, before we go any further?' Gust asked.

'Business people.'

The girl wasn't saying anything now; she sat watching them.

'You've been having problems,' said Gates.

'Have been?' said Gust. 'Who said they were over?'

'It's a risky life you're leading,' said Gates, 'I don't know if you quite realise.'

'Are you part of the risk?'

'That's what we need to talk about.'

'We heard about your girlfriend,' Lena said.

Gust put his fork down. 'How did you know about that?'

'We might go into that later,' Gates said. 'Meantime let's talk about that shoot-out with Manny Farb in Soho. Your problems at Marly's piano bar. The copper from Poland Street. Spaulding.'

Gust waited.

'Spaulding's after you for murder, did you know?'

'He should have looked further back.'

'Why should he bother if you fit?'

'That's right,' said Gust. 'I'm convenient.'

'Did you know two Russians died the other day?' said Gates. 'Violently. Maybe you read about them.'

'I didn't,' said Gust. 'I haven't time for the papers.'

'Have you ever heard of a man called Draper?'

'No. Should I have?'

'Never mind,' said Gates.

'These particular Russians,' said Lena, 'I think they'd have interested you.'

'Don't let's get ahead of ourselves,' Gates said. 'He doesn't know anything about that. Let's consider his other problems, such as Marly's.'

'I wasn't going to just sit there and let them top me.'

'Of course not,' said Gates. 'And you certainly didn't.' He took out a case of Havanas and Gust lit a Casterbridge.

'Those things are really disgusting,' the Dziadek girl said.

'They're not a taste,' said Gust, 'they're a habit.' He blew the smoke downwards, but she coughed just the same; most people did.

Gates rolled his cigar about in his fingers. 'You've got other problems still which perhaps you don't even know about.'

'I haven't got room for any more.'

'Make some,' Lena said.

'The name Hawley mean anything to you?' said Gates.

'Hawley the paymaster?'

'That's the one.'

Gust wasn't going to tell Gates how much the name meant to him; he either already knew or he didn't. 'He got shot up in a south London drugs deal that went wrong and he hasn't operated in the UK since. He works out of Turkey these days, he can't come back here, there's a murder warrant out on him. That's all I know.'

Gates put his cigar down. 'I fancy an armagnac, how about you? Lena will have another.'

'A large one,' she said.

'Large ones are the only ones Lena knows,' said Gates. He smiled bitterly.

'I'll just have scotch,' said Gust.

Gates ordered the drinks. 'I'm much more up to date than you are,' he said. 'Hawley was in Britain no later than today, did you know that?'

'No,' said Gust. He had no intention of going into that.

'I'm surprised he hasn't been in contact,' Gates said, 'because I hear he's very interested in you.'

If you only knew how interested, thought Gust. 'Well, naturally I'd like to hear about that.'

'You might,' said Gates. He drew on his cigar. 'I went into a business deal with Hawley recently. Refinancing. I'm beginning to think now I made a mistake; I think he's trying to screw me.'

'That's what villains normally do,' said Gust. 'Like to tell me what sort of a deal?'

'No,' said Gates. 'And then you've got just one more person to worry about; I'll ask you again. Draper. Are you quite sure you've never heard of him?'

'Name means nothing to me at all.'

'Then we'll keep it that way.'

'I think it's time you told me what all this is about,' Gust said.

'I'll tell you what I feel like telling you,' said Gates. 'Meanwhile, let's go back to those two Russians I mentioned. I'm not surprised you haven't heard of them, they didn't exactly make headlines. But there was one interesting fact that was never reported at all; when the bodies were found they each had a new British passport on them.'

'How did you come to know that?'

'I've got contacts,' said Gates, 'and that means something to you, passports, doesn't it?'

'Some passports might.'

'There were a thousand of them in this case. Stolen.'

'I don't feel like talking about them right now,' said Gust. The conversation was turning out the way this caper had all along, with his never understanding more than two thirds of it.

'No,' said Gates. He laid his cigar in the ashtray. 'On the whole I wouldn't expect you to.' He leaned back in his chair. 'Lena and I are staying at the Royal Garden.

Why don't you come round for a nightcap? We could finish the rest of this discussion there.'

'All right,' said Gust, 'I just have to go to the heads.'

He stood up, and Lena stood up with him. 'I have to go too,' she said. A waiter saw them coming and whipped open a door invisible in the leather wall, which it matched.

'Me to the right,' said Gust when they got out there, 'you to the left.'

'Why?' she said. 'There's no one about.' She grabbed him by the arm. 'I want to fuck you,' she whispered in his ear. 'Now. It's as simple as that. And don't say you don't want me, I'm coming all over the place.' She exuded a harsh animal smell. 'All right,' she said, 'I'll clean up in here. We'll do it at the hotel.' She disappeared through a door marked ladies in four languages.

When they rejoined Gates he didn't look pleased. Compared to his previous easy-going behaviour he looked grim, and Gust realised that he had guessed what Lena had been saying outside and was used to it, which didn't mean he had learned to like it.

'Now I'll tell you what I brought you here for,' he said.

'I think I've already guessed,' said Gust. 'You want those passports, only I don't know where they are.'

Lena came back and sat down without saying anything.

'I think you do know,' said Gates. 'Anyway, I'm hiring you to find out.'

'Use someone else. I've got enough on my plate.'

'There isn't anyone else,' said Gates, 'and you've got every reason to find them, the bother you're in. Also I'm paying good money.' He pulled out a pack of currency. 'Here's five thousand; that's just half, a deposit. Count it. Go on. People in here count money all the time, they're gamblers.'

Not being able to mention Sladden, not being able to say he knew bloody well who had the passports, not being able to make a single slip or knowing where any of these people fitted together, Gust knew he was playing way out of his league. He was a robber, not a conman, but he counted the money anyhow and put it away. *After all*, he thought, *I might even get off the hook if this goes on, buy a house, stay clean.* He knew it would never happen; he wasn't even sure he wanted it to happen. If he ever did buy a house he would soon be back in trouble, or else he would just sit in it and brood over Petal.

Besides, playing with men like Gates and Hawley, this would only be a very quick hand. What he thought as he picked up Gates' money was, bricks, blood and bank-notes don't get on; they never did, they never had.

They nearly did it in the lift, but Dziadek managed to wait until they had emptied the minibar and checked that Gates was in bed. Then she took him to her room; as soon as they were in there they locked onto each other, leaning against the door. After Petal the last thing Gust wanted was sex, and bile came up in the back of his throat.

'You come on like a dead fish. You're not gay, are you?' she said at one point. 'That would be just my luck.'

But when she did get him at it she didn't know what had hit her. 'Easy,' she said, 'don't rush it. Christ, when did you last have a fuck?'

'I've forgotten,' he said, because he didn't want to remember.

'Get this top cover off the bed or I'll soak it,' she said. 'Dont finish all the chocolates in one mouthful, suck me off first.' She spread her legs open as far as they would go and exposed her clitoris between splayed fingers; it tasted like a daiquiri made with a hand-grenade.

'Why me?' he said.

'Because I like it rough. I only had to look at you, I always know.'

'Doesn't Gates care?'

'He won't like it, he never does, but he won't say anything.'

'What made him so quiet?'

'Who cares?' she said.

When she finally fell asleep he slid out of bed, picked her bag up and took it to the bathroom. Inside he found a new British passport containing an exit stamp at Moscow airport and an entry stamp at Heathrow dated three days ago. He looked at the serial number on the passport and recognised it.

He wasn't surprised. Whoever Sladden worked for must have arranged it. He wondered what Gates would say if he knew that, and knew who Sladden was. In turn Gust wondered who Draper was, but he had never heard of him, although Gates had; Christ, it was like a Chinese puzzle. He flushed the lavatory, replaced the passport in the bag, shut it, put it back on the floor and got into bed, staring upwards in the half dark until the girl woke up and started fondling him again.

He pushed her off. 'You're not Czech. You're Russian.'

'What difference does it make?' She yawned. 'I could sleep for hours, but I can't keep my hands off you.'

'I bet you forget people in half an hour.'

'Of course I do.'

They made love again.

Next time she woke she lit a cigarette each for them. Gust told her, 'You know very little about me.'

'What does that matter?'

'Did you know before I met you what Gates wanted me for?'

'No. He just said he wanted to see you; he doesn't tell me everything.'

'Do you tell him everything?'

'Of course not.'

'While we were eating you said you knew what had happened to my girlfriend. Did you know that I'm conducting an inquiry of my own?'

'No I didn't.' She looked amused.

'Try and behave like a human being for once,' said Gust. 'I'm looking for the man, or more likely two men who killed her, probably with a baseball bat or an iron bar. Her name was Petal Chang. Would you like to tell me more about that?'

She hesitated. 'I'd never heard of her until Richard talked about her.'

'If I believed you that would be one thing, but I don't. Try again.'

'I might have vaguely heard of her before that. Very vaguely.'

'That's better,' said Gust. 'It mightn't mean much to you, but I've got this passion to find out who killed her. If you can give me any ideas on that I've got a piece of information for you.'

She thought about it. In the end she said, 'You'd better try Hawley.'

'That makes sense,' said Gust. 'This time I want to make sure I hit the right people.'

'Do you know Hawley?'

'We've met,' said Gust. 'The atmosphere wasn't good.'

'Hawley's a monster,' she said, 'and I've met some.'

'He hurt you, did he?'

'His men hurt me for him,' she said. 'He can't do it himself any more, not since he was shot.'

'Going back to Petal. You're sure it was Hawley?'

'He told Gates about it. They meet quite often.'

'Are you saying Hawley was there when Petal was killed?'

'He was there. Two other men did the killing.'

'Can you describe them?'

'No.'

'Why not?'

'Because I've never met them.'

'And that's all you know?'

'It's better than nothing, isn't it?'

'Yes,' he said. 'Much better.'

She turned away from him, and to Gust it was as if they were just two pieces of rock in the bed. Two men, she'd said. He did a mental inventory of Hawley's men: the thin man, George, the Giant ... or Stuart and Dingo? Yes, his money was on Stuart and Dingo. Realising who had killed Petal gave him no thrill of revenge or hatred; it was just the truth, and therefore it could be acted on.

Lena turned back to him. 'What was this information you said you had for me?'

'It's about your passport.'

'How do you know anything about my passport?'

'I looked through it while you were asleep.'

'I might have expected someone like you to go through my things. Anyway, what about it?' She was curious, not angry.

'I know that passport,' said Gust. 'It's red hot, in fact I'm surprised it hasn't caught fire, because those stolen passports Gates is interested in, you're travelling on one of them, did you know?'

It was as if he had disturbed a viper. She was out of bed like a whiplash, and for a moment he thought she had gone mad.

'Who's done this to me?' She was talking to herself, not him.

'I don't know,' he said, 'but whatever stroke it is you're pulling over here, it's washed up.'

'Wait till I talk to Gates.'

'Don't go near Gates,' said Gust, 'he's fucked as well. Get dressed and get out of the country if you can, but don't try using that passport.'

'Who set us up?'

He couldn't tell her that; there were a lot of things he couldn't tell her. 'I know parts of this the same as you do,' he said, 'only I know parts that you don't. If you get out of this in one piece you'd better find out which load of villains you're working for and which ones are taking

you for a sunset ride, and you'd better get to grips with
the fact that you and Gates are being watched minute by
minute, probably filmed, that's all I can tell you.'

'Fuck Gates. And you've got your nerve even telling
me about this passport – you've as good as told me that
you know who's got the rest of them.'

'Then you'll have worked out that they're no mates of
yours,' said Gust, 'and whatever I've told you, it's
because I don't want to see you go down for thirty years
or maybe even get topped; so, if you've got any grati-
tude, tell me what business you're in with Gates.'

'I can't discuss that with you or anybody.'

'Well, it must be something really heavy,' he said, 'the
people you've got after you. You can't afford a single
mistake with them, don't I know it. Right now they're
probably letting you run to see where you lead, but they
could wipe you up any time.'

'Do you know who they are?'

'They're what you call the state security police; pity
you didn't know it in time.' He got off the bed.

'Where are you going?'

'Away,' said Gust, dressing. 'The people who are
watching you are watching me.' When he was ready he
opened the door. 'Good luck.'

'Can I contact you?'

'Not a chance.'

He left the hotel through a fire exit that the cleaners
were using, thinking of how she had thrown herself on
him, in a way that seemed no more than bad acting now,
in the light of dawn. He thought of her sex, her dry
sphincter when she wanted him to take her doggy-
fashion, her nipples the colour of rust. He thought she
was the worst fuck he had ever had and it left him
anxious, unsatisfied, every nerve in him shrieking raw-
edged; what was someone like that compared to Petal?
He looked up at the white sky. Nothing.

'Nothing!' he shouted to himself. 'Nothing! Nothing!'

29

He had to get down to Brockley. He needed a car; that was as far ahead as he could think as yet. After that, once he had got the money back from Johnny's, he didn't know what he was going to do.

He hadn't time to wait for a bus, so he found a taxi to take him back to Soho. He went up to Christine's flat and knocked. There was no answer, so he broke in. The flat was empty. He went into the bedroom and checked his gun, loading a new clip. He was tired, and lay down on the bed. *Just for a minute*, he thought. He didn't know when he would get the chance to sleep again.

When he awoke with a jerk it was dark; he had overslept. Christine still hadn't been back and the clock by her side of the bed said half past seven. He felt dirty and unshaven but he had no time for a shower; he had to find a car straight away, which meant it would have to be nicked. Night was falling and people were going home, but he knew he stuck out on the manor like a sore thumb and what he didn't need was a copper watching him get into the wrong driving seat.

He walked up Wardour Street where the cars were parked bumper to bumper, but none of them was what he wanted; they were all K- or L-registered, too conspicuous, too bugged with alarms, too big, too fucking new.

Finally he settled for a Peugeot on a meter opposite the Prince, a six-year-old 205 diesel, black, dusty and anonymous with a rear-end dent. It would do; it would have to do. He decided against breaking into it, so he bought a pint in the pub opposite and stood drinking it in the doorway while he waited for the owner, knowing he wouldn't be long unless he wanted to be towed away. It was half past eight now but the street still wasn't emptying in spite of the rain that had started falling again; Soho never really emptied. He watched the crowds on the pavement. When the owner did arrive everything would have to be done quickly; too bad it would have to be in the middle of a crowd. He just hoped the owner wasn't a woman.

He didn't have to wait long. An introspective-looking young man with steel-rimmed glasses and a collapsible umbrella stopped beside the Peugeot, feeling in his pocket for the key; but before he had found it Gust had crossed the street against the traffic and was on the pavement behind him. The young man had the key in his hand and was putting it in the lock. Gust waited till the door was open and said, 'Don't even squeak,' but the young man automatically opened his mouth to shout. Gust hit him, not hard; just the same the young man fell into Gust's arms like a deadweight load of feathers. Gust pushed him into the passenger seat. It took him a moment to start the car but that didn't matter; no one even turned round. He whipped the car round the corner into the entrance of Duck Lane, pulled the young man out and sat him behind a row of industrial rubbish bins. The young man started to recover and Gust said, 'You'll be all right.' The young man said, 'What happened? I was going to meet my girlfriend.' Gust put a twenty in the young man's top pocket and said, 'Sorry about the headache, have a drink.' He drove off.

He didn't think about anything after that except getting to Brockley. He thought about times with

Johnny, about the piss-ups at the Old Tiger at Lee Green; how they had taken the dogs out into the park at Brockley Rise, bombed out of their brains. He remembered the night he had gone up there with the leash of one of the dogs looped round his wrist; he had bent down and whispered to it as it strained away from him: 'Look, on the horizon there, see the fox?' That did it; the animal tore away with him towards that loping shape in front of the setting moon two hundred yards away on the horizon. Gust tripped and the dog dragged him through the mud with Johnny shouting, 'Don't let go of him, he's worth ten grand!' and himself yelling back. For once, for a short while, he had been happy in his own world with his own people in the warm, wet feel and smell of the summer night on the edge of the city.

Now Johnny was dead; and yet even though he had been killed in front of him he still couldn't believe that Johnny wasn't going to open the door when he arrived. 'Don't be stupid,' he muttered. 'What? The door opened by a ghost?'

He turned the car radio on and found he was listening to some weird kind of play. A woman said something, but it was drowned out by static.

A man's voice explained, 'I've been here for a long time now. I have to be on my own for a long time.'

Gust switched the radio off and drove down the Old Kent Road, realising how stupid he had been to believe that he would ever get through what faced him intact, that he would somehow pull it off.

The familiar turning came up on his right, and he drove up the edge of the park. He reached the house, drove past it, parked and got out. By chance the moon was in the same quarter as the night he and his ex-wife Cheryl had got back there after their wedding; walking back up the pavement he recalled how he had got her frillies off but then had to endure her tongue for the rest of the night. Plans. That was what she always wanted to talk about, going on about money. What was he going to

do about money? Pull a job. More money? Pull a job.
But I'm talking about long-term. Ah for Christ's sake
shut up.

He neared the house and thought, *If there's anybody in
there it'll be their unlucky night.* What was the name of
Johnny's woman? Shirley. *You can bet I won't find her
here, she'll have fucked off.* Johnny,' he whispered, 'watch
my back wherever you are.'

There wasn't a light showing, yet that was no reason
why the house need be empty. He stood in the street
against the sharp edge of shadow where the moonlight
finished and rubbed the sweat off his hands on his jeans;
then he slipped the gun out of his pocket.

'There's two to be paid for,' he whispered to it, 'let's
get to work.' Even if they weren't there here they would
come. 'We'll wait for them.'

He looked out across the park opposite. It was very
quiet. Groves of trees stooped immobile in the dark and
beyond them London came to an end; there was just the
M2 roundabout and then vague clusters of white and
orange light after that, far out south towards Swanley.

He ran silently up the steps to the house keeping to
the moon-shadowed side; there were eight of them, and
he had used them so often that he knew them as if they
were his own. He went up to the front door and put his
ear against it; he thought he heard movement in the
house that was not from the dogs' annexe, although they
could hear him and were moving about too.

He also knew it was possible that Hawley, Gates,
Sladden or even Spaulding were in there. He removed
the loose brick in the wall by the door and pulled out the
spare key on its piece of twine. In the deep silence even
death would have sounded noisy, and now he was
certain he heard muted sounds in the main house. He
said to himself, *Go in*, so he turned the key. The dogs
immediately started whining, so he stood still with his
back against the inside of the front door, hardly breathing, with his gun out.

Yes, Shirley would be long gone. He imagined her packing and getting out fast, ripping off whatever she could carry. He hadn't liked her drunk and he wouldn't like her sober; that time he had met her with Johnny he had marked her down as a loud-mouthed pisspot good for spending his money and nothing else.

But what he had to do first was go to the kennels and try to calm the dogs down. He was no animal lover, but remembering the care Johnny had taken of them it shook him when he came in from the darkness of the passage from the house and opened their door. They were in a bad way, whining with hunger, and as soon as he was inside with them they erupted in a mad chorus of howling and barking. Dirty, unfed, their flanks streaked with excrement and blood where they had snapped at each other, their ribs sticking out, bang went the money they were insured for; Johnny couldn't have got a policy on them for a tenner now.

When they saw Gust they flew at him, pushing their faces into his hand, sniffing, licking at him as if he were food himself; but the state of the dogs was, to Gust, only a symbol of the whole insult of Johnny's death, as much a part of it as the bullet that had killed him.

He squatted amongst them. He told them as they licked at his face and coursed hungrily round him: 'Johnny's murdered, so that's our world gone.'

He didn't know what to give them, so he just gave them water and threw whatever food on the floor that he could find in the bins. Then, when their hunger was satisfied, he opened their door and said, 'See if there's anybody in the place, then, go on.'

The dogs streaked away into the house and he turned back into their quarters. There was no question of turning a light on; he had to make do with the near dark, the light coming in from the street; he hadn't a torch.

'So the money went to the dogs, Johnny,' he muttered. It was unlucky money; he had given it to Johnny to look after, and Johnny had lost his life for it, so that to Gust it was tainted money. But no one else was going to have it; Johnny had done his best, leaving that message for him when Hawley must have been coming for him, and he was going to get it back.

He knelt down and raked the litter out of the dogs' kennels, but found nothing. He thumbed a flame from his lighter, shielding it, and searched each square foot of the floor, but it was concrete with just a grating in one corner for swabbing out that joined the main drain, and there was nothing under there either.

He turned to the feed bins; there were four of them. They were too heavy for him to tip over on his own quietly, so he started unloading the contents onto the floor by hand. He had almost finished with the first when he heard all the dogs whining in the house upstairs. He ran through to the hallway and up to the second floor. The dogs were jammed together in a mass, barking, standing on their hind legs, scratching at a door on the landing. He pushed past them and tried the handle, keeping his body to one side, but the door was locked. He pointed his gun at the door and said, 'I'll give you five seconds to open up, if not I'll blow it open.' He counted to five and nothing happened, so he chanced the noise and fired at the lock point-blank, then put the boot in.

He found himself in a spare bedroom. At first, having nothing but the lighter flame to illuminate it, he thought it was empty, but the dogs rushed past him and started nosing at a trussed-up bundle on the floor by the window, lying half under the drawn curtains. Gust put his pistol away and felt for his knife, slitting the cords and the blanket that covered the bundle from head to foot, and saw Shirley's face, her eyes wide with terror, her mouth gagged with a wad of cotton-wool. He pulled the gag out and she started to scream, but Gust clapped his hand over her mouth.

'I'm not going to hurt you,' he said. 'You know me, I'm Johnny's friend, calm down.'

She recognised him and nodded, and he took his hand

away. When she sat up he saw that her clothes were torn, her legs bare and shoeless; she had also been hit in the face. 'Christ,' she said, sitting up, 'I thought no one was ever coming.'

'Who did it?'

'Two men.'

'Did you know them?'

'No. They jumped me in the street the night after you and Johnny left; I got bored waiting and went back to the disco.'

'These two men,' said Gust. 'Was one of them big by any chance, the other small, the big one in a pink suit?'

She nodded. 'That's them.'

'That's Stuart and Dingo,' said Gust, 'they seem to go for women.'

He was going to tell her she was lucky to be alive, but there was no need because she said, 'They wanted to kill me, but they were interrupted. They got a call, the fat man had a mobile phone.'

'You hear any of it? You know who called them?'

'They called him Hawley,' she said. 'Where's Johnny? What's happened to him?'

He couldn't see any point in telling her. 'When did you last see him?'

'How do I know?' she said. 'He came back once, he said just to drop something off, and left again. I don't know when it was. I've been here so long I don't even know what day it is.'

'It's Saturday.'

She worked it out slowly. 'Then that must have been on Tuesday.'

That was the day before Johnny died, the day he left Gust the message.

'Where is he?' she repeated. 'Did you go out together after I'd gone? What happened?'

'We just went for a meal,' he lied, 'that's all, a Chinese in the West End. We split afterwards, he said he had things to do.'

'Why didn't he come back? Why hasn't he called me?'

'I don't know, he must be busy.'

'He could still have called me.'

'Maybe it was something he didn't want you involved in.'

'Involved?' she said bitterly. 'Look at me.' She had found her handbag on the floor and was trying to see her face in its mirror by the light from the window. 'I'm involved all right.' She rubbed her wrists. 'And what about you? What were you doing with him?'

'I tell you, we just went out for a meal.'

'I don't believe that was all. Why are all the men I know liars? What did you talk about that night?'

'I wanted him to look after something for me.'

'Money?'

'Maybe, why?'

'If it was money they took it,' she said. 'Thousands of quid in fifties, it was in a hole under one of the dog-bins; I was there when they found it. They made me show them everything in the house, that was why they wanted to kill me; the fat one said: no witnesses. They've turned the whole place upside down, smashed everything. Still, you're here, and I suppose Johnny'll be back sometime.'

'Sure he will.'

'You don't really believe that, do you? I can tell. He's left me.'

'Of course he hasn't. Why should he have?'

'Sometimes I didn't treat him right,' she said, 'and then he'd leave and stay away for days, that's nothing new. But this time feels different, I don't know. Anyway, I'm sorry if the money was yours.'

'I'll get it back.'

'You'll be lucky. They're hard men.'

'Not to a bullet. To a bullet they're tomato paste.'

'I'm starving,' she said. 'Shall I make us something? There's stuff in the deep freeze.'

He shook his head. 'I haven't time.'

'What's the hurry?'

He didn't want to tell her that they could be having visitors any moment. 'I've got things to do. You can't stay here either on your own like that.'

'I'll be all right. Anyway, I've got nowhere else to go.' The dogs swarmed round her, licking her. 'Anyway, let's hope lightning doesn't strike the same place twice.'

How wrong she was. He waited for her while she went to the bathroom; then, in the light of the moon which was waning now, they went downstairs. 'Come and help me shut the dogs up,' she said, as if it was just any old evening.

Later he couldn't understand why she should have bothered to go down to the street door with him at all. She could just as well have said goodnight to him at the top of the stairs and gone to bed, and although downstairs would have been lively, at least she would have been well out of the way. She probably just went down to the door with him out of habit.

Gust was luckier. For no reason except that its door was open he looked into the ground-floor room where he and Johnny used to sit; the room where they had talked the night they went up to see Manny. Therefore he was invisible from the street door in that second when Shirley took the bullet through the heart as she opened it. The impact threw her right the way down the hall, but she was already dead when her head hit the wall by the bottom stair.

Part of Gust's mind couldn't believe what he saw, but the rest of it had no difficulty. Gun in hand he went deeper into the curtained darkness of the sitting room to wait till he could get a line on the open street door; but right now, although he was safe, he was at right angles to it. He stilled his breathing and hoped he could get this over with before the neighbours started an uproar; everyone around must have heard the shot and lights were probably going on in the houses round about already.

He heard two voices on the path. 'You cunt!'

'I thought it was him, Stuart,' said Dingo, 'and I wasn't taking chances, not with him. OK, so it was the bird. Still, she had to go. You said no witnesses.'

'You fucking psychopath!'

'Anyway, Gust's in there,' said Dingo, 'I heard his voice. I told you it was worth coming back for another bite. Anyway, I don't feel safe with him around.'

Even as he was waiting to attack them Gust sensed it was reckoning-time, time to tot up a bill whose total told him he had nothing to look forward to. He was the professional gambler who had got fed up with gambling. Win or lose, the future wouldn't change anything, so that whether it brought victory or defeat no longer mattered; all he wanted was to play out this one game and leave the table. So that was what reaching the end of the line meant. He found that it was cold living in a fog, even a red fog.

None of that had any effect on his actions, though. He needed to urinate, so he walked soundlessly to the blind corner of the door and pissed out of it from such an angle that the stream was all the two men could see. He heard it pattering onto a pair of shoes and the pink man swore.

'You! Gust! You dirty bastard!'

'You'd better come in,' said Gust. 'You're drawing attention to yourself.'

'You come out!'

'No use arguing,' Gust said. 'You can't kill me if you can't see me.'

'Fuck you,' said the pink man.

'Good idea,' said Gust. He went back into the sitting room and used his gun to smash a windowpane. He heard both their steps pounding along the outside wall while the glass was still crashing, running to see what had happened. Gust doubled back to the front door. When he reached it he leaned round the edge and shot Stuart in the back of the head just as he was drawing back from the hole in the window. The head erupted in a shower of pink and grey mud. Dingo was just behind the pink man, but he was beat on the table.

Gust took his gun away from him. 'Get inside the house. Move. I want you alive.'

'You're not going to kill me?'

'Wrong,' said Gust. 'I only need you alive for thirty seconds.' He pushed Dingo indoors and shut the street door behind them.

'Can't we kosher this up?'

'Try praying,' said Gust. 'The priest in Parkhurst said it worked wonders.'

Saliva rolled down Dingo's lower lip and hung on his chin like a yo-yo at the end of its run. Without the pink man he looked even thinner than the night they had pushed Gust into the Jag, and a dark patch was forming in the crotch of his trousers. He farted wetly in his terror, and liquid shit bubbled out of him. 'Gates and Hawley know we're here,' he shrieked. 'They're parked in the next street; if I don't ring in they'll know.'

'Who fucking cares?' said Gust. He lined Dingo up against the wall beside Shirley's body and hit him, watching him fall across Shirley's body. 'I never thought you'd come in so useful,' he said. He went outside and found his money in the pink man's tussore jacket; then he went back in and put Dingo's pistol in his hand, afterwards kicking it away again and across the floor. 'Try arguing your way out of that when you get to court,' he said.

He ran back to the car and left the street as the first carload of heroes was turning into it behind him. In his mirror he saw neighbours in nightclothes cautiously coming out of their front doors.

30

Gust made for the coast. He got onto the M2; once he was down at Folkestone he could jump a ferry. He knew people at the docks, ex-cons, crew members who could work him on board for money and pass him off as one of theirs; there was always a way. He felt like winding this little motor up as far as it would go, putting the accelerator through the carpet, but there was no point in driving like a film sequence; the last thing he wanted was a john.

The motorway stretched ahead and London slipped into an orange glow behind him. He had the money, also the money from Gates, pressed against his thigh in his trouser pocket, all the money that had never done him any good. It was a quarter to two in the morning and there was little traffic except the lines of forty-tonners pounding down to the port in the slow lanes; but once he was past the Swanley turn-off and saw that the two pairs of headlights that had been with him for a while now were still with him he increased his speed to ninety and kept it there. But he was only driving a 205, while the first motor behind him was a Jaguar, likely enough the one the pink man had bundled him into. The car immediately behind that was a Mercedes, and either of them could see the Peugeot off without even trying.

He overtook a long string of trucks, six, seven, eight

234

nose to tail, and stayed in the centre lane. Ahead there were road works which had narrowed the motorway to a single file and would delay all of them; there was also a lay-by sign.

But the road works turned out not to matter, because before he reached them the Jaguar pulled out alongside him in the fast lane, and Gust saw Hawley in the front passenger seat with George at the wheel. As the Jag kept pace with him Hawley's window came down and he aimed a pistol; but before he could fire it Gust slammed his brakes on, which made the second car veer out, almost hitting the central divide to avoid the first. Gust saw that Hawley was still trying to get a shot off at him. He couldn't, but he fired all the same, and Gust's offside front tyre exploded. He lost control of the car even though he had his foot flat on the brake, and the shoulder of the motorway raced up to meet him. But even as he saw it he was through it, mounting a steep embankment into a hedge at the top, where the car buried itself and died. He got out running, wiping blood off his face where it had hit the steering wheel.

They couldn't follow him except on foot; no driver in his right mind would try following him up that embankment. So he had a start.

But a start to where? He found himself running across a ploughed field. In the starlit darkness augmented by an aura of distant lights he sensed that it was vast; there was no sign of a hedge anywhere ahead of him. There was only one object darker than the night in front, reaching up into the sky, a high tension pylon; looking up he saw cables high above him. With wet earth dragging at his feet he reached the base of the pylon and stopped to listen; a long way behind he heard voices. He still had his gun but he wouldn't need it; there was no point having a gun now.

He looked at the pylon. It was ringed off by a fence, but that was no obstacle to what he was going to do. It was an easy decision really, because there was nothing

else he could do. He couldn't run for ever, so he started
to climb the pylon.

When he was halfway up, his eyes used to the dark
now, he stopped to look back at the motorway. From
where he sat, astride a girder seventy feet up, he could
see clear over the hedge, beyond the wreck of the
Peugeot, and most of the way down the embankment. In
the silence he could still hear voices, but just as he was
straining to see how far Hawley and Gates had come he
was distracted by a revolving blue light higher up the
motorway and the wail of a siren groaning to a stop in
the lay-by. Gust laughed, and kept on laughing till he
reached the top.

31

It was daylight now, and he had been sitting at the top of the pylon for a long time.

He found himself thinking back to when he was eleven, living with his mother in Welling after his father had been killed in a jail riot, in a road with two hundred houses like theirs in it, each with a garden at the back; and that was when Janey Smith, the Gusts' divorced neighbour, a big woman who was always singing and joking, killed herself one early morning in June. That was the day, when he saw her body from the top of the wall that separated their gardens, that he knew the wrong people would always go down.

The body was not lying in the grass but leaned outward from the taut rope at an angle of forty-five degrees like the statue on a bowsprit, feet pointed inwards and dragging in the grass on their uppers, the face averted.

There is an equality between have-nots that no slack-jawed royal will ever know; no hand waving from a limousine inspires awe like a human being dying at the bottom of her garden under an apple tree. No music on earth, played in no matter how vast a cathedral by however great a master, can match that kind of grief and sense of isolation; the onlookers, himself among them, could still read the resolve on her face as the police and the ambulance crew cut her down. Her features, distorted by the shock as the rope shortened her fall, had turned white in the dawn chill. Death had not worked as an artist. She had died with the seams of her stockings crooked, and she still wore the apron she put on to do the housework.

What had been the last straw for her?

Even aged eleven Gust knew that she wasn't a woman meant to be childless, divorced and to live on her own. But until he found her there under the summer leaves she had pointed outwards at the end of the rope, hanging motionless over the grass all night, in a distant loneliness so great that finally nothing mattered any more.

Once she was gone, when the ambulance had taken her away from the white flowering weeds, from the earth, her neck stretched taut, then everyone began inwardly to pray for her, even Gust. They couldn't have done it before, any more than they had felt able to help her while she was alive, because she gave them no chance. She always cheerfully parried any attempt neighbours made; and evidently, while she was alive no black suit could be taken down off its hanger, no best shoes polished yet, no memory evoked nor tear shed.

But once she had taken her great step off in the garden, tying the rope to the branch and jumping off the packing case, then 'Abide With Me' could wheeze from the out of tune organ in the granite church at the street corner. The prayers were intoned by a replacement priest with chronic sneezing fits. He wiped his nose on his surplice, croaked his way through the service and didn't know anyone in the street. But at least he was aware that the street had gathered to mourn and that nobody wanted any homilies, and he made as creditable a job of the ceremony as he could; nor had he created any difficulties about burying a suicide.

Anyway, she was buried with respect, and that was enough.

Gust had never managed to talk to anyone, not even Petal, about what it was like to find Janey leaning into the rope like that with her carpet-slippered feet turned inwards at six o'clock that sunny morning; it killed his summer, and other things in him too. When they left the church his stepfather took him down to the Gunners at the corner and bought him half a mild which he drank outside slowly, thinking of her in her old checked skirt, and remembering that at the same moment he found her he had heard a cuckoo calling in the apple tree where she had died.

Then almost at once after her death trouble began for Gust too: there were quarrels at home and his stepfather left. He was separated from his mother and went to stay with his gran, who had problems enough of her own; but over the years of his childhood she explained as much of life to him as she knew, which was a good deal, something that he never forgot and which he tried to repay as the end of her own life fell due.

But in the months that followed the Smith suicide people had trouble in one house after another until in the end the whole of their part of the street broke up. He never tried to explain it because he had no words for it, but he did know that the first face he ever really understood was his dead neighbour's; in his dreams he still sometimes edged up to her among the flowers under the tree with the birds singing and stood there before he woke in a state of shock. The rope was tied in the same slipknot that she used to pull her laundry tight when she packed it up in a sheet; he touched her gingerly, wanting to undo it, as if that might bring her back to life, but she was so cold that she scared him, and the rope was too deeply sunk in her neck. He went round to look at her face because he wanted to touch that too, but he found he couldn't; it was too changed.

Anyway, he had never mentioned it, not even in jail where time passes so slowly that the inmates tell any kind of story to while it away. But he had never completely sponged it out of his mind, and here it was, back again.

He returned to the present. 'When you're ready,' he said aloud, 'grab the cable, do it in one, don't hesitate; you'll only make a mess of it otherwise and it mightn't be fatal.' (This is the only life we ever had or ever will have.) Now that he was close to it he could see that things were going to be more difficult than he had thought; it was going to be worse than being executed because there was no one to get him into position. He moved closer to the terminal that would kill him when he touched it; looking down, he saw a crowd of people gathering round the base of the pylon shouting and looking up at him.

He didn't even know why he had waited as long as he had, except that part of him didn't want to go through with it. Even though he knew he had no alternative, elements in him still persisted with what had now become only the ghost of life. But he set his face against all that, against ghosts: *I can think as long as I like, but the longer I live the longer I shall have bad dreams.*

He was even taken with a burst of hilarity at one point and shouted back, waving at the people below: 'Hey! Even a duke gets diarrhoea, you know! We've all got to go, mate!' He doubted if they could hear him, but what did that matter?

It was ridiculous. He had got himself into this absurd position, quitting his shape, the only one he had ever had; inevitable or not, it was an idiotic solution. It didn't feel real, but then nor did anything else, and after all, Petal no longer had any shape either. Anyhow, it was better than going back to jail; he would be vulnerable in jail. Hawley, Sladden, Gates, or someone acting for them would knock him off; it just depended on who got to him first.

The other night, he remembered, he had heard on the radio at Petal's (could it only have been the other night?) that six hundred thousand people died in Britain every year; he wondered if they too, Petal too, had all thought and felt the way he was thinking while it was happening to them. That seemed to help.

He moved along the cable, balancing a hundred and eighty feet above the police and firemen with death next to his hand, and gazed across the fields as far as the motorway. The sun shone, bright and cold; the traffic glittered and sparkled in the distance under a blue film of exhaust.

He thought, *It's strange, I'm not just an ordinary suicide, if there is such a thing, I'm not doing it to get attention. I'm doing it because there's nothing else to be done.*

The people below him, the luminous sky, the fields, the high tension cables beside him, the steel construction he held onto, none of it seemed real. He felt the same false relief of a bankrupt, freed of his anxieties because his life had been wound up. He was already dead; he was down there in the fields before he had even hit them. Reality was already a long time ago, and he experienced a sensation in which the daylight itself had turned dark.

'Maybe it would be easier if I had a bottle of scotch,' he said, and grinned. He looked up at the sky. It was clouding over and the wind had risen sharply, but the sun was still shining; it was a brilliant November afternoon. Indeed it looked as if the whole universe had been sandblasted, scoured until it glittered, newly forged; at that height the wind snapped and plucked at his jacket, whipping his jeans round his legs. The people on the ground peered up at him against the sunlight, shading their eyes; everyone except Sladden, who had his camera going.

The lens of the camera, watching him, caught the sun and Gust watched back, imagining what would have happened if Sladden had caught up with him, or if Hawley had shot him in the hedge back at the motorway and he hadn't died. Things could only have turned out one way, and once he was in hospital, supposing he was still alive, sooner or later Sladden would have appeared.

'I've come to get a statement from you.'

'I've nothing to say.'

'You'd better talk while you can, you're badly hurt.'

'It was meant to be worse still, wasn't it?'

'Let's have a statement. Come on, they say you're fit to make one. I've got a draft here, some questions.'

'If I answer them what happens?'

'You can change your name, go abroad, anything you want. Say Australia. Australia's OK.'

'Down under?' he would have said. 'Six foot under, you mean. You hoped Hawley, Gates, Dingo or Stuart would write me off but it didn't turn out like that, so you're going to have to do it. I wouldn't get a mile from this hospital in case I went running to the tabloids, you'd none of you get a night's sleep with me alive.'

'You're raving. You kept your side of the bargain, we're keeping ours.'

'I don't believe you, nor would you if you were in my place.'

'All we want is a statement.'

'But once you've got it I'm brown bread. Now I'm tired, fuck off, the deals are all off.'

'A man like you, the deals are never off.'

'They are. Next time you see a dead man have a good look at him, Sladden. They all look the same, they don't care about deals any more, they just look as if they were farting in your face.'

'You'll have to cooperate. If you don't you'll go back to jail.'

'I'll never do that.'

'You will if you don't help us until we've finished with you, and if you think you're in danger out here, that's nothing to what you'd be risking inside.'

'I know that.'

'You'll have to trust us then.'

It was a hand he could never have won, and when he had lost it he would have turned his face to the wall and started laughing, reliving his years with Petal, talking to Johnny and the Irishman, and beating his head against the head of the prison hospital bed, pissing himself laughing over old jokes and riotous times, and he would have gone on doing it until someone came along with a needle and put him to sleep.

But up here he was on the brink of a sleep that no Sladden could break.

Up here on the pylon everything was better, cleaner. It was his life till he lost it; he didn't want any more bother with Sladden and he was ready to pay. He leaned out and shouted, 'You! Sladden! Can you hear me? Why don't you come up and join me on the live wire?'

Nobody down there could hear him because of the wind and he turned his back on them, laughing in his frozen hands. 'All these people think of is their mortgages,' he said. 'It's incredible. I'd never have believed it if I wasn't here watching it. Petal and I are worth ten thousand times more to each other than they are even in the state we're in.'

There were even more people clustered around the pylon now; Draper had arrived with Ricky, bumping across the plough in a four by four. He had a loud hailer with him and yelled up: 'All right, come on down now, Gust, that's enough!'

'He's not going to,' said Sladden, 'that's a racing certainty.'

'Any press around?'

'No, thank Christ. Not that I can see even them scrambling up there for an interview.'

'What a fuck-up.'

'Not if he jumps. It's if he doesn't.'

'Why don't we just disconnect the power line and go and get him?' said a keen-looking young copper.

'And disconnect a quarter of a million customers?' said Draper. 'What's your name, sonny? Remind me to put you in for the order of the lead balloon, you obviously don't know what dropping a bollock means yet.' He shouted up at Gust: 'That's enough now, come on down, stop farting about!'

'Not a chance,' said Sladden, gazing through his viewfinder. 'He's standing up there laughing at us, taking the piss.' In fact they could hear Gust's laughter at times, when there was the odd change of wind.

'All he's got to do is touch that terminal,' a fireman muttered, 'and wham!'

'We'll have to go through the motions of trying to get him down alive,' Draper said.

'No need to try too hard,' said Sladden.

Draper turned to the station commander. 'Can't you get your big ladder up to him?'

'The ladders are ready,' said the fireman, 'but by the time they're in place he'll have passed us coming the other way. Seeing us coming'll only speed him up; I've seen it happen.'

'He hasn't any choice anyway,' said Ricky.

'That makes me feel great, that does,' said Draper. 'There are times when I really don't know what I'd do without you, the way you cheer me up.'

'You're not worried about Gust,' said Ricky, 'you're worried about balls-ups.'

'Come and see me in my office tomorrow,' Draper said.

'I've had two more calls through,' said the station commander. 'We can't stay here for ever.'

'I realise that,' said Draper, 'but there's a priority on this, we've still got things we want to ask this lunatic, only of course we can't unless he's in one piece.' He looked at his watch. 'All right, five more minutes, and then up you go anyway, shit or bust.'

Gust was shouting something, but the wind had turned in the meantime so that they couldn't catch it.

'Get that net ready,' the local police inspector told his men. 'Not that it'll do much good,' he added to Draper.

'Jumping from that height he'll like as not go straight through it.'

'I'm resigning after this,' said a constable who was holding one edge.

Gust gave up shouting at them. He couldn't have made any of them understand what he was thinking anyway, even if they could have heard him; besides, the wind was too strong, rising to a roar, and it was getting dark. 'It takes a long time to realise it's no good shouting at the dark,' he said. 'It's only the last second that you get any message back, if you ever do.'

He wished he had started out knowing that, not that it made any difference now. His position now was like that of old people, like his grandmother, where the people around them, if there were any, just wished they would die and get on with it. They weren't interested in the departing babble of a lifetime's knowledge, and it wasn't often these days that the last vision of earth that the dying took with them was even a caring face. For dying sets a person apart from those who can't bear to think they're mortal, so that the far side of knowledge in the end amounts to no more than a handful of earth thrown onto a box by people anxious to get out of the rain, which in London at least has a habit of falling on the newly dead.

So at this height, standing on enough current to run the Underground, Gust put things to himself as he saw them; the only real sorrow he felt on leaving was that his friends had died for no reason except that they had helped him.

Johnny.

Petal, dying under a hail of blows from a baseball bat.

In any case, going out, he could have told them: *Eternity? There is none. What we went through was it. What never was is not, and never shall be, and what we were told would be never could have been.*

They found that on him later, scribbled on the back of a lunch menu.

'What's that mean?' said Ricky, reading it as they walked back to the cars afterwards, and Sladden, indifferent anyway because he had a disease which he knew would kill him said, 'Who cares? That's the end of Gust, cheapest way out. What do you think, Spaulding? You're a detective.'

But Spaulding turned his back on them.

Gust's mood had changed. He felt sick, lonely and afraid now, and he was flagging. He shaded his swollen face against the sun, which was low on the horizon, and watched the world roll into the evening. On the ground people were still shouting up at him, others were looking at their watches, but he ignored them.

'What's the point of knowing the truth,' he said, 'when it's too late to do anything with it?' He made a last effort to think back, but because he couldn't frame his thought in a way that made sense, thinking had become like a madman's monologue.

'The tide has taken me into its hands,' he said, and at least he could see forward now, even if the view was new and strange. With his arm hooked over the cable and his fingers an inch from the terminal, he was already back where he would rather be anyway, dancing with Petal in the Eclipse, forever turning with her round the floor; she seemed more tangible to him now than she had ever been.

It had been a difficult hand to play but he had managed it; everybody managed everything in the end. It could never have been an easy game for him even if he had been dealt all the aces, not that anybody ever was.

He understood for an instant what it meant to be in two worlds, alive and dead; to be someone different, better, cleaner, unthreatened, unaggressive, unafraid. Weight fell off him that he never even realised he had been carrying because he had carried it all his life; this strange experience seemed to enable him to accept his fate. There could be no peace without death's acceptance; purity had to be achieved in the absolute.

He said: 'The fog's lifted.'

It was true. He could see all over again. For the first time since Petal's death his mind was working; he saw everything as it was, undistorted. At last he could see Petal again as she had been the day they had decided to live together and gone out to celebrate with Johnny; she was running into the Diadem now. He still had the set of keys to the flat that she had given him, and he pulled them out of his pocket, balancing on the cable, to look at his name engraved on the silver tag.

Gust.

Gust? he thought. It was like talking about a stranger. *Who was Gust? Who cares what he knew?*

It was exactly what the impatient people at the foot of the pylon were saying.

Petal, Johnny, the Irishman: you'll find them again.

But he didn't think so. He felt panic instead, his clothes flapping at him. Sure that it was true in a way, he shouted down into the darkness against the wind which was blowing harder than ever: 'I was innocent!'

His right hand, which he had never before felt so much a part of him, crept towards what was going to happen to it. 'It's what I've always said to you whatever we were doing,' he told it, 'there's no turning back. One day it has to happen to everybody.' But even so the mystery of his own end awed him; he had never been as close to it as this.

He gazed at the world. 'Don't look at it too long,' he warned himself. 'Don't think about that any more now.'

He made up his mind. 'Slipping off the edge of the possible,' he said. He grasped the cable, said *I trust you*, and was catapulted outwards away from the pylon, shocked and rigid, at a sharp angle, a hurtling blot of rags against the sky. His eyes were dried to nothing by the voltage and he shrank like dried flowers as he flew; his jacket, which he had opened on his way up the pylon, was buttoned up wrong. But the words, as he turned over and over in the dark air, were still on lips that had fried to his teeth: *I trust you*, and the next day, if he had been there to see it, he would have picked up the paper to see his face there, had a good laugh and jumped on a bus to drop off at the Diadem:

'Me a celebrity? That'll be the day.'

But the real shock of the current was going into the Diadem so fast that the wind was tearing his hair out, and hearing the girl behind the bar saying as he went through the door: 'Hullo Gust, message for you,' and then, her voice changing to a scream: 'Look out!'

The door of the Diadem slammed shut, striking him with the force of a battering ram.

He fell face down, making a crater in the ploughed earth, and everything was silent after that.

Nothing at all happened after that.